THE HAUNTING OF TYRESE WALKER

J.P. ROSE

ANDERSEN PRESS

First published in 2022 by
Andersen Press Limited
20 Vauxhall Bridge Road, London SW1V 2SA, UK
Vijverlaan 48, 3062 HL Rotterdam, Nederland
www.andersenpress.co.uk

2 4 6 8 10 9 7 5 3 1

British Library Cataloguing in Publication Data available.

ISBN 978 1 83913 240 7

Printed and bound in Great Britain by Clays Ltd, Elcograf S.p.A.

In memory of my mum,
who soars with the eagles
and rides on the waves of the ocean,
touching my cheek as she dances in the wind.
I miss you.
You told me I could, and I did . . .
This is for you.

Shadow Man, Shadow Man, him come get you,
Shadow Man, Shadow Man, him come take you . . .

1

August
Jamaica

'How much longer *now*?'

Tyrese let out a long, loud sigh, making certain his mum heard. He didn't want to be here. Here, underneath the beating sun. Here in the middle of nowhere. And here because his mum hadn't given him *any* other choice. That thought twisted inside him and his gaze prowled angrily along the landscape. 'Mum! *How long*?'

He flicked a glance at her. Having never been the most confident of drivers, she kept her eyes pasted to the narrow, uneven road. 'I'm not sure, honey, it's further than I remember – but we should be there quite soon.'

'You said that, like, forty minutes ago!' Tyrese turned his head away, continuing to watch the outside world go by.

He dangled his hand out of the car window, tracing invisible circles with the tips of his fingers on the hot metal door of the Jeep. They'd been driving for over three hours – his mum getting lost and going too slowly – travelling away from Kingston up the steep winding roads where the clouds wrapped around the mountains like a thick white ribbon. There they'd been greeted by a vivid blue sky and it had felt to Tyrese as if he'd entered a secret land above the earth. A smouldering, scorching earth, the heat gluing itself to him, making him feel uncomfortable as it clasped around like a snake strangling its prey.

He'd given up wiping the trickling sweat off his face which tasted of salt. It was supposed to get cooler up the mountains, though the further they drove through the rainforest, the hotter and more humid it seemed to get. The breeze only teased him, bringing nothing but billows of warm air.

Even the cold can of Coke they'd bought at the airport had quickly turned warm; the ice cream he'd been so looking forward to had within minutes melted all over his hands, down his favourite T-shirt, running on to the car seat to leave a gooey mess everywhere. Now the whole car smelled of strawberry swirl and butterscotch ripple.

There'd been nothing good since he'd stepped off the plane, though there'd been nothing good *before* he'd got on the plane . . . nothing good for a *long time*. He just hated it all.

A sudden flutter cut through the line of Tyrese's faraway gaze and his stare followed a huge red bug with spindly black legs land and hitch a ride on the door. He quickly drew his hand back in at the same time as the Jeep swerved sharply, sending Tyrese sideward.

'Sorry about that, Ty,' his mum apologised chirpily, only just avoiding the large goat darting across the track.

More used to seeing her avoid buses and trams, Tyrese watched it disappear behind a bush. He suddenly felt more homesick than ever.

The Jeep slowed and his mum pulled up by a grove of

trees. Smiling, she turned to look at him. 'We're here! And can you smell that, Ty? That's ginger lilies. Oh, I love that smell.'

Tyrese's nose filled with the strong, sweet scent. He stared out at the twisting stretch of shrubs and plants which made the whole place feel like it was surrounded by a thick, towering green prison wall. He could hardly get his words out. 'Here? *This* is it?'

'Yes, it's gorgeous, isn't it? To be this far up in the mountains, is so lovely.'

'Where's Grammy's house?'

'Just there, through those trees . . . See it?'

Swivelling around in his seat, Tyrese felt some trapped sweat squishing round the top of his legs and between his butt cheeks. He took off his glasses and wiped away the smears with the bottom of his T-shirt.

Running his fingers through his light-brown Afro, he bit down on his lip. It was worse than he thought it was going to be. How could his mum think *this* was lovely? There was nothing. Just trees and more trees. Why weren't they staying near a town or village, or even near some of the brightly painted coloured houses he'd seen perched on the slopes of the hillsides when they'd passed the coffee plantation? Why would she bring him here, up in the mountains by a forest, miles from anywhere?

Fighting back his tears, feeling them catch at his throat, Tyrese glanced down at the no signal bar on his phone. 'I don't even know why we had to come.'

'You know why, sweetheart. We need a break, don't we?'

His mum smiled, tilting her head. Her cheeks were pinched red, her face shiny as if it'd been glazed in cooking oil and her hair seemed like it was trying to escape from the clutches of its messy bun.

Tyrese knew she wanted an answer, but he stayed silent, watching yet another bug land on the Jeep. All he wanted was to be at homc. Back in his bedroom on his own, just the way he liked it.

'And besides, Ty,' his mum continued, smiling again, 'Grammy and your cousin are really looking forward to seeing you. It'll be fun . . . Come on, there she is! This is going to be wonderful.'

The familiar knot in Tyrese's stomach told him otherwise, and memories like distant voices called on the wind.

2

Unsticking the back of his bare arms from the hot, sweaty leather seat, Tyrese stepped out of the Jeep, and the sun hit with a slap.

'Ty, now, don't forget we're here for the whole of the summer holiday.' His mum grabbed his arm gently. 'So try to make an effort, baby.'

He shrugged one shoulder, doubling it up to scratch his ear. 'Or what? We'll go back home?'

'Sweetheart, there's no need to be rude, I'm just asking you to try.'

Slipping his trainers back on and not bothering to answer her again, Tyrese trudged towards the bright green house with sun-bleached pink shutters where Grammy was standing on the porch waving with both hands.

He hadn't seen her since the last time he visited Jamaica, just before his fourth birthday. Not that he could really remember, and whenever they'd tried to FaceTime Grammy, the signal always dropped. But he recognised her from the photos they had hanging up in the kitchen at home. Though she looked older. She was reed-thin, hunched up, her skin smooth for someone her age, and she wore a light blue head wrap which matched her blue dress. Dark circles like ink smudges rested under her brown eyes. They twinkled, and a large smile was drawn across her face.

Walking carefully down the wooden porch stairs to greet them, Grammy's arms stretched wide. 'Tyrese! Patty! Tyrese! Come, let me give you a hug. It's *so* good to see you both! How was your flight? Oh, Tyrese, look 'pon you! What! Look how tall!' Grammy cackled and hooted. She called over her shoulder: 'Marvin! Marvin! Dem here! Quick, dem here!'

His mum beamed. 'How are you?'

'Everything is everything. Me good.' Grammy beamed back.

The hug was tight and long. With Grammy's arms around him, Tyrese watched a boy appear from the side of the house by the swing bench. His hair was freshly braided in zigzag cornrows. He wore faded blue trousers, a striped T-shirt just as washed-out, and his trainers looked slightly too big for his feet, tied with colourful neon laces.

'Marvin, say hello to Tyrese,' Grammy encouraged.

Wiping some crumbs off the side of his mouth, Marvin revealed a grin. '*A long time me nuh si yuh, Tyrese. Weh yuh ah seh, wah gwaan?*' he said quickly.

Stepping away from Grammy's surprisingly strong embrace, Tyrese looked at his cousin. They were the same age, their birthdays only a month apart, but he'd only ever met him once and that had been ten years ago during his stay at Grammy's. 'Excuse me?'

'*A long time me nuh si yuh. Weh yuh ah seh, wah gwaan?*' Marvin repeated but then he burst out into laughter as loud, warm and crisp as Grammy's had been. *'Bwoy, you don't know how fi chat Patois?'*

Grammy clipped Marvin on the back of the head gently. 'You're too chatty, Marvin. Of course him not know how to speak Patois.'

Rubbing his head and still laughing, Marvin stepped nearer to Tyrese. '*Me forget, yuh an English bwoy. A Manchester bwoy*! You want me to speak English for you, *Manchester bwoy?* Then I shall be the King of England.' Marvin put on a silly accent and, taking hold of Tyrese's hand, shook it. 'How do you do, Tyrese? How nice of you to come.' Then he burst into loud fits of giggles.

Grammy frowned. 'Stop teasing, Marvin . . . It's fine, Tyrese, come, take no notice of him. Now, say sorry, Marvin. Come now!'

Marvin shrugged. 'Just joking.' And he spun round to look at Tyrese's mum.

She grinned. 'It's lovely to see you again, Marvin,' she said, giving him a hug despite the blistering heat.

'Aunt Patty, do you know how to speak Patois?'

She winked at Marvin, her blue eyes becoming brighter as she stood fanning herself with the bottom of her grey linen shirt which seemed to swamp her tall, slender frame. 'No, your uncle tried to teach me a few times but in the end he gave up. I think I was a very bad student.'

'So, how come he didn't teach you Patois, Tyrese? You never want to learn? You not a Yard man at heart?' Marvin giggled again, turning back to look at his cousin.

Tyrese dipped his gaze to the ground. He could feel his

heart beginning to race. Why couldn't everyone just leave him alone? Why did his stupid cousin think it was funny? Once again, he wished he was back at home in the safety of his bedroom.

'I don't know what the joke is,' Tyrese whispered, already annoyed by how much Marvin laughed, especially as he didn't think there was anything at all to laugh about.

'Why, were you a bad student too, dat it?'

'Whatever,' Tyrese mumbled.

'You want me to teach you? I can! Maybe I'm a better teacher than your dad!'

Tyrese's jaw jutted. He stared up at his cousin. 'Don't talk about my dad like that. Just leave me alone, yeah.'

Marvin raised his eyebrows, glanced at his aunt Patty, glanced back at Tyrese. 'Sorry, Ty, I only meant your dad—'

'. . . I don't care what you meant,' Tyrese snapped, interrupting his cousin.

'Tyrese, that's quite enough!' his mum said, flushing a deeper red. 'Marvin's only having a bit of fun. It's no big deal.'

Tears weren't far from Tyrese's eyes. He spun around to glare at her, but he didn't say anything.

The silence hit down harder than the heat. It sizzled away until Grammy broke it.

'*Lawd Gee*, Marvin! *Nuh trouble trouble, til trouble trouble yuh.* Stop causing mischief, now hush, say no more!' She turned to Tyrese, squeezed his hand. Smiled. 'Why don't you go and get yourself freshened up, Ty? Marvin can take you to your room . . . Oh, and, Tyrese, welcome back to Jamaica.'

3

Having taken a quick shower to freshen up, Tyrese sat on the single metal bed in the guest room. He didn't know which was louder, Marvin's singing coming from the kitchen or the noise of the insects outside making it sound like the whole of Grammy's house was surrounded by rattlesnakes.

He yawned, rubbing coconut oil between the palms of his hands, careful not to drop any on his clothes. He glanced at the time: four p.m. He already felt so tired. Maybe he should lie down? The large pillow *did* look so comfy and inviting, but he hated going to sleep. Sleep only meant he'd dream, and dreaming meant he'd be taken back to his old life: to the life he'd had before that day in March at Manchester airport when his mum had met him at the arrivals lounge, her face burnt with tears, a whispered scream of pain as she told him the news.

He hated remembering, he hated *that* memory. It gnawed away at him like a disease. And when he did wake, the instant his eyes fluttered open, he was hit all over again with remembering what he'd lost . . . Yes, to sleep, to dream, would only be to wake, and realise there were no more yesterdays, only today.

He yawned again. Well, he'd just stay awake, that's what he'd do. He'd go for a walk. It was better that way, and he was fine as long as he didn't think too much.

Chewing on his lip, Tyrese fought to push everything out of his mind. He massaged the oil through his Afro and, gulping for air, blinked away the prickling behind his eyes.

Standing, he grabbed his baseball cap and headed for the door, but his breath caught like he'd stepped outside on an ice-cold winter's day. On the bedside cabinet was a photograph. Him and his dad. Smiling. Laughing. His mum behind the camera, telling them to keep still, stop giggling, stand straight. The last photo of them ever taken.

He pounced. Diving at it as if he were plunging into the depths of the ocean. Grabbing and turning the frame in his hand to find the clips, to tear the photo out of its white wooden frame, which he dropped on the floor with a clatter.

A tight pain in his chest.

He crumpled the photo in his hand, squeezing it, taking the very life out of it.

'What's that, Ty? Everything OK?' His mum appeared at the door, smiling, worry outlining her words.

Tyrese quickly pushed the photo into the pocket of his shorts. 'Nothing. Just rubbish.'

Her eyes flickered with suspicion but she held her smile. 'Fancy coming for a snack before supper time? Though I need to warn you, Grammy's cooking enough for an army and then some.'

‘No thanks. I’m just going to go for a walk. Have a look around.’

‘Well, that’s good, I’m glad you’re going to get some fresh air, a bit of exercise. Just be careful, Ty, OK? Don’t go too far . . . are you sure you’re all right?’

Using his foot to quickly tap the empty photo frame under the bed without his mum noticing it, Tyrese clenched the photo tighter in his pocket. He shrugged. ‘Yeah, course, why wouldn’t I be?’

—

Quickly stomping along the dusty track, past the chicken pen and away from Grammy’s house, Tyrese kicked at every stone and stick in sight. But nearing the top of a steep slope, he slowed down, the heat gripping him, making it seem like he was dragging a sack of rocks behind him.

He squeezed his hands into fists, shut his eyes. He’d give anything not to feel like he did. He couldn’t believe his mum really expected him to spend the *whole* summer here. It was all because she’d listened to his stupid counsellor, Jonathan or ‘Johnny’ as he always liked to be called.

Johnny knows best, sweetheart. Johnny has dealt with this kind of stuff before. Johnny says time away is the best thing for you. Johnny thinks getting out of your bedroom and going to see family is just what you need right now.

Well, it wasn’t Johnny who was stuck here. It was him. He let out a long, audible groan at the thought and opened his eyes.

Looking around, Tyrese suddenly realised how far he’d

walked. The sun was beginning to go down. Wisps of mountain mist rose slowly, although the heat in the forest still sat wet and clammy like an unwelcome guest.

He couldn't see Grammy's house at all now. The track he'd come along wound up the mountain, disappearing round the corner. Everywhere was so silent. He couldn't even hear the insects any more. Plants and shrubs that Tyrese had never seen before grew waist-high along the narrow track. Strange-shaped trees with enormous gnarled trunks covered in green and yellow moss surrounded him, reaching up and weaving together to block out the sun, leaving only a gloomy, fading light.

He glanced at his watch. 5.25 p.m. Should he turn back? No, that would mean having to speak to everyone. He just didn't want to deal with that.

Swatting a mosquito that looked like it was getting ready to take a bite at his arm, Tyrese continued heading up the track, though he'd hardly gone a few more paces when he heard a twig snap.

He stopped, listened, quickly glanced around, but hearing nothing more, he continued, passing a fallen rotten tree cloaked in giant fungus and teeming with woodlice.

He stopped again, certain he'd heard the crunch of footsteps behind him.

Turning around, Tyrese expected to see his mum. There was nobody there, although he called out anyway: 'Mum? Mum, is that you?'

Nothing.

Just the faint call of a bird high up in a tree . . . What was that smell? He sniffed. Smoke. It smelled as if someone had been burning wood. Frowning, Tyrese shifted his stare. Then he heard another twig snap, only closer this time. His gaze danced through the trees. 'Marvin, if that's you, it's not funny, OK? *Marvin?* Marvin, just come out from wherever you're hiding, yeah.'

He licked his lips, tasted the dryness of his mouth. All he could hear now was the sound of his own breathing. Even the bird was silent. It felt like the quietness was closing in on him like a rising tide.

Scanning the forest again, he was careful not to let his gaze wander towards the dark corridor of trees. Maybe he should just go back to Grammy's after all?

About to head off down the track, something caught his eye . . . There, through the thick wall of palm and eucalyptus trees. What was it? He pushed his glasses further up his nose, squinted, his heart lurching. There was something moving in the patch of shadows . . .

4

Not wanting to make a noise, Tyrese kept still. Fleetingly, he wondered if he should just make a run for it, but curiosity overrode his initial fear. He stepped towards the edge, looking down the steep forested mountainside, the creeping mist weaving upwards.

For a moment, Tyrese felt like something was staring back at him. The sense he wasn't alone tapped into his imagination, slipping it into endless possibilities.

A shape darted through the trees. Startled, he jerked back, holding his breath as if somehow that would protect him from whatever it was.

His eyes stayed locked on the mountainside, and although there was nothing moving now, Tyrese caught sight of something else. Hidden behind a broken tree which leaned against a jutting out boulder – like a blister erupting from the face of the mountain – Tyrese could see something dark and solid.

Puzzled, he quickly scanned the descent. Then, careful not to get his feet tangled in the twisting plants which snatched at his ankles, Tyrese began to climb down the side of the slope, using the blue mahoe trees for balance.

Getting to the boulder, he stopped. Concealed within the tall ferns and between the fallen tree and the rock, he saw that the dark and solid shape was in fact a long stone slab sunken in the undergrowth.

Tentatively he moved closer to get a better look . . .

A neglected grave.

Frowning, he glanced up the mountainside. Strange to have one here. Why would anyone want to have a grave on such a steep slope, hidden from everyone?

Everything about it looked homemade; the tombstone, misshapen, and even though he couldn't make out the inscription which had mainly been worn away, he could still see the remains of some letters which had been crudely and unskilfully chiselled into the stone.

Tyrese pushed his glasses up. The grave was choked by creeping vines, and lichen and moss spread across it but there was something else carved into the stone. Kneeling, he began to rub away the heavily ingrained dirt, then leaned back on his heels examining what he'd revealed.

Although faded, there was no mistaking what he was looking at. Carved into the stone was a large, simple etching of a snake in a circle devouring its own tail. There was something unsettling about it, and once again a sudden uneasy chill scurried down his spine, spider-like. His gaze darted around once more and he swallowed. It sounded too loud in the quietness. And maybe it was his imagination, but had the air just become stiller? Heavier? Like the aftermath of a fire.

Slowly, Tyrese stood and began to edge away, but a sound of rustling coming from the bushes had him spinning round and scrambling as fast as he could back up the slope and through the blue mahoe trees to the track at the top.

Panting, he let out a relieved sigh, brushed himself quickly off, wanting to get back to Grammy's as soon as he could.

'Ty?'

'Mum!' He jumped at the sound of her voice right behind him. 'Mum, did you have to sneak up on me like that?'

His mum rested her hands on her hips, catching her breath. 'Sorry, I didn't mean to . . . Are you all right, Ty? What were you doing down there?' She peeked over the edge. 'Oh my goodness, you could have fallen, look how steep it is.' Concern rippled over her face and a thin film of sweat sat above her top lip.

'It's not that steep.'

'It is, and I'd rather you didn't go off like that.'

'I thought you wanted me to get some fresh air,' Tyrese muttered sullenly.

'I do, but you don't know the place yet. It's so easy to get lost. Look how dense the trees are, you could've ended up walking round and round in circles for hours.' She pushed back her fringe. 'Are you sure you're OK, Ty?'

'I'm fine.' He wasn't in the mood to talk but it didn't stop his mum wanting to have a conversation. It never did.

Her face became animated as she launched into an unwanted speech. 'You know, I'd forgotten how amazing this place is. Can you imagine having all this nature right on your doorstep all the time? It makes a lovely change from the Salford Quays dockyards, doesn't it?'

He didn't think it did. He just wanted to go back home to Manchester. So he just shrugged, shoving his hands in his pocket. Then he felt something. The photo. He'd forgotten he still had it.

As soon as his mum glanced the other way, Tyrese pulled out the crumpled-up photo and quickly dropped it behind him, where it rolled down the slope.

'Come on, let's go, it gets dark much earlier here,' his mum said, turning back to him and resting an arm round his shoulders. 'And, Ty, when we get back, try not to get so upset when Marvin or Grammy talk about—'

'. . . OK, I get it,' Tyrese said quickly, knowing *exactly* what she was going to say.

They began to walk back down the track but Tyrese glanced over his shoulder towards the trees on the mountainside. Even though it was hot and humid, he shivered, his skin tingling. Why couldn't he shake off the feeling that something or . . . *someone* was watching him?

5

Although it was barely nine o'clock it was already pitch black. The thick forest was now just a silhouette against the night sky, which was scattered with only a few pinpricks of stars and a half moon sitting low. But it was still hot and Tyrese could feel the trickle of sweat slinking down the back of his neck.

He headed to the porch. It was lit by a small electric lamp which attracted dozens of insects, their dark bodies crawling over it, blocking much of its light. 'Hi, Grammy, I was looking for you,' he said politely, watching her untie a small hessian sack full of rice.

She looked up and gave Tyrese a wide grin. Even in the dim light, he could see her eyes shining as she looked at him. 'Oh, Ty, just the boy. What a tonic it is to see you standing there. Me so happy you've come for the holiday. You've made an old lady very happy.'

He couldn't help smiling, he couldn't help feeling bad about the way he'd behaved earlier and he couldn't help wishing things were different. But as much as he didn't want to be here – and he didn't – he had to admit seeing Grammy was lovely.

'Grammy,' Tyrese said, kicking at the floor at nothing in particular, 'I just wanted to say, I'm sorry, yeah. You know, for getting annoyed with Marvin earlier. I shouldn't have done it.'

He waited for her to say something, but she just walked up to him, and took his face into her hands. They were soft and smooth, as if she were stroking his face with cotton. He could feel them trembling. 'Ty, there's no need to apologise. Me understand. If you need to shout and scream, well, this is the place to do it. You a here amongst people dat love you. We all want to help you get through this.' She paused and sadness traced her smile. 'Oh, Ty, one day you'll be able to feel the warmth of the sun again, me promise.'

Tyrese nodded in answer, chewed on the inside of his cheek, hoping that she wouldn't say anything else.

'You are a brave boy, Ty.'

He looked at her. He didn't *feel* brave. He didn't quite know *what* he felt, but he wanted everyone to stop saying it.

As if Grammy had read his mind, she winked at him. 'You're probably fed up with hearing dat, but it's true. You're brave, just like your father.'

He pulled away. He wasn't going to be rude, she was his grammy. But he didn't want her to be like everyone else. To be nice to him, then try to trick him into talking. Just like Jonathan always did. Well, he just wasn't going to go along with it. There was nothing to talk about.

He watched her take a handful of rice and start sprinkling it all over the porch. 'What are you doing, Grammy?' he asked quickly, hoping to distract her, though he was actually interested.

'What me do every night,' she answered, taking another large handful from the hessian sack.

Tyrese raised his eyebrows. The only time he'd ever seen anyone sprinkle food all over the ground was either when his mum fed the birds or when his dad had sprinkled salt on the path when it was icy. He quickly shut down that thought, and took a deep breath, focusing even harder on what Grammy was doing.

'But why, Grammy? I don't get it.'

She turned her full attention on him. 'It's to keep us all safe.'

'With rice?'

'Yes, darlin',' she nodded. 'Me a keep the good duppies in and the bad ones out.'

'Duppies?'

'You must have heard of duppies, Ty, I'm sure your dad must have talked about dem . . . They're what you might call ghosts.'

'Ghosts?' Tyrese repeated, almost doubting what he'd just heard. 'You mean like ghosts of dead people?'

She nodded. 'Sometimes dem a the angry souls of the dead who are so troubled they rise from their grave and walk the earth, though others are just demonic beings sharing our world . . . Duppies are everywhere, Ty, and some of dem need a little more attention than others. A lot of the wicked ones like to cause a whole heap of trouble at night, but if you sprinkle rice around the outside of your house, then the duppies will have to gather every grain, one by one . . . By the time they've collected it all, the sun will be rising and dem will lose most of their power.' She shrugged, seemingly in acceptance of this fact.

Tyrese quickly blinked and stared at her. *Duppies.* Grammy was joking, right? There was no way she was being serious. 'No, what's the rice *really* for, Grammy?'

Tilting her head, her eyebrows snapped together. 'Me just tell you, Ty, it's to keep us all safe.'

Tyrese studied Grammy's face, waiting for it to burst with lines of laughter.

'I know you're just teasing me.'

Grammy picked up the bag of rice. 'No, Ty. I would never joke about keeping you safe. Everyone who lives on the island knows this is what you have to do.'

'*Everyone* can't believe that,' Tyrese said with a chuckle, still expecting her to say she was kidding.

Grammy shrugged. 'Well, if they don't, it's like dem saying they don't believe in the sun and the moon. Just ask Marvin, him will tell you about the duppies. Him knows.'

A thought came to mind. 'Grammy, whose grave is that?'

'What grave?'

'When I went for a walk, I went really far up and there's a grave hidden on the mountainside.'

Grammy seemed to miss a beat, she bristled before answering. 'Me don't know what you're talking about.'

'There's a grave and—'

'. . . *And* nothing, Ty,' Grammy cut in sharply. She held his arms and his stare. 'Stay away, understand? Don't go up there, especially not alone.'

His words swung with unease. 'Why? Why can't I go there?'

She gave him a tight smile. 'Just . . .' she stopped, as if searching what to say. 'You don't want to get lost, do you? So promise me you won't go there again, *ever* . . . *Haad ayse pickney nyam rackstone.*'

Tyrese grinned. 'What?'

'Hard-eared children eat rockstone. It means, children dat don't listen learn the hard way . . . Remember dat!' She handed Tyrese the bag of rice. 'Come, me can't let the chicken stew burn. Be a good boy and finish this for me, but make sure you sprinkle it all around good, especially at the back.'

She smiled again, shuffled away, leaving Tyrese on the porch holding the bag.

Grammy *really* expected him to go around sprinkling rice? He smiled to himself, but nonetheless he walked down the two wooden stairs on to the grass, making his way around the back of the house where it was even darker.

Although Tyrese knew he was only a metre or so from the front door, he suddenly didn't feel as confident. His gaze swept towards the blackness of the forest. But then he shook his head. This was stupid. What was he even doing? He loved Grammy, but scattering rice? Nope. It was totally crazy. And with that thought, Tyrese dumped the rice in the metal bin and made his way quickly back inside.

—

In the early hours of the morning, Tyrese lay in bed, fighting sleep. His eyes were so heavy but no matter how exhausted he was, he kept forcing himself awake each time he dozed off. The heat didn't help. It was so sticky, his whole body was covered in sweat, making it feel like he was stretched out on the wet earth.

His mind wandered to the grave concealed on the mountainside. He couldn't understand why anyone would place a tomb there, whose family would want a grave hidden in such a remote place. And Grammy, well she'd looked so anxious when he'd asked her about it. Maybe it was true that she was worried about him getting lost, but it was odd that she'd snapped at him like that.

Thoughts of the grave were suddenly interrupted when over the noise of the fan, Tyrese heard the sound of the window opening. Must be his mum, though he couldn't see her, it was too dark, but he felt irritated that she'd come into his room to check on him like he was still a small kid. She was always fussing, and he squeezed his eyes shut, not wanting her to know he was awake. She'd only want to talk, ask him if he was all right, worry that he wasn't asleep. So he lay as still as he could until he was sure she had gone.

Fully awake now, Tyrese sighed, wishing again he was back in his room in Manchester. Something told him this was going to be one long summer.

6

It was early Sunday morning and the sun burned through the open window whilst Tyrese got dressed. He'd woken up with the worst headache he'd ever had. He also felt strange, like he was dazed. Perhaps it was jet lag, or maybe the pollen from the flowers which were directly outside his window had triggered his hay fever? He had no idea why his mum had come in and opened it, she knew he liked it closed at night.

Annoyed, Tyrese slammed it shut. He frowned. On the top of his finger there were droplets of blood trickling out from three small pinpricks. Puncture marks on his skin. What was it from? They looked too large for mosquito bites and they didn't itch either. Perhaps a spider bite? He'd read about stuff like that. Though the thought of it was gross. He didn't even want to go there.

He shuddered, wiped away the blood but immediately winced, a sharp pain hitting the back of his eyes. He pinched the bridge of his nose. His headache was getting worse and he still had to unpack. He contemplated leaving it until later but he didn't want his mum to come in, start to fuss and unpack for him.

He let out a long sigh, grabbed his red sports duffle bag, flung it on the floor, unzipped it and took out one of his shirts.

Opening the tall cedar wardrobe and trying his best to ignore the pain in his head, he reached for one of the padded coat hangers. As he did, his hand brushed against a light blue pinstripe jacket. He gasped and stepped quickly back, recognising it straight away. It was his dad's.

Memories rushed in. He squeezed his eyes shut like he could block out his thoughts by closing them. But he snapped them open when the strong scent of the aftershave his dad always wore hit his nose like a cloud of dust, seeping out from the fabric. The smell of vanilla and woody tones surrounded him, as though his dad was standing right next to him.

'*No!*' Tyrese shook his head. His heart pounded and he banged the wardrobe doors, closing them with force, as if he were trying to lock in a wild animal.

Taking large gulps of air, he spun around, leaning his back against the wardrobe. He felt something scratch his neck and, still gasping, he glanced down and saw a large, black centipede crawling out of the small gap between the wardrobe doors, on to his shoulder. He flicked it away in disgust.

'Hey, cuz, I'm sorry if . . .' Marvin appeared at the door, but no sooner had he begun to talk, he trailed off, staring at Tyrese. '. . . Ty, you OK? Ty?'

Tyrese was struggling too much to answer. His chest was tight and his heart raced so quickly it made him dizzy.

'Ty?'

'I can't breathe! I can't breathe!' Fighting for air, Tyrese could hear the panic, the fear in his own voice.

'Ty, shall I go get Aunt Patty?'

Tyrese shook his head and took another slow, deep breath, like Jonathan had told him to, concentrating hard on steadying his breathing. He refused to cry. *He would not cry.* And he certainly didn't want his mum to come, she'd only start fussing. But the panic attacks which he'd had since March made him feel like he was choking, like he had something wedged in his throat.

They frightened him . . . they made him feel like he was *dying*. But they also made him feel stupid, like he was weak, like there was something wrong with him. Though there was no way he was *ever* going to tell anyone that, especially not his mum. No way at all.

Breathing in through his nose, he glanced at Marvin, who was frowning at him. 'I'm OK. I'm fine now.' He tried to smile. 'Really, it's OK.'

'What happened, Ty?'

He shrugged at his cousin. 'Nothing. Just . . . just asthma,' Tyrese said, lying. 'Don't say anything to my mum though, yeah?'

Marvin seemed surprised. 'You have asthma? Grammy never said.'

'Why would she?' Tyrese snapped, wishing now he'd used a different excuse.

His cousin pulled a face. 'Doesn't dat affect your running, though?'

A cloud rushed over Tyrese. He'd been trying really hard *not* to think about his running . . . He'd loved it. It was all he'd wanted to do. He'd even dreamed of smashing the national record at the middle distance 800 metre schools' athletic championships this year. And he'd really believed he'd had a chance. He'd trained hard, preparing for the season, for the race, for the sound of that starting gun. Nothing else had mattered, but then in March, the world he'd known had been kicked upside down. Nothing would ever be the same, and he doubted he'd ever put on his running shoes again. What was the point? What was the point of anything now?

Tyrese glanced at his cousin again. He hated lying and now he was going to have to lie some more. 'No, it didn't, I was fine . . . Anyway, it doesn't matter, I'm not going to bother competing, I'm done with it.'

'Why?'

He shrugged, adding more untruths to his story. 'I dunno, I guess I got bored of it.'

Marvin looked like he wanted to say something but he just shrugged. 'OK. Anyway breakfast a ready. Oh, and, Ty, sorry about what I said yesterday. Me never meant to *vex* you.'

Tyrese nodded. 'Yeah man, no problem.'

'You see, already you sound like you're a Yard man!' Marvin laughed, which made Tyrese smile.

'I'm sorry too, I shouldn't have said what I did.'

They smiled, nodded to each other. Then Tyrese tied his laces as Marvin jumped in front of the mirror, grinning.

'Grammy thinks we look alike . . . What you say?'

Wanting to make an effort, Tyrese put his glasses on and stared at his cousin. He'd always been told how similar they looked. He couldn't see it though, apart from in one photo Grammy had sent him last year, and looking at his cousin now, he still didn't think they did. For a start, Marvin had a smaller face than him, thinner, although Tyrese had to admit their slight sticky-out ears and round-tipped noses were the same. But unlike him, Marvin had a dimple in his smile. 'No, I don't think so.'

'Is dat because I'm too handsome?' Marvin laughed again, then pulled a face and struck a pose.

Even though he'd been angry at Marvin yesterday, Tyrese couldn't help liking his cousin. 'So, how come you're here at Grammy's?' he asked while strapping his watch back on to his wrist.

'Most of the time me live here because my dad, well, he likes to do his own thing,' he said, looking at Tyrese in the mirror. 'But me don't mind, cos I love being with Grammy.'

Tyrese got up and threw his towel on to the chair. It missed and slipped on to the floor. 'Do you ever see your mum any more?' He'd always wondered about this, but his parents had never really explained.

'No. She gone. Left. Don't think she's coming back . . . Anyway,' Marvin said, changing the subject, 'come, Grammy have cooked.'

Knowing exactly how it felt to be made to answer prying questions, Tyrese decided not to say anything else. And almost knocking over the large potted aloe plant in the corner, he followed Marvin along the hallway in silence, noticing the small pinpricks on his finger were beginning to bleed again.

—

'You all right, Ty? Gosh, you look tired, why don't you have a sleep after you've had something to eat?'

His mum was sitting at the kitchen table, which was heaving with food. Why did she always do that? Treat him like a kid in front of people. It was embarrassing.

'Me hope you're hungry, Tyrese. Help yourself,' Grammy said, gesturing towards the ackee and salt fish, callaloo, fried Johnny cakes, plantain and yam.

Tyrese felt his mouth water. He sat down in Grammy's small, whitewashed kitchen, wanting his grammy to think well of him, especially after yesterday. 'Thank you, it looks amazing, I love ackee.'

'Then you'll have to be quick if you want any,' Grammy added. 'Marvin will *nyam* his as well as yours if you're not careful. Him like his food!' She cackled and took a large bite of homemade hard dough bread. 'But I always tell him, *wha' sweet nanny goat a go run 'im belly.*'

'It means, what's nice now, may hurt you later.' Marvin chuckled, his mouth full.

'True. True.' Grammy clapped, delighted. 'Me always used to say dat to your father, Tyrese. Him loved his food too . . .' She paused for a moment, her eyes so full of warmth, Tyrese couldn't hold her gaze. 'Me a tell Marvin earlier how much you look like your father when he was your age. You and Marvin both do. You look less like cousins and more like twins,' Grammy said. She dropped her voice. 'And when me look at you, Ty, it's like your dad's sitting there.'

Tyrese felt his chest beginning to tense again. He held his cutlery tighter, wishing Grammy would stop talking.

'He was one of the brightest stars in the family, you know.' She paused once more and looked serious, then turned to Marvin. 'You see dem eye glass Tyrese wears? Shows him smart, just like him father.'

Marvin giggled and Tyrese couldn't help laughing a little too. He felt the pull in his chest subside.

'They're just glasses, Grammy, it don't mean him smart.'

'Nonsense, dem there cos him read him book,' Grammy said firmly.

Marvin winked at the same time as spooning another large helping of callaloo on to his plate. 'We're going to go to Buff Bay this morning, Ty.'

Grammy tutted. 'Dat was supposed to be a secret, Marvin, you get too excited, me told you not to say anything . . .' She glanced at Tyrese. 'But him right, the whole family are wanting to see you, Tyrese. Everyone's so excited you a here. Dem have a surprise planned.'

Hardly containing his enthusiasm, Marvin bounced up and down in his chair. 'Out and bad, Ty, it's going to be really cool! We'll be able to go on the beach.'

'You know your dad loved surfing at Buff Bay when he was growing up,' Grammy said.

'Can we just stop talking about him all the time?' Tyrese snapped, before he could stop himself.

They fell silent and all that was left was the buzzing and clicking of insects from outside.

Tyrese could see his mum giving him an intense stare, her face flushing redder. This wasn't how today was supposed to go. He knew his mum wanted him to behave, to be happy, to be pleased he was here, but he just couldn't stop the fire building in his chest, the tears threatening behind his eyes.

'Ty, remember what I said about getting upset?' His mum touched his hand gently. 'And what Jonathan said about you getting plenty of rest?'

'I'm fine, I've just got a headache because you opened the window last night. It's probably hay fever,' Tyrese muttered, frowning.

'I didn't come into your room last night. It must have been Grammy.'

Grammy shook her head. 'No, me didn't come into your room.'

'Well, someone did, yeah. I heard them, and the window was wide open this morning.' Tyrese glanced at Marvin, who shook his head too. Then he caught Grammy looking at him strangely, worry rubbed into her eyes.

7

It had just gone eleven o'clock. On the drive to Buff Bay, Tyrese sat in the Jeep jammed between the hot metal door and several large bags packed with Tupperware boxes full of food which Grammy had made. As usual his mum drove far too slowly down the winding, uneven, potholed roads. There were steep drops on one side without any guard rails, and coffee plantations, houses and farms on the other. Rolling mountains rose up like giant waves, surrounding them.

Besides being squashed up he also had to sit listening to countless rounds of his mum, Grammy and Marvin playing *I Spy*. Nobody was able to guess Grammy's object, largely because she'd spied it over forty years ago when she'd been in Kingston. The game went on for ages, their laughter so loud it put Tyrese on edge, like he'd just bitten through a piece of ice, making his headache worse. Then with the game *finally* finished, Grammy and Marvin started talking non-stop: . . .

'Me remember being a young girl, dem always used to say . . .'

'Lawd, what was the name of dat lady who . . .'

'Let me tell you, she a badmind, dat day when . . .'

'Me think she was taller than . . .'

Their conversations just went on and on like a babbling stream. And Tyrese felt ill. Though it was more than that. He still felt weird, almost as though he wasn't quite part of what was going on any more, like he'd stepped outside of himself.

He groaned loudly as the singing started, put his hands over his ears, rolling his eyes. And every time his mum looked at him in the driver's mirror, he turned his head, pretending he hadn't seen.

—

'Pull over here, Patty. It's dat house, there,' Grammy directed, pointing to a large white villa which was surrounded by bright red and yellow flowers and several banana plants.

'You'll meet *all* your other cousins, Tyrese. Me know dat they can't wait to meet you. Hope you still got room in your tummy, dem have been cookin' up a feast for you. Your belly will be rollin'!' Grammy laughed, turning around to look at Tyrese from the front seat.

Everyone got out of the Jeep and carried the bags towards the house, and Tyrese could see the balloons and streamers decorating the garden. There was even a large banner with his name on it tied to the branches of the breadfruit tree.

He threw a glare at his mum. She should've known that he wouldn't have wanted this. She should've told Grammy that he didn't like surprises, not like this, anyway. Not when everyone would want him to talk, to smile, to think, and he didn't want to do any of those things. He couldn't. He didn't want to be asked over and over again if he was all right and told how brave he was.

He stayed back, shook his head. 'Mum, please, do we have to do this? I don't want to see anyone.'

Unfastening the top button of her blouse, his mum smiled. 'Tyrese, you heard Grammy, they're expecting us, and they're excited to see you.'

Tyrese could feel his mouth becoming dry and his heart was pounding faster than if he'd just finished running a race. 'Why didn't you just tell Grammy I wanted to stay at her place, that I didn't want to come here?' he said, trying his best to keep his voice down so Grammy wouldn't hear. He really didn't want to hurt her.

'They'd already arranged the surprise, it would've been rude . . . Look, they've even got a banner with your name on. Oh, and see the balloons over there? Your name's on those, too. Look what they say: *Welcome Tyrese* . . . It's so kind that they've done this for you. Come on, Ty.'

Tyrese walked slowly down the white pebbled path and, as he got nearer, he heard the sound of soft reggae playing in the garden: Ken Boothe's 'Everything I Own'. One of his dad's favourites . . . He frowned . . . Well . . . he thought it was. For some reason he couldn't quite remember properly – suddenly everything seemed muddled in his head, like his mind was sitting in a thick mist.

The music was cranked up louder.

Then just as though a cold wind was blowing, Tyrese trembled. He wanted it to stop. He wanted them to turn off the music and stop. He couldn't do this. He *couldn't.* It was as if the song was spinning him round and round, whirling him back to that day, like he was a time traveller; to the sights and sounds and smell of the airport, to his mum's words when she met him off the plane after his trip to Athens in March. '*Tyrese, I need to tell you something. I'm so sorry but something terrible has happened . . .*'

'What! Wow!' Marvin bounced towards him.

The sudden distraction from his cousin helped Tyrese pull away from the dark well of his thoughts and get back in touch with the here and now. Fighting tears, he took a deep breath, feeling a lump leap into his throat.

'Yes, Ty,' Marvin continued. 'Look at all *dat!* Red snapper, Jerk chicken, rice 'n' peas! Race you to the fruit punch!' Laughing, Marvin set off running towards the glass bowls full of punch, leaving Tyrese standing with his mum. To his side, he heard voices. He looked around and saw a sea of strangers: aunties, uncles, cousins he'd never met, only seen in photographs, all looking at him, smiling, waving; welcoming him, coming towards him, like a wave ready to sweep him away and push him under.

Retreating, Tyrese stepped back, shrinking away from the house and his relatives. 'Mum, I just can't do it. I can't.'

'Ty, please, come on. They're all waiting.'

'Mum, don't make me do this, *please.*' He didn't want to be rude. He didn't want to feel like this, but he couldn't help it. He just wanted it to all go away.

His mum reached out, stroked his face, her bottom lip

beginning to quiver. 'Ty, just come and say hello . . . *Please*, honey. They've gone to a lot of trouble . . . You might enjoy it, and who knows, it could be fun. Sweetheart, will you just try?'

'Sorry, Mum.' He swallowed his tears and he felt like he was falling with no one to catch him. 'I can't . . . I can't . . . Grammy, I'm really, really sorry.'

'Tyrese, ya all right?' Grammy asked, walking towards them.

Before he could stop himself or think about what Jonathan might say, or take in Grammy or his mum's worried expressions, Tyrese turned and started to run towards the bay.

'Maybe I should go after him?' he heard his mum say. 'I don't know how to help him.'

'The boy's just hurting, let him blow it out on his own, Patty. After all, you can't catch a storm.'

—

Sprinting down a narrow sand path, passing the beach hut cafés and kiosks, Tyrese found himself on a deserted part of the beach. He stood by the restless, crystal waters of the Caribbean Sea, holding his breath, trying to stop the cry from deep inside. He covered his face with his arm, screaming into the crook of his elbow: '*I hate you, I hate you, I hate you, I hate you!*' Then he leaned forward, rested his hands on his knees, trying to slow his breathing which panted out noisily, closing his eyes while the warm ocean wind fanned his face.

He thought about the party. He really hadn't wanted to

be rude to anyone, or be ungrateful for the surprise, but he was happier on his own. That was why he preferred being at home so much. He could just lock himself in his bedroom, shut everyone out. He didn't see anything wrong with that, even if his mum and Jonathan did. Although it hadn't always been like that. He'd loved hanging out with people, having fun, talking. But not any more. To Tyrese, everything seemed have begun and ended on that day in March.

His mum had said *this* trip might make him feel better but, if anything, he felt worse. Since he'd woken up this morning, nothing was clear, nothing was making sense. Like life was speaking a different language to him. He didn't even feel like himself any more. It was as though the stitches of a tapestry were unravelling, leaving nothing but a pile of threads.

He hated feeling like this. Why couldn't he just turn back the clock?

He sighed. The blood had rushed to his head and he opened his eyes, blinked away his tears, straightened up. Then, with the sun sitting leisurely in the sparkling blue sky, Tyrese knocked away his thoughts, as he so often did.

Even though the heat was blistering, he took off his trainers and decided to walk along the shore. He certainly didn't want his mum finding him. What would she say when he went back? He didn't even want to imagine.

Heading towards the palm trees at the end of the curved, narrow sloping beach, Tyrese could smell the salty ocean. Smooth blankets of warm air washed over him. The sand was scorching but there was something about the fine stones and dark grey sand running through his toes which he liked. It made him start to relax. He stopped gritting his teeth, unclenched his fists, the tension in his body floating away like petals in the wind.

Walking on, he made his way down another small sandy path, through a grove of palm trees. Although the sea was only a few metres or so away, Tyrese suddenly couldn't hear the waves of the ocean breaking any more and the air was cooler here, cold even, which surprised him. But he welcomed the breeze, listening to the creak of the palm trees overhead as they moved in the wind. Other than the noise from the trees, there was a strange silence, a roaring quiet, as though he were listening into a seashell.

He looked around. Tucked behind the palm trees, on the edge of the beach with an uneven road running behind it, was a brightly painted beach diner with ocean-rusted metal tables and chairs outside. The yellow wooden shutters were closed and the place was empty, although a chalkboard drilled crookedly on to the brick wall listed a wealth of Jamaican dishes.

About to move away, Tyrese glanced around again. Odd how the wind here was beginning to strengthen, because the day had seemed so calm a moment ago. Although it was August, hurricane season, so he guessed storms could start quickly without much warning. He glanced up, watching the sky dull from blue to grey, pillowy dark clouds growing and hovering above him. In the distance he heard the faint rumble of thunder.

'Tyrese. Tyrese.'

He caught his breath. What was that? He was certain he'd just heard his name being whispered. It wasn't his mum's voice. Perhaps she'd asked his relatives to help look for him. Why couldn't everyone just leave him alone? Well, he wasn't going to answer.

'Tyrese. Tyrese.'

His head shot round. That wasn't coming from behind him any more, it was over there by the trees. He peered in that direction, although he couldn't see anyone. Maybe it was just the wind *sounding* like his name. It had to be that. What else could it be? His skin started to prickle. But why, if nobody was there, did he feel like he wasn't alone any more? Like there was someone watching him?

'Ah!' Tyrese let out a loud yelp as he banged his toe on something hard and sharp. Looking down to see what he'd bashed his foot on, he saw a dark object jutting out of the sand. Then he shuddered as a mass of thick, black, squirming centipedes wriggled out from under it.

Kicking them away, Tyrese pulled at the object. He saw it was a box. A rusting metal box. The size his mum kept her jewellery in. He dusted the sand off the top. The metal was dented as though it had been weathered and beaten by the rocks. He quickly glanced around again before starting to pull at the edge of the metal lid, slowly easing it open . . .

8

The lid creaked open. Tyrese gawked at the contents of the box which caused gooseflesh to run up and down his body. Cold fear flushed him hot and cold. He scrambled away, throwing the box on the ground like he was holding a handful of blazing coal.

He fell backwards, dropping hard on to the sand and almost hypnotically he continued to stare. Inside the box was the photograph of him and his dad, the *exact* photograph he'd thrown away down the mountainside near Grammy's. He could see the signs of where he'd furiously scrunched it up . . . How did it get here? What was going on? This must be a joke, right? Somebody's idea of a stupid joke.

His gaze darted around but it soon landed back on the box which was now filled with the writhing, shiny black centipedes. His stomach turned as he watched them start to eat each other.

He edged away some more, though not looking where he was going, he knocked into something.

'Come wid me.'

Tyrese jumped, scrambling around to see a bearded old man glaring, looming over him. His grey hair twisted in thick short locs, his hollow face covered in dirt, his dark eyes dancing with anger.

'Did . . . did my mum send you?' Tyrese muttered, noticing how the old man's yellow stained fingernails were ringed with earth.

The old man laughed, although it was rolled in meanness. His stare fixed tightly on to Tyrese. 'Nuh.'

Alarmed at the way he continued to glare, Tyrese tried to get up but the man pushed him back down, holding on to his shoulder. He struggled, fought to twist out of the grip but it only got tighter. 'Get off me! *Just get off me!*'

Cracked lips smiled at Tyrese. The old man bent his face so close to Tyrese's that he could feel his wiry beard touching his skin, smell the strong sickly odour dancing off his breath like mist.

'Him come, him come and take you.'

Trembling, Tyrese stared back. 'Who? Who will?'

The man released his grip and looked around, whispering his words. 'The Shadow Man.' Then the corners of his mouth turned up into a horrible grin, showing the gaps in his mouth where his teeth had once been. He put out his hand. 'Come wid me.'

Shaking his head, Tyrese started to back away, wondering how he could get up and run without the old man grabbing him again. 'Just stay away from me, yeah? . . . *Stay away*.'

'Him want you. The Shadow Man want you.' Rasping, the old man's hand moved even nearer like a slithering cobra.

'Just leave me alone!'

The man roared with laughter and started to chant, his eyes rolling back.

'*Shadow Man, Shadow Man, him come get you,*

Shadow Man, Shadow Man, him come take you.'

Tyrese took his chance, scrambled up, darted past, running down the path faster than he'd ever run in his life. He stumbled through the grove of palm trees and even though he wanted to see if he was being followed, he was too terrified to look back. Breathing hard, he continued to head along the beach and it was only when he got to the sandy narrow path that he dared to slow down . . .

'Tyrese! Ty!'

Catching his breath, Tyrese looked up and saw Marvin coming towards him, waving. He raised his hand but didn't say anything. His lungs felt on fire. He inhaled deeply through his nose, blew out through his mouth. What had just happened back there? Who was that weird old guy?

Noticing his hand trembling, Tyrese wiped the sweat away from his forehead.

'Ty!' Marvin called. 'You OK, Tyrese? Everything good? Grammy was worried. We all were. Everyone's been looking for you. Where you go?' Firing questions, his cousin came to a stop in front of him. 'You've been gone three hours, you know.'

Still shaking, Tyrese took off his glasses, and used a tissue from his pocket to wipe the grains of sand away which had collected along the bottom of the black plastic rims. 'I didn't know I'd been that long. I'm really sorry.'

Marvin smiled. 'It's OK, you're here now, but Aunt Patty, well, she was crying when she couldn't find you . . . You sure you're all right? *Bwoy*, you look mash-up. Is it your asthma again?'

'Yeah, yeah it is,' Tyrese said, remembering the lie he'd told Marvin earlier. Then he saw his mum running down the path. He groaned to himself. Now he was going to have to face her.

'Tyrese! Ty!' She hadn't come to a stop before she started talking, nagging, fussing. '*Please* don't go off without telling me where you're going. Remember what Johnny said?'

How could he forget? Especially as she reminded him so often. 'Yeah, I know, *I should check in before I check out*,' he said, thinking how much Jonathan's – *Johnny's* – sayings always sounded like a car bumper sticker. He glanced at her. 'But I am sorry, yeah . . . and I'm sorry about the party, I hope I didn't ruin everything, but I . . .' He stopped talking, the photograph in the box springing into his mind. It didn't make any sense. Maybe . . . He searched around in his thoughts for reasons . . . *Maybe* it wasn't the same photo he'd thrown away, after all. Maybe he hadn't looked at it properly and it was just some random photo, not a picture of him at all. Nothing to do with him. Yeah, yeah, that was probably it, and he was just being stupid, letting his imagination mess with his head.

Shrugging, he brought his attention back to his mum. 'I . . . I just needed some space. I *really* didn't realise I'd been gone for so long.'

'OK, but come on, let's go and find Grammy,' his mum insisted. 'She was worried.'

They hurried up the sandy path with Marvin slightly in front of Tyrese but as they went to cross over to the house, Tyrese called out to his cousin. 'Wait! Hey, Marvin! Marvin, wait up . . . What do you know about the Shadow Man?'

Marvin stopped walking. Tyrese noticed his cousin's whole body stiffen as he turned around, a look of dread scraped across his face. 'Where you hear dat name from?' Marvin said in a low voice.

'Er . . .' for some reason Tyrese's stomach tightened like he'd said something wrong and he decided that it was probably best not to say anything about the old man. 'Just someone,' he answered.

His cousin stepped forward, closer, giving a tiny shake of his head, squinting from the dazzling rays of sunlight. 'No one says dat name.'

'What name?' Grammy's voice came from behind Marvin. She looked first at Marvin, then saw Tyrese. 'Oh, Ty. Thank goodness. We were so worried.' Pools of relief welled in her eyes. 'Me so glad to see you're OK. But is dat why you ran off? Him teasing you? Calling you a name?'

She hobbled up to Marvin. 'Is dat what you were doing, mmm?'

Not answering, Marvin looked down at the ground.

'Marvin, me say it again, what name is Tyrese talking about? Don't let me put on me mad hat, Marvin. Speak now!'

Seeing that Marvin wasn't going to answer, Tyrese owned

up. 'It's not his fault. He hasn't done anything . . . I asked him about the Shadow Man, Grammy.'

Grammy held on to Marvin's arm. She stared at Tyrese. He could see the same alarm in her eyes as Marvin had shown. 'Talk and taste your tongue, Tyrese,' she whispered.

Tyrese looked at Marvin, hoping he would explain. Marvin gave a tight smile. 'It means "Think before you speak", Tyrese. No one says dat name, *no one* mentions him . . .'

9

The noisy buzzing and clicking of insects cut through the air as the sun rose. It didn't feel like a Monday and although it was just gone five-thirty in the morning, already the heat felt crushing. The air was hot and dusty and under his mosquito net, Tyrese yawned, listening to the clatter of pots and pans coming from the kitchen. His mum had mentioned how early Grammy got up, and she wasn't kidding. Still, it didn't matter because he couldn't sleep anyway.

His head rested on the large fluffy pillows, clammy sweat sat on the back of his neck as if he'd been training. He'd only slept a little because each time he *did* find himself falling to sleep, he'd shaken himself awake, then lain there thinking about the old man. Thinking how Grammy had got angry when he'd mentioned the Shadow Man and how the journey back to her house had been made in silence, which had been worse than the chatter and games on the way there.

His mum had told him that Grammy was quiet because she'd been worried about him, but it hadn't been worry he'd seen in her eyes when he'd mentioned the Shadow Man, it had been fear. The same fear she'd shown when he'd mentioned the grave on the side of the mountain.

Seeing Grammy so troubled had caused a sense of dread to sit in his heart, and although Tyrese knew he was being stupid, by once more letting his imagination taunt him, he'd lain all night on his wrong side, not wanting to turn towards the window where the dark twisting silhouettes danced, thinking that someone was looking in.

Yawning widely again and stretching, Tyrese felt his foot touch something soft. Puzzled, but feeling too tired and lazy to bother looking at what it was, he moved his toes to feel it again. Something soft . . . feathers? No, because Grammy had put sheets on the bed for him, and not a duvet. A hankie? A sock? No, because he'd had neither.

It baffled him and he pushed himself on to his elbows, kicked off the sheets, looking down towards his feet . . . There was something there, though he couldn't work it out. He prodded whatever it was with his toes. Not liking the sensation, he curled them back almost straight away.

He had no idea what it could be.

Reaching across to the bedside table, Tyrese fumbled for his glasses, grabbed them quickly, sitting up further.

Still puzzled, he leaned forward to get a closer look, then jumped back and tumbled off the bed with a loud thud.

A moment later he heard footsteps coming along the corridor, then a small knock, before the door opened.

'Ty, are you OK? I heard a bang.' Looking to where Tyrese was sprawled, his mum frowned. 'What happened? What are you doing on the floor?'

Tyrese continued to stare at the bed. His mum followed

his gaze. Four curled-up furry bodies with dark powdery wings lay on the crisp, white sheets: dead moths the size of saucers.

'Oh God, look at that!' his mum said, sounding quite chipper.

'Where did they come from?'

His mum picked them off the bed and threw them in the waste paper bin. He hoped she wouldn't see the broken photo frame which he'd chucked in there yesterday. She'd only start complaining.

'I've no idea, Ty. Moths like to hide in dark places, so I guess under the sheets is perfect. *Was* perfect.' She laughed. 'Maybe the smell of your feet killed them off, Ty!'

'That's not funny,' Tyrese flared. They made him feel sick. There were just too many disgusting insects here, another reason why he just wanted to go home.

His mum raised her eyebrows. 'Ty, calm down, I'm only joking.'

The thought they'd been there all night was horrible, but then Tyrese remembered he'd eaten a biscuit in bed last night. He'd shaken the sheets to get rid of the crumbs. They hadn't been there then. So where had they come from? When did they crawl in?

He got up from the floor. 'You don't think it's strange that they're there?'

His mum placed the sheet back on the bed. 'Maybe unpleasant, but not strange. We're in the countryside, Ty, these things happen.'

His mouth was dry. He felt another headache start behind his eyes. Piercing. Burning.

'Don't look like that, Ty. They're only dead moths. OK, big ones, but that's all. Perhaps this room hasn't been slept in for a while and that's why they're in here . . . Anyway, I better go and help Grammy with the breakfast . . . I tell you what, how about you go for a run later, before it gets too hot? You always talked about how good it made you feel.'

He stayed silent, only stared, not wanting to say anything that might turn into an argument.

'Or maybe you and I could go for a walk later,' she continued. 'Explore, perhaps even drive up to the top of the mountains. That would be so much fun. We always used to enjoy hiking, didn't we?'

'It won't be the same, will it?' He bit down on his lip.

Tyrese watched his mum's face drop. Her shoulders slump.

'We still need to do things *together*, Ty . . . make our own memories, that's what Jonathan said, remember?' She paused, twisting the ring on her wedding finger. 'I'm so proud of you Ty, and Dad would be too, if he was here.'

'But that's the thing, Mum, he's not, so how would you know?' he snapped. 'Look, can we just stop talking now?'

'Sweetheart, I know it's hard. I know how you feel.'

He buried his head into the crook of his arm. He didn't want to look at her, he didn't want to look into her eyes, because for some reason it made him cry, and he thought that was stupid and he didn't want to feel stupid, not on top of everything else. 'You don't know how I feel. You don't!'

'Then talk to me, Ty, *please*. Please let me help you. I just want to know you're OK.'

'*That's all you ever ask me!* That's all *anyone* says to me. *Are you OK, Ty, are you OK*, like a thousand million times . . . Well, I'm fine!'

Crying, Tyrese dropped his arm and looked at his mum, picturing her sitting next to him in Jonathan's office, encouraging him to talk about his '*feelings*'. But he hadn't. He'd always just sat looking at the view of Old Trafford football stadium, making himself think about music, homework, gaming, what he was going to have for dinner, *anything* but talk. Pretend what had happened in March wasn't real. That's what he'd told himself, because talking about it made it true, and he really, really *didn't* want what happened in March to be true.

'Ty, I'm sorry . . . Look, why don't we just try to make the most out of being here, hey? It's funny, because the first time I ever came to Jamaica, I remember that your dad—'

'. . . Mum, *stop*!' Tyrese yelled. He scrunched up his face, closed his eyes. 'Why can't you just *stop*? I hate it when you do that! I hate it when you start talking about things I've asked you not to . . . Just *go*. Just get out of my room, Mum! *Get out! Get out! I hate you! I hate you!*'

He opened his eyes in time to see her hurry off, but not before he'd seen the glint of her tears. He clenched and unclenched his fists and kicked the chair, sending it on to its side, spinning across the room. He hadn't meant to upset her. He *really* hadn't. And what was weird was that he didn't *actually* know where that anger had come from. It was as though the anger had been in charge of him, like it had a life of its own.

He'd spoken to Jonathan before about getting upset, annoyed, snapping too quickly, clapping back, being rude, even. 'Puddle jumping', Jonathan had called it. Jumping in and out of his emotions. But he'd never been angry like this before. *Never*. And he hated knowing that he'd made her cry because even though she'd tried to hide it from him, he knew she'd done a lot of crying this year. His stomach lurched at the thought. A wave of nausea washed over him.

He'd never tell anyone this, *especially* Jonathan, who wanted to know everything he was thinking. But her tears, well, they made him feel odd, they made him want to run away. Every time he saw them, he felt scared, helpless, but most of all he felt useless. Useless, for not being able to make things better for her.

Standing in the middle of the bedroom, his chest rose and fell rapidly. He didn't want to think about it. Couldn't.

Sighing, he peeked at the dead moths in the bin, then grabbed his towel off the chair to go for a shower. He might as well, he was wide awake now. But he frowned, noticing the pinpricks on his finger had now become three large pus-filled blisters, looking angry and swollen. They were disgusting, infected, and he still didn't know what had caused them. He squeezed his hand into a tight ball, not wanting to look at his finger any more.

Getting to the door, a soft clunking sound made Tyrese

stop and turn around. He stared in the direction of the noise. He shrank back, watching as the moths appeared at the top of the bin, fluttering their wings as they came crawling out. Then, for some reason, the words of the old man at the beach came rushing back into his head . . .

'*Shadow Man, Shadow Man, him come get you,*
Shadow Man, Shadow Man, him come take you.'

10

'Ty, come! You're too slow! Come, Manchester *bwoy*, is dat all you got!' Marvin rode ahead on his bike and glanced over his shoulder at Tyrese.

'Slow! I don't think so!' Tyrese called back, laughing. He hadn't planned to go on a bike ride with Marvin but when his cousin had suggested it, he'd jumped at the chance. Anything to get away from his mum.

Winds from the night before had broken trees and branches, and jackfruit, ackee and kola nuts lay scattered across the ground from where they'd been picked off the trees by the gusts. Tyrese sped around them, imagining it was an obstacle course, head down, eyes watering, feeling the wind.

Flawless blue skies hung over him and hummingbirds flitted through the forest which stood tall on either side. He pedalled hard, hearing the clang of the bike's chain as it jumped into action. His thighs burned from the effort. The wheels bounced over the rough terrain, his whole body shaken about. Potholes and stones made it hard to go faster and Tyrese felt like he was not only battling Marvin but also the heat which pulled him back, stealing the energy out of him.

'Hey!' Further down the hill where the forest faded on

one side into a grove of banana trees, Marvin came to an abrupt halt in front of Tyrese, the back tyre of his bike lifting up off the ground as he slammed his feet on to the stones. Almost crashing into the back of him, Tyrese looked over to see who Marvin was calling to.

There was a girl on a sandy track by a large clearing. She was short and her pink T-shirt stretched across her rounded tummy, and for some reason she was spinning and twirling around, waving two metallic blue pom-poms about in the air. Her mop of red hair was curled, tied in a satin yellow ribbon under a large white floppy sun hat. And Tyrese wondered why her whole face was covered in thick, white cream.

'Hey yourself, y'all,' she said, panting slightly, smiling broadly.

Marvin pointed to the pom-poms. 'What you ah do?'

The girl – who looked around the same age as them – began to walk over. 'Practising. My dad wants me to get into the cheerleading squad. Apparently, that will make him real proud of me.' She rolled her eyes and gave a half-smile. 'So I set myself a target to practise for at least two hours a day.' Her American accent bounced through her words.

Marvin nodded. 'But how come you're way out here though?'

She pointed down the sandy track. 'There's a construction site along there. Behind those trees. Daddy owns it and he's building a hotel there.'

'*Your* dad's the hotel developer?' Marvin sounded as surprised as the girl suddenly looked.

'You know him?'

'Kind of. He came to our house a couple of times to introduce himself, he wanted to talk to local residents about the hotel he's building, though Grammy wasn't very happy about it.'

'Yeah, he builds hotels all over the world.' She sounded apologetic. 'That's why I'm here. As it's the summer vacation, I just go where he goes. It's his turn to have me.' She shrugged.

Tyrese didn't think she looked very happy about it. But he totally got why. He knew exactly what it was like being forced by a parent to go somewhere.

'Your parents divorced?' Marvin asked.

She shrugged again. 'Since I was a baby. What about you? What are you doing here?'

'Me live here, and my cousin, he's just visiting us . . . Oh, I'm Marvin and he's Tyrese.'

'Ellie-Mae.' She smiled again. 'They're cool. Pretty retro,' she said, looking at their identical red push bikes.

Marvin was glowing with pride. He grinned, his eyes shining as he sat on the bike with its long padded high-back seat, high-rise handlebars and different-sized wheels. 'It's a Chopper. I restored dem myself, dat's what me like to do, restore things.' He smiled shyly. 'They belonged to my dad, and Tyrese's dad when they were young.'

Tyrese flicked a glare at Marvin, though he didn't say anything to his cousin. He just took his hands off the handlebars, and began to count backwards like Jonathan had told him.

'Why you've got dat on your face?' Marvin said, staring at the thick white smudges across her cheeks and around her nose.

From underneath her sun hat, Ellie-Mae laughed. 'My mom got my dad to promise that I wouldn't get bright red and sunburned. She's worried it'll spoil my chances of entering any of the Miss Texas pageants when I get home.'

Sweat dripped into Tyrese's eyes, trickled along the top of his lip and sat in the corner of his mouth. He licked it away.

'So are you going to show us?' Marvin asked.

Ellie-Mae looked at Marvin and crinkled her nose. 'Show you what?'

'The thing you're practising.'

She shuffled her feet, grinding her shoes in the dust. 'I'm not very good. Well, that's what everyone at school keeps telling me.' She pulled a face.

'I'm sure you're great,' Tyrese said warmly.

She laughed. 'I'm not and, you know, I'm OK with that, it's Mom and Dad who seem to get disappointed. I don't even *like* cheerleading, and as for the beauty pageants Mom enters me for . . .' She rolled her eyes again. 'Well, they are not cool at all.'

'So why do it? Do they make you?'

'Nope, but . . .' She looked at Marvin thoughtfully as if she'd never been asked the question before. 'I guess . . . I guess I do it for them really, to please them, make them happy . . . I'd rather be in the wrestling team any day, but I don't think Daddy would like it, I dunno.' She grinned. '*I wouldn't want my princess rolling around and around in a leotard*,' Ellie-Mae said as she impersonated her father. '*Only hogs and hippos roll around on the ground, not young ladies* . . . He also thinks girls aren't any good at wrestling. Go figure!'

'Him right, girls *aren't* good at wrestling, and they definitely wouldn't stand a chance against *any* boy. Even if he's made out of a twig!' Marvin roared with laughter and Tyrese playfully shook his head at his cousin.

Ellie-Mae's eyes lit up. 'Is that so?' She grinned.

Marvin crossed his arms. 'Too true.'

'There's only one way to prove it, Marvin.' She spat on both of her hands then laughed. 'One round. That's all it'll take . . .'

11

Squashed underneath Ellie-Mae, Marvin banged his hand on the ground in defeat. As she began to giggle, so did Marvin. Their peals of laughter rose up into the sky, mixing with the waves of heat. She rolled off him and looked up at Tyrese, who stood chuckling.

'That was *actually* awesome, Ellie. Banging,' Tyrese said, genuinely impressed.

'You want to come and have something to eat with us at my grammy's?' Marvin asked.

Ellie stood, dusting off some soil from her T-shirt. She pointed to herself, which made Marvin laugh. 'Me?'

'Well, who else?'

Ellie's eyes twinkled once more. Tyrese glanced at his cousin, who looked seriously crumpled now, his T-shirt stained with sand and sweat, his trousers covered in grass marks. He looked more like he'd wrestled ten people rather than one.

'For real, Marvin? Really? Yeah, I mean, that would be so cool. No one's ever invited me to their house before.' She shrugged once more.

'We can wait here for you to go and tell your dad,' Marvin added.

Ellie looked behind her at the track leading to the building site, then curled her lip. 'Nah, he won't even notice I'm gone. He's too busy . . . Oh wait, here he is now . . . Daddy?' Wearing a cowboy hat and standing six foot tall with an extra three inches of cowboy boots, Ellie's dad shouted angrily down his phone. '*You said that yesterday, and if I don't have them, make no mistake, I'm going to sue your behind . . .*'

Tyrese watched him. His over-tanned skin was turning pink with annoyance, a muscle in his jaw visibly pulsing as he clenched it, and even his long moustache looked like it was curling with irritation as well.

'Daddy?'

Still on the phone, Ellie's father reached into his trouser pocket, pulled out a large roll of Jamaican dollars and pushed the money in her hand. His small green eyes were piercing. 'Here, take this.' He looked her up and down and shook his head, covering the mouthpiece on the phone. 'Ellie Mae Thomas, what have I told you about keeping yourself looking neat and tidy? You know what your momma's like. She'd be disappointed if she knew I was letting you walk about looking like that . . .' He waved her away, concentrating again on his phone call, his accent as strong as his daughter's. '. . . *I need to know what the hell is happening about these shipments . . .*'

Ellie's shoulders dropped. Tyrese watched her glance down at her clothes; her pink T-shirt along with her elastic-waist shorts were covered in dust. 'I don't want money, Daddy. I said, *I don't want money*!' She raised her voice to be heard over his phone call. 'I just want to go to their house. Can I go to Marvin's house?'

He nodded, not really listening, giving Tyrese and Marvin the quickest of smiles as if he was saving on time. Then he stopped, frowned, and stared at Tyrese, then at Marvin before looking firmly at his daughter, clicking his fingers several times to gesture Ellie over.

He covered the mouthpiece of the phone again with his hand. 'Hang on, young lady, you can't just go off with people. For a start I don't know where you're . . .' Though Mr Thomas suddenly trailed off as he regarded Marvin properly. Tilting his head, he frowned even deeper, wagging his finger at him. 'Remind me.'

'I'm Mrs Walker's grandson. The bright green house at the top by the stream, you came to see my grammy about—'

'. . . shrimp curry,' Mr Thomas interrupted. 'That's right, isn't it? Now I remember. Of course. She might've hated the hotel plans, but my God, she served me up the best shrimp curry I have ever tasted. How is your grammy by the way?'

'Oh she's . . .'

'. . . *So I don't want to listen to any more bull about why I haven't got this damn shipment and let me be clear* . . .' Mr Thomas launched back into his phone conversation, leaving Marvin's reply hanging.

'So, Daddy, can I go to Marvin's? Daddy?'

Mid-tirade, Mr Thomas just nodded, dismissively waving Ellie away again.

Tyrese blinked, the sun streamed into his eyes. He turned, staring into the dense forest, hearing Ellie's dad shout down the phone as he marched off.

'Parents can suck,' Ellie muttered.

Marvin kissed his teeth. 'Yep, mine can.'

She giggled. 'What about your parents . . . Tyrese?'

Tyrese didn't answer, he kept his stare focused on the forest, forcing himself to take a step closer to where the trees met the path. He rubbed his head, the sharp pain of his headache returning. He listened as hard as he looked. Like yesterday on the beach, everything felt too still. And the smell . . . It was the same as in the forest above Grammy's. Bitter, like old wood smoke from a fire. So weird.

He looked at the branches of the trees, which were bent and twisted together, forming peculiar shapes. Even though it was barely midday, it seemed like a darkness had wrapped round him, the shadows of the forest creeping out to touch, and once again, it was if someone he couldn't see was watching him.

He pulled his gaze away from the trees, took a deep breath and turned to Ellie, feeling the effort of his smile. 'What were you asking me?'

'I was just asking, what about your parents, are they cool?'

Tyrese thought about how annoyed he'd got with his mum earlier, but he simply shrugged his shoulders. 'Yeah, my mum's great, though she does treat me like a baby, which drives me crazy.'

'What about your dad?'

Ignoring the question, Tyrese turned and hopped on his bike, riding away up the hill.

—

It was over half an hour later that they neared Grammy's house. The journey had taken *so* much longer than they'd expected. The heat felt like it was driving them back as if it were a gust of wind and the mountain track they'd sped down earlier, now seemed impossibly steep.

'Are you sure you don't want a ride, Ellie?' Tyrese asked as he pushed his bike along the potholed track. 'You can.'

'Thanks, but actually . . .' She sounded embarrassed and looked shyly at Marvin and Tyrese. 'I don't know how to. Mom and Dad were always too busy to teach me. But I don't mind if you guys want to ride on ahead.'

'No way, we wouldn't leave you. But I can't even call my mum to come and pick us up,' Tyrese said, part apology, part gripe. 'I haven't had a signal since I've got here. What's the point in having a phone if it doesn't even work?'

'I prefer it. I like that no one can contact me,' Ellie answered.

Tyrese was surprised. Although he'd pulled away from most, if not *all* of his friends this year, that didn't stop him liking the ping of notifications from social media, letting him know what was going on. But now, he didn't even have that.

Flicking off some sort of yellow bug which had landed on his hand, he gave Ellie a sideward glance. 'Why?'

'It stops the kids in my new school sending me messages,' she said, her Texan accent stronger than ever.

'Like what?'

'You know, poking fun, making nasty memes about me, saying stuff on Facebook. Just throwing shade. So I don't ever want to get a cell signal again.'

She laughed nervously and Tyrese glanced back at Ellie. 'I'm sorry, that's horrible.'

She smiled gratefully and they continued in silence for a while, with Tyrese still trying to shake off the feeling that someone was watching.

'Wait, hold up.' Marvin came to a sudden stop by a long stony path which ran alongside a stretch of large juniper trees. He looked excited. 'Me want to show you something, Ty. Come.'

'Seriously, if it means walking even further, yeah, count me out. I just want to get back. I feel like I'm going to melt.'

Marvin grinned, his dimple on his cheek prominent. 'Come on, Manchester *bwoy*, it's not dat hot.' He winked. 'It won't take long. It's down here.'

Tyrese laid his bike on its side. He and Ellie followed Marvin, walking along the mountain path, thankful for the shade from the dense trees which formed a canopy as though it were a green painted ceiling above them.

They battled through a sea of plants and trees until they came to an exposed rock face.

'*There*,' Marvin announced, looking delighted. 'See there,

Ty. Those initials are our dads', Nathan Walker and Linford Walker . . . Grammy told me every year they'd come here and write their name and the date. It was their secret place . . . And even as adults, every time your dad visited Grammy, they kept up the tradition.' Marvin grinned. 'See dat one, dat's from when they were kids. It's dated thirty-five years ago.'

Tyrese stared at the craggy rock of the mountain. All over it was graffiti. Dates. Initials. He stepped forward, put his hand on it, and sharply drew breath.

He closed his eyes and even though it should've been cold to the touch, Tyrese felt a warmth in his hand, imagining his dad writing on it. And just for the briefest of moments, he didn't feel like he was touching the rock – Tyrese could feel his dad's hand touching his, palm to palm.

He gasped.

'Ty, Ty, are you OK?' Marvin asked after a moment.

Tyrese pulled his hand away, tucked it under his arm. 'Yeah, I'm fine,' he said breathlessly.

'This is so cool. Look at that one,' Ellie uttered. 'It was done at the end of last year, but whose initials are they?' She pointed.

'They're *mine*. Mine, Mum's . . . and Dad's.' Tyrese swallowed hard. 'He must have done them on his last visit,' He stepped even nearer, peering at it in detail. His stomach knotted as he touched and traced the letters gently with his fingers.

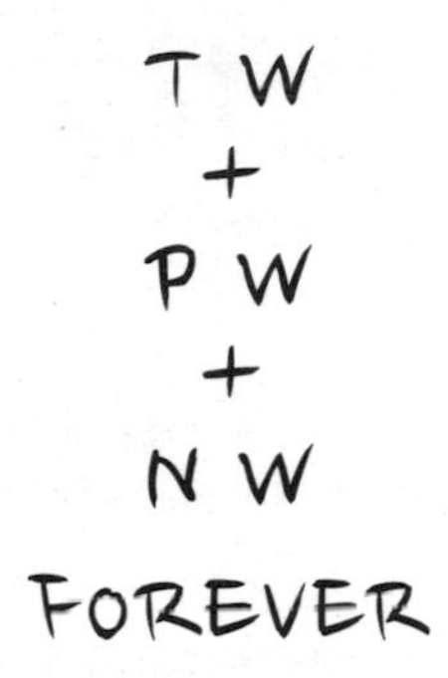

He quickly pulled his hand away again: his body jolted and he gritted his teeth, feeling like a paper ball had scrunched up inside of him. Backing away from the rock face, a storm rumbled through his veins. 'This is stupid, look at it. It's just some dumb writing. Let's go.'

'I think it's lovely,' Ellie said. 'Where's your dad now?'

Tyrese stared at her hard, gulped down his sharp words, then marched off, though it didn't stop him hearing Marvin and Ellie talking behind him.

'Is he all right, Marvin? Did I say something wrong?'

'No. It's OK.'

'So why's he upset?'

'Ty's dad died in March, and he doesn't like to talk about him.'

12

Brushstrokes of cloud streaked the sky. Exhausted, but finally at Grammy's, Tyrese rested his bike against the broken white fence. The strong minty pine scent of eucalyptus sat in the air.

He couldn't get the graffiti out of his head. Why did Marvin have to go and show him that, what was the point? Had his cousin *really* thought he'd want to see it? Ellie had said it was lovely, but there was nothing lovely about it, about here, about anything. All he really wanted to do was forget.

'And you're sure your grammy won't mind me coming for lunch?' Ellie looked between Marvin and Tyrese.

Marvin beamed broadly at her. 'No, she'll be happy to feed you. And like your dad says, Grammy cooks the *best* shrimp curry in the whole of Jamrock!' Marvin laughed. 'Come.'

Ellie followed him into the house with Tyrese trailing behind, the storm still brewing inside him.

'Grammy, me have a visitor for you . . . *Grammy*!' Marvin called loudly.

Grateful to be greeted by the cool air in the house and the smell of Grammy's cooking drifting along the hallway, Tyrese walked down the hallway, looking forward to that first sip of ice-cold ginger punch.

They made their way to the kitchen where Grammy was just finishing mopping the cream vinyl floor tiles. His mum was putting some dishes away, quietly humming to herself.

'This is Ellie-Mae, her dad is building the hotel down the hill. Oh, and he thinks your curry is the best ever and now Ellie wants to taste it,' Marvin said enthusiastically, jumping over Grammy's mop towards the fridge, and bringing out a large pot of rice and curry. He put it on the side. 'Oh, this is my grammy, Ellie.'

Grammy plonked herself down in the chair, rubbing her swollen legs. 'Well, it's a pleasure to meet you, Ellie-Mae.'

'And this is Aunt Patty, Ty's mum,' Marvin added.

'Lovely to meet you, Ellie-Mae.'

'Thank you, it's lovely to meet you too.'

'Is that a Texan accent I hear?' Tyrese's mum said, her eyes shining.

'It is, ma'am. I'm from Austin, Texas.' Ellie sounded as proud as she looked.

'Ellie's a wrestler. She's really good,' Marvin boasted.

Taking a sip of water from the glass on the side, Tyrese's mum smiled. 'Really? That sounds like it must be fun.'

'It's one of my favourite things to do. That and math,' Ellie said, twirling the ends of her red hair between her fingers.

'Maths?' Tyrese's mum's laugh gently drifted around the kitchen. 'Well, you're a girl after my own heart then, Ellie. I read mathematics and physics at university. That's where I met Tyrese's dad.'

Tyrese looked down at his trainers.

'Was he doing math too?'

'No, chemistry. We actually met when we joined the university rowing club, neither of us were very good though, so in the end we joined the sailing club . . . Now *that* was fun.' Tyrese glanced at his mum and he saw her beaming, it was almost like he could see the memories replaying in her eyes.

'In fact, we loved it so much, we spent our honeymoon sailing around the Caribbean islands. Anyway . . .' His mum quickly took another sip of water and he noticed her hands were trembling.

Ellie stood shyly by the entrance of the kitchen next to Tyrese, until Marvin waved her in.

'Make sure you pile her plate up good, Marvin, give her some plantain while you're at it, but wash your hands first . . .' Grammy fussed warmly. 'Ty, come and sit down.'

Tyrese smiled at Grammy but then he did a double take, inhaling sharply, folding his arms tightly against his body. 'Why have you got those out? I didn't even know you'd brought them with you.' He glared at his mum, who was now standing by the small, plastic fan, looking like she was trying to stop herself from melting.

She glanced in the direction of the scrapbooks lying on the table. 'I just thought they'd be nice for Grammy to see, don't you think?'

Stealing a quick look at Grammy, Tyrese knew it was a question he didn't want to answer. There was no way he wanted to upset Grammy again, but he didn't think it was anywhere near nice. His mum had no right. How could she? He didn't want *anyone* looking at them. They were *his* scrapbooks . . . his and Dad's. He'd hidden them at the back of his wardrobe at home, which meant she'd gone into his room without asking even though he'd pinned a sign on his door saying *Private*.

He glanced again at Grammy, who saw him looking. She gently placed her fingers on the books. 'There are some lovely photos in there, Ty. And all those articles you've saved about the charity walks you and your dad did, well, dem a wonderful. And you both raised all dat money for the hospital dat always looked after him so well! Gosh, me so proud of you. How much did you raise altogether?'

Tyrese could almost feel the anger towards his mum entering his body. His face began to tingle and his throat felt dry. This was all her fault.

'Tyrese. Your grammy's talking to you. Don't be rude, please.' His mum gave him a curt nod.

His heart beat faster. 'I [illegible] er . . .' He shrugged.

'*Tyrese*' His mum prompted him again. 'Tell Grammy.'

He tried to think. It was so weird: he couldn't actually remember how much it was. But how was that possible, he'd even been presented with a jumbo-size cheque and his photo had gone in the paper, hadn't it? Even *that* seemed unclear. It was like he was peering through fog.

He rubbed his temples. 'I can't remember.'

'Don't be silly, you know exactly how much you raised, Ty.'

But he didn't. He *didn't* know and he couldn't even start to guess how much it was.

'The heat makes me forget too. Dat, and old age,' Grammy said warmly. 'Don't worry, Ty.'

Tyrese stared at his mum, she stared back and they stayed silent. He ran his tongue along his teeth as if he was wiping the swear word he was thinking out of his mouth. He didn't understand why he'd forgotten how much he'd raised, but he didn't understand either why his mum had thought it was all right to take his personal belongings. He muttered under his breath, 'They were private. You didn't even ask me.'

'Let's not do this now, Ty,' his mum said calmly, smiling at Ellie, who smiled back widely. 'But I'm sorry, Ty, OK? Though I'm sure your dad would have wanted us to show them to Grammy.'

'*Don't!* Don't say that! You don't know!'

There was a tense hush and only the stove-top coffee maker hissing away on the low flame made a sound.

Tyrese blinked and he was surprised at how loud his voice had been. He hadn't meant to shout. He moved his gaze to Ellie. 'Ellie, I'm sorry.'

Ellie smiled but she didn't say anything. Gently, Grammy picked up the scrapbooks from the table, holding them out for Tyrese. 'Here you go, why don't you put dem back in your mother's room, darlin'. And maybe you'll be kind enough to show me some other time and talk about all those marvellous things dat you've done.'

He mouthed a silent *Thank you* to Grammy before scurrying out of the kitchen.

13

Holding the leather-bound scrapbooks, Tyrese stomped through the back door. He dropped them with a bang on the decking, then threw himself on to the swing bench which was just below the window of his room. Swiping the cushion off the swing, he kicked his heels down on the white painted bench and lay there panting, listening to the song of the insects, losing himself in his thoughts.

Minutes passed before he started to feel calmer and he slowly sat up, picked up one of the scrapbooks, placing it in his lap. He hadn't looked at it since . . . well, for a long while now. And taking a long, deep breath, Tyrese opened the book at the first page.

Blinking rapidly, he gazed at the headline of the small cut-out newspaper article he'd stuck in so carefully. It was dated only ten months ago.

Hero father and son raise money for local hospital

Tyrese read on, ignoring the slight catch in his breathing, the prickle at the back of his eyes. He touched the clipping and found himself having to chew on his lip to stop the tears.

His dad had been in and out of hospital all his life for routine procedures and check-ups, nothing Tyrese had ever been concerned about. His dad's blood disorder had been so much a part of their lives that when his dad had told him he was going into hospital that final time, he hadn't really dwelled on it. He'd assumed everything was going to be all right. And now, now nothing was all right.

He held his head, rocking, willing his thoughts to disappear. He didn't want to think about it. He didn't want to picture that day. Angrily, he wiped his eyes, glancing back down at the scrapbook on his lap. This was stupid, why was he even looking at it?

He threw it back down on the decking and pulled a face as he watched a large coiled black centipede come squirming out from underneath the other scrapbooks. Almost immediately, he jerked his head around: he could smell smoke again. That was weird, where was it coming from? He knew Grammy hadn't lit a fire and there were no other houses for miles around, yet the stench was so strong.

Once more he smelled the air, then realised it was coming from his room.

Careful to keep his balance, Tyrese kneeled up on the swing, peeking through his bedroom window. Plumes of thick, dark smoke crept through the gap between the doors of his wardrobe, twisting out like writhing serpents. 'Oh God! Fire! *Fire!*' he bellowed, jumping off the swing, sprinting back into the house and into his room. 'Help! Help! Mum! Grammy!'

'Tyrese, what's going on? Tyrese? Ty!' A mixture of his mother's voice and his grammy's came from behind him.

Breathless, he spun around to look at them, pointing towards the wardrobe. 'Fire! Quickly!'

'What, where, Ty?'

'There . . . there . . . In the . . .' But he trailed off as he looked back at the wardrobe. No smoke. No flames. No smell of burning. 'I . . .' He spun on his heels to stare at his mum. 'I saw smoke coming out of it. *I did.*' He ran across and flung open the wardrobe doors. It was empty. What was going on? He couldn't understand it. There was smoke. There was, there *was*. He knew what he saw, what he smelled. Then he thought of something.

'The jacket. The jacket's gone.'

'What jacket, Ty?' Grammy asked.

'The light blue pinstripe jacket of Da . . . Da . . .' It felt like the word was burning his tongue.

'Of your dad's?'

'Yes,' Tyrese spluttered, wiping his tears and runny nose on his sleeve.

Grammy's eyebrows knitted together in a frown. She glanced quickly at Tyrese's mum, then looked back at Tyrese. 'There's never been a jacket in there, Ty,' she said softly.

'But I saw it! I saw it, Grammy. It was his jacket. The jacket he married Mum in. It's the one in all their wedding photos.'

'Ty.' His mum spoke almost in a whisper. 'That's impossible, sweetheart . . . that was the jacket your dad was buried in.'

Tyrese could feel his head beginning to pound and he put his hands over his face. 'No, no, don't say that!'

'Ty, baby, I'm only saying that because you must have got mixed up, maybe . . .'

'. . . Maybe what, Mum? Because it was there! *It was!* I know what I saw.' He dropped his hands and stared at his mum but he held them together to stop her seeing him trembling. Once again he felt strange, like he was half awake, half asleep. He didn't know what was happening to him and all he wanted to do was be back in the safety of his bedroom.

His mum looked at him sadly, touching his forehead. He jumped away.

'Oh my God, I'm *not* ill, Mum! I haven't got a temperature!'

'I just think that you're not sleeping properly, Ty, and that makes a difference. You know it's a well-known fact that if you *don't* get enough sleep, you get irritable, lose concentration, and you can also hallucinate as well, start seeing things that aren't there. How much *have* you slept in the last couple of weeks, Ty?'

He caught a glimpse of Marvin and Ellie looking at him from the doorway of his bedroom and felt a wave of embarrassment. 'I dunno, maybe only a couple of hours a night,' he muttered truthfully.

His mum's eyes turned a deeper blue, clouding with concern. 'Oh, Ty, that would do it. No wonder you're feeling strange and seeing things. No one could survive on that little sleep. None of this is real, baby.'

He could tell by the way she was looking at him that she

wouldn't believe him, no matter what he said. It felt like he couldn't think straight any more. What was happening to him? He knew what they must think of him. Maybe his mum was right, how could it be real if no one else saw it? And like night creeping in, snatching away the light, doubt began to darken and overshadow Tyrese's thoughts. In that moment, he realised he no longer knew what was real and what wasn't any more.

—

It had gone dark, and with Marvin, Ellie and Tyrese having helped Grammy prepare the vegetables and marinate some goat meat for tomorrow's stew, Tyrese stood alone on the porch to get away from all the chatter.

Beads of sweat sat around his neck. His heart beat too fast, his legs twitching as though he'd been chilled by a crisp December morning. He took a long deep breath in and leaned forward, pressing his head against the wooden pillar of Grammy's porch, feeling the splinters rub against his skin.

The sound of the tree frogs and crickets filled the air, while the cicada bugs screamed a noise so shrill his headache pounded all the more, sharp and painful, making him feel sick.

From where he was standing, Tyrese could see tiny flashes of light flickering in the forest: fireflies, looking like someone was turning fairy lights on and off.

Letting out a sigh, he massaged his temples. His anger towards his mum was still there, whirling silently in the background of his mind.

While they'd been having supper, Grammy had whispered

in his ear, '*Quarrel never has a good word.*' He didn't want to quarrel, but he didn't want to feel like this, either. He just wanted to feel like he used to.

Tears pricked as a reminder of how life had changed and he quickly gulped down a sob, not wanting anyone to hear. Once again Tyrese wished he was back at home, alone in his room, shutting everyone out. Shutting out that day. Shutting out the last time he'd seen his dad alive . . .

'Tyrese, your mum's taking Ellie home now.' Grammy and his mum appeared with Ellie and Marvin behind them, talking together like old friends as Marvin excitedly told Ellie all about the different bikes and mechanical toys he'd salvaged and restored.

'Ty, you all right?' His Grammy stared at him, sounding worried.

'Yeah . . . I've just got a headache. I think Mum's right, I am tired.'

'Then you stay here with Grammy, Marvin and I'll drive Ellie back,' his mum suggested warmly.

Tyrese's nod came before his words. 'OK, but, Ellie . . .' He paused, pushing up his glasses and feeling awkward. 'I'm *really* sorry about before. And I was thinking, why don't you get your dad to drop you off tomorrow, then maybe Marvin and I could teach you to ride our bikes?'

'Really? I mean, wow, wow that would be amazing. Sure.' Ellie's face seemed to light up as much as the fireflies. 'Thank you . . . and you don't need to apologise, it's cool, I get it.'

They turned to go, but Grammy beckoned his mum back.

'Patty! Patty! Make sure you do your windows up when you drive Ellie home.'

His mum smiled. 'Why?'

'It's dark.' Grammy's tone was serious. She glanced up at the night sky and the dappled silver crested moon gazed down at them. 'The backroads here in Jamaica are well-known to be hunting grounds of duppies. Though you might be all right, the moon a shine bright tonight, and a lot of them are afraid of it.'

Although he was exhausted, Tyrese grinned. 'Hunting grounds, Grammy!'

'It's not a joke, Tyrese,' Grammy said firmly, 'let me tell you, there's nothing funny about a duppy.'

She pursed her lips and Tyrese spluttered out a melody of laughter. He hugged Grammy hard, and she hugged him back before she hobbled inside.

'I'll see y'all tomorrow then,' Ellie called, getting into the car with Marvin

'Yeah, see you.'

Tyrese watched his mum drive away, the lights of the Jeep fading into the night, and for some reason the broken, hidden grave on the mountainside trickled into his mind.

He stared round. It seemed like the forest had darkened suddenly, the fireflies vanished and the insects silenced. He shivered, hurrying inside after Grammy.

14

A few minutes after his mum had left with Marvin and Ellie, Tyrese decided to get ready for bed. His headache had worsened and the crushing pain drove down from the top of his skull to behind his eyes, feeling like it was attacking the bones in his face. He'd never had migraines before, only since he'd come to Grammy's.

He sat on the edge of his bed, listening to the sound of a welcome rainstorm, but it was still unbearably hot. Yet again he could feel the tingling of sweat on the back of his neck, a coating of perspiration on his stomach. The only part of the house which seemed to feel cool was the floor. He wriggled his feet against the cold tiles, enjoying the feeling.

Trying to empty his mind from unwanted thoughts, Tyrese glanced up, watching a small fly land and go round and round on the blades of the ceiling fan. Then he watched the silk tree branches – like fingers – tapping at the window while the wind groaned, rattling the panes like it was trying to get in.

He looked about the cream-painted room. Although the furniture was old, Grammy kept everything neat and tidy, pretty. A large blue sewing box sat in the corner with an unfinished crocheted scarf lying on top. He'd lost count of the scarves she'd sent him: red ones, blue ones, pink and yellow ones, so many. *Why you live somewhere so cold? This is to keep you from freezing, Tyrese,* she'd written in her letters. It was as though Grammy was worried Manchester would turn him into a block of ice.

He smiled to himself but flinched at the sight of a large, thick centipede slithering quickly across the floor.

'*Tyrese, Tyrese.*'

Tyrese whirled round, peering out into the darkness to where the voice had come from.

'*Tyrese.*'

A chill clutched at his throat; the voice no longer sounded like it was coming from outside, but from within the room. His body froze and he only dared to move his eyes.

'*Tyrese, Tyrese.*'

His heart lurched, fear spiked and whined inside him.

He held his breath.

Something had just touched his leg . . . There it was again, the smallest of touches, brushing slowly against his ankle. He sat motionless. Then a thin gasp seeped from him as he felt the mattress underneath him lifting up . . .

. . . No, *no*, no, he had to stop himself from doing this. He was just being stupid. It was his mind playing tricks again. It was probably that disgusting centipede he'd just seen, crawling on the back of his leg, and as for the mattress, well, he obviously just imagined it. There was no one here and he was going to prove it. He was going to *prove* to himself he knew what was real and what wasn't. He was going to prove he wasn't beginning to lose his mind.

Sliding off the mattress, Tyrese kneeled on the floor, bending forward to peer under the bed.

The old man from the beach stared back at him.

'Tyrese, child of the Shadow Man, child of the darkness, what will you give him when him come take you?' Baleful laughter spewed out, his mouth leaking with drool. His gnarly hand, bulging with veins, gestured towards Tyrese. His grin widened, spreading across a thin-fleshed face, rotted and hollow. His eyes were sunken into their sockets, and they had no pupil – only the whites remained. Still, they seemed to glare sightlessly at Tyrese. He rasped and cackled.

'*Shadow Man, Shadow Man, him come get you,*
Shadow Man, Shadow Man, him come take you.'

Struggling to breathe, too terrified to move, Tyrese opened his mouth to shout for help but nothing came out. The old man's hand reached nearer, the tips of his broken yellow fingernails grazing across the back of Tyrese's arm.

Managing to scramble away, Tyrese pushed himself against the wall.

A noise from the hallway: Grammy singing outside the door.

'Grammy! Grammy! Help me! *Help!*'

The door swung open and Grammy, clutching her peach-coloured night robe around her, hurried in. 'Tyrese, Ty? Lawd have mercy, what's happened?'

'There's someone under the bed.' His voice shook, his words a hush. 'The old man's under the bed, Grammy.'

Grammy blinked, a vertical wrinkle appearing between her eyebrows. Her mouth hung open loosely but she quickly composed herself and glanced towards the bed. 'No, darlin', there's nothing there, except a whole heap of fresh air.'

Tyrese tugged at his pyjamas, shook his head. 'There is, *there is*.'

'No, Ty. Look, let me show you then,' Grammy said, reassuringly shuffling across the room, reaching for the cotton bed sheet.

He grabbed her arm. A piercing scream left his mouth: 'No, Grammy, don't, don't! *Please.* He's under there. He's under there.'

'Oh, darlin'.' And she bent down and lifted up the sheet. 'Look, nothing, Tyrese.'

Tyrese stared. All he could see was the wall on the other side and a pair of trainers he'd kicked under there. 'But he was, he *was* there, Grammy! You've got to believe me, he was there.'

'Well, darlin', there's nothing there now, Ty.'

She sat on the bed and Tyrese continued to kneel on the floor. 'What's happening to me? What's happening, Grammy?' Tears dripped into his lap. 'Help me, Grammy, please help me.' He felt her stroke his head.

'Oh, Ty, tell me what's going on.'

'I can't, I can't.'

Grammy leaned forward and wiped his tears with the palm of her hand. 'Ty, you don't have to deal with what happened to your dad on your own, darlin'. Your mum and me are here. Don't let that storm inside destroy you.'

He stared into her eyes. 'But I don't want to think about it, none of it. And the last time I saw Dad just goes round and round in my head, Grammy. I wish I could go back and change things, if only I could've shown him, told him that . . .' He stopped, unable to think about it any more and buried his face in his hands. Tears seeped through his fingers.

'Oh, Ty, *please* talk to me.'

'Talking won't change things though, will it?'

'No, not the past, but how you see the present, Ty, how you see yourself, how you walk into the future . . . *Di darkes part a di night, a when day soon light.*'

Tyrese looked at her for an explanation.

'The darkest part of the night is when daytime is coming. It means, there's hope even in the darkest of hours, the light will come. Don't give up, Ty.' Grammy's eyes glinted with the beginning of tears. 'Me know it hurts but don't run from your feelings, Tyrese, because wherever you run, darlin', dem will be there waiting for you.'

He tapped his head. 'In here, Grammy, everything feels so messed up.' Then he covered his face with his hands again, unable to look at her but his words rushed out. 'I don't know what's going on any more. I know it's stupid but I'm scared – but I don't really know of what, and all these weird things are happening, yeah. I don't know how to stop it. I can't tell what's real any more. Like the old man, Grammy, the old man and that rhyme.'

'What rhyme, darlin'?' She pulled his hands gently away from his face and helped him on to the bed next to her.

'The Shadow Man, he's coming to take me.'

Grammy swayed slightly, clutching tighter on to Tyrese's hand.

'Hello, we're back!'

Tyrese heard his mum calling from the hallway. 'Please don't tell Mum about this, she'll only worry. *Please*, Grammy.' He grabbed her hand.

Grammy didn't answer. A deep frown was carved into her brow.

'Grammy?'

'Sorry, darlin', I . . . I . . .' She sounded breathless and once more Tyrese could see fear in her eyes, and noticed she was trembling. 'What . . . what did you say?'

He shook his head. 'Nothing.'

Looking distracted, Grammy, kissed him on his cheek, got up, hurried towards the window, twisting and locking the bolts on the window frame.

'What are you doing, Grammy?'

'Nothing for you to worry about, Ty,' she said hesitantly, 'just . . . just keeping us all nice and safe . . . now come, get some rest.'

Grammy left the room and Tyrese glanced across to the bolts on the window. A sharp fear pierced into his heart. He listened to the sound of Grammy's slippers swishing away along the corridor and he fought to keep his mind away from the old man. Then for some reason Tyrese found his thoughts drifting back to that day in March when he and his mum had driven home from the airport in the car. The day he'd found out.

He'd felt numb, he'd felt lost, he'd felt pain, he'd felt unable to breathe, he'd felt an indescribable ache, a feeling he didn't even know was possible. And his stomach twisted as he remembered his mum's tears along with his screams, which he could almost still hear . . .

'You should've called me! Why didn't you just phone me, Mum, and tell me? I would've flown back, I could've come home.'

'Ty, I did what I thought was best, I didn't want to tell you when you were in Athens, and I certainly didn't want you to fly back having to deal with this on your own. I thought it was better to wait. I'm sorry, Ty, I was trying to protect you. And Dad and I both knew how important this competition was to you. He would've wanted you to stay.'

'But you should've told me sooner, Mum! You should've told me. I shouldn't have been running some stupid race instead of coming home.'

'Honey, I just wanted you to have a couple more carefree days, and coming home wouldn't have made a difference, it was already too late, Dad's heart attack was so severe, he'd died within minutes.'

'Stop, stop, stop! Don't say that! I hate you! I hate you!'

. . . But the truth was he didn't hate her. Tyrese hated himself. He hated how he felt. He hated thinking about the last conversation he'd had with his dad, but above all else, he hated not having him around.

He fought his scream, pushing out all thoughts but then he noticed his bed sheet was smeared with red and realised the three unhealed blisters on his finger had popped and were once more trickling with blood . . .

15

The early morning sky held shades of bright blue. Tyrese, Marvin and Ellie stood by Grammy's small guava orchard on the wide track behind her house. Tyrese smiled, trying to pretend everything was fine. His mum had commented at breakfast about the dark circles under his eyes – she'd wanted him to go back to bed. But he knew he wouldn't have been able to go to sleep and he hadn't wanted to just lie there thinking. Even now he was fighting to keep his thoughts focused on what he was supposed to be doing.

'Are you sure you're all right, Ty?' Ellie asked. 'You're not saying much.'

'I'm fine. Thanks,' he said, hoping he didn't sound like he was snapping at her, especially after what had happened yesterday.

'You don't have to do this if you don't want to.'

Tyrese smiled again but his head was beginning to throb. He wanted to seem normal, be normal, act normal, but he felt far from normal. It was like he wasn't quite here, as if he was watching himself through a window. 'Really, it's OK . . .'

'But I don't want you to—'

'. . . Ellie! Just *stop. Please,*' Tyrese cut in, sharper than he'd wanted to. 'I said I'm fine, so just please, *leave* it, yeah.' There was an awkward silence, then, trying to sound cheerful but thinking he sounded *way* too high-pitched, he added, 'Anyway, are you ready? Shall we do this?'

Ellie glanced between Tyrese and Marvin, then carefully sat on the bicycle which they were holding for her. Her eyes twinkled and she positioned herself on the seat.

'Hands on the handlebars, and for now keep both feet on the ground.' Tyrese smiled. 'You comfortable?' Marvin asked.

She nodded, grinned broadly, looked at Tyrese from underneath her floppy sun hat while Tyrese bent down beside her, winding the foot pedals to the perfect point.

'Now put your foot here and whatever you do, just keep pedalling. Got it?' Tyrese said.

'Got it.' Ellie stuck her tongue out in concentration, frowning, and started to pedal.

The bike lurched forward, and Tyrese and Marvin ran along on either side of her, holding the seat to steady the bike.

Breathlessly, Marvin yelled, 'When we let go, keep pedalling.'

'Don't let go!' Ellie screamed in laughter.

Tyrese and Marvin ignored her and let go anyway.

'Keep going, Ellie! That's it! You can do it!' Tyrese yelled, watching the bike wobbling over the bumpy stony path. 'You've got it! Keep going, keep going!'

'Yo, Ellie, you look good!' Marvin hollered.

But unexpectedly Ellie swerved – avoiding a fallen mango

tree branch – and fell with a hard bang in an awkward heap on the ground. Tyrese sprinted across to her. 'You OK?' he asked, noticing the graze on her knee. 'You did great though, look at how far you got.' Smiling, he pulled her up.

Grabbing her hat off the floor, Ellie rubbed her knees and elbows. 'I don't know if I can do this, y'all, look at me.'

Marvin snorted. 'Well, I guess your daddy's right: girls aren't good at wrestling and it looks like dem aren't good at riding bikes either.' He winked, eyes full of mischief, and burst into laughter. 'Come, wrestling queen, try again. You got this, Ellie.'

Over the next half hour, Ellie tried and fell off, tried and fell off, with Tyrese sprinting across to her each time to pick her up, before returning to stand under the shade of the trees, watching, shouting encouragement while he battled to empty his mind. Then the moment came they'd all been waiting for: instead of falling off, Ellie pedalled in a large circle, making it back unscathed to where Tyrese and Marvin were clapping her on.

'Yow, *tun up*! Dat was great, we knew you could do it.' Marvin fist pumped the air.

Gasping, Ellie could hardly get her words out. Her hair stuck to her forehead with sweat, like it had been glued on. She jumped off the bike, dancing around, laughing. 'That was awesome . . . Thank you! And even if I am melting from the heat, y'all, I don't care, this is the best vacation I've *ever* had.'

Marvin nodded. He grinned at Tyrese, who nodded and hoped the smile on his face looked convincing.

'Marvin! Marvin, cum yah, yuh still nuh cleaned out di chickens! Dem nah clean out themselves!' Grammy called from the house.

'OK, coming!' he shouted back cheerfully, setting off towards the chicken coop.

Still slightly out of breath, Ellie linked arms with him. 'I'll help if you like . . . Ty, are you coming too?'

Tyrese glanced at them, thought about it. He was pleased for Ellie, she'd done great, but he wasn't in the mood to chatter away with her or his cousin. The disquiet he'd woken up with this morning had grown, crushing him. Now his body, his very muscles, felt jittery, like he was caught up in a cold blast of air. No matter how much he tried, he couldn't stop his unwanted thoughts rotating round and round in his mind at high speed. 'I'll catch up. Just give me a minute to put the bike away, yeah?' he said, making up an excuse to be on his own.

They walked away, leaving Tyrese to slowly wheel the bike across to the fence under the shade of the mango tree. His gaze wandered towards the forest-covered mountains which stood sentry over Grammy's house.

He yawned widely.

Thinking he'd heard a cry, Tyrese snapped his mouth closed, craning forward, eyes roaming the landscape.

Shrill screams floated down from the mountain. Instinctively he stepped back. Then he watched as a pandemonium of parrots soared and squawked across the treetops. He let out a sigh of relief, shaking his head at his jumpiness, but just as he'd convinced himself it was nothing, more terrifying screams filled the air.

And this time, Tyrese was certain they sounded human.

His heart pounded and quickly he looked over his shoulder to see Ellie and Marvin disappearing around the corner. He yelled after them, 'Wait, wait, yeah, I'm coming,' and without looking back, he sprinted over to catch up.

—

The evening held a brutal heat. Tyrese sat quietly on the bench in front of Grammy's house, trying to braid one side of Ellie's hair as they waited for her dad to arrive. Though he could see he wasn't doing a very good job, the blisters on his finger were getting larger and it hurt, like he'd banged it with something heavy, making it painful to use.

Ellie, was wearing an orange T-shirt and shorts, which had the unfortunate effect of attracting a lot of flying bugs. She swung a grin at Marvin, who was busy braiding the other side of her hair. 'I thought Texas was hot but now I'll never complain about it again. Could you imagine having to work in this heat? Or exercise, even!' She moved her eyes to glance at Tyrese. 'Could you, Ty? Could you run an eight-hundred-metre race in this?'

He shrugged, not wanting to go there.

'Marvin told me how awesome you are, and you've broken, like, so many school athletic records. That's way cool . . . And, wow, it's pretty neat that your dad coached you. I couldn't imagine Daddy knowing how to teach anyone even to run to the front door.' She swiped a large bug off her top and giggled. 'When are you racing again, when you go back to school after the vacation?'

Tyrese felt like someone had punched him in his stomach. He bent forward, wrapping his arms around his middle. The picture of his dad standing, cheering, waving, arms open, waiting to greet him by the finishing line screeched into his mind . . . Though he didn't want it there, he didn't want to see it, think about it. He just wanted all those thoughts to leave him alone but the snapshot stayed, burning like a furnace.

Unable to answer Ellie, Tyrese gulped for air but it seemed to catch. He felt like he was suffocating. He scratched at his throat. Sweat dripped off him, his chest felt heavy, like the weight of water rested on it. And no matter how much Tyrese tried, he couldn't stop himself crashing, spinning into an attack.

'Ty, is it your asthma? Ty?' Marvin sounded panicked. He put his arm around his cousin's shoulders as Tyrese's lungs searched for air.

'He needs his asthma pump,' Ellie said, just as panicked. 'Has he got a pump?'

'I don't know.' Marvin yelled behind him: 'Grammy! Aunt Patty! Grammy, quick!'

Moments later Grammy appeared. 'What in heaven . . .' Seeing Tyrese gasping, she trailed off. 'Marvin, what's happened?'

'Me think it's his asthma, Grammy.'

'Asthma? Tyrese doesn't have asthma.' She bent down, rubbing his back. 'Tyrese, look 'pon me. Your mother has told me about your panic attacks. Are you having one now?'

Tyrese managed a small nod.

'OK, darlin', so me want you to try take slow breaths ... You hear me, just breathe slowly ... Dat's it. Good boy.' Grammy continued to rub his back and Tyrese felt the clutch on his breath subside. He exhaled, feeling his chest lose its tightness. His shoulders relaxed and Grammy watched him for a moment. 'What brought it on, Ty?'

'I think it was me.' Ellie sounded worried. 'I was talking about his dad. I'm really sorry.'

Grammy reached out and held her hand. 'Don't apologise, dat's a good thing, Ellie-Mae. He'd be pleased you were talking to Tyrese about him. Him would like dat.'

'Well, I don't.' Tyrese wiped his face, feeling embarrassed, weak, stupid, that he'd had an attack in front of Ellie and Marvin. Now they knew it wasn't asthma, they probably thought he was a liar when all he'd really wanted to do was be normal, *feel* normal. 'I already told you, Grammy, there's no point, and I tell Mum and Jonathan that all the time. I mean, it's not like he's here,' he added, trying not to seethe at Grammy.

'You're wrong, Tyrese. Him here. But you just have to learn different ways of seeing him now. Don't shut him out.' Grammy smiled at them all. 'Fight the darkness an' look to the light.'

'The light?'

She stroked Tyrese's face. 'Your light is the way you loved him, and the way him loved you. Hold on to dat, because *remember*, it's the light which will guide and protect you in your darkest hour.'

The beep of a horn startled Tyrese and he watched the insects caught in the headlights of Ellie's dad's large four-wheel drive coming down the track.

Calling out of the driver's window, Mr Thomas came to a speedy stop in front of them. 'Ellie, come on, make it snappy, honey, I've got things to do!'

'Do I have to?'

'What was that?' He leaned further out, the brim of his cowboy hat tipped up over his eyes. 'Speak up, Ellie, only skunks and armadillos whine and complain.'

Getting up from the bench, she shot him a hard stare. 'No, they don't. That's not even a thing, Daddy. Who even says that? You're so embarrassing.'

'Just get in the car, Ellie.'

'Whatever.' Then she waved to Tyrese and Marvin and Grammy. 'Bye, guys.'

'*Inna di morrows*.' Marvin laughed at Ellie's puzzled face. He grinned. 'I'll see you tomorrow.'

As Tyrese watched her go, a sense of dread swelled in him like a sudden fever, and the feeling that something terrible was about to happen gripped his heart.

16

It was late the same evening and a summer storm was getting up. Tyrese stood at the kitchen sink, slowly drying the dishes, trying to ignore his headache as he listened to his mum, Grammy and Marvin chatting away at the table.

'Ty?' his mum called over. 'What's that game you and Dad liked playing? You know, the one where you have to describe a word without actually saying it? It always ended up with you two rolling about with laughter. I was telling Grammy about it . . . Ty?'

Even though he didn't want to join in the conversation and he didn't know why his mum insisted on talking about stuff he didn't want to, Tyrese automatically reached for the memory. But it wasn't there. He frowned, searching his thoughts. This was crazy. He should be able to remember, but all he had was a haze . . . Come on, he *had* to think. But a pain in his head stopped him, making him flinch. 'I dunno,' he muttered.

'Ty, you *do* know. Don't be like this again.'

Tyrese scowled at his mum. 'I'm not being like anything, I *can't* remember.'

He began to feel panicked. The more he tried to search

for the memory, the more lost it got, as if it had been snatched away, inaccessible, ensnared in the very heart of a tornado.

'Tyrese, honey, you know it's OK to talk about things,' his mum said warmly, turning her full attention on him. 'Jonathan really wanted you to start talking more about Dad.'

'I've just told you, I can't remember!' Tyrese's voice cranked up a notch.

As it so often did, his mum's face flushed a deep pink. 'Ty, listen to me, sweetie, just because someone's died doesn't mean we have to stop talking about them. Dad dying . . .'

'. . . Don't say that! Don't say that!' He put his hands over his ears. 'Stop it! Stop it! Stop it! *Stop it!*'

His mum stood up, came towards him, opening her arms to comfort Tyrese, but he backed away as if her touch would sting. Once again the image of the last time he saw his dad smashed into his mind. The room felt as if it was spinning. A glow of fire burned in Tyrese's stomach, exploding like a raging inferno. For a moment the kitchen faded to black, for a moment, his thoughts eclipsed as though they were blocked by the dark side of the moon, and for a moment he thought he could hear yelling and screaming in the distance, and it sounded like his own voice.

Then as quickly as it had fallen, the screen of confusion was swept aside, leaving Tyrese back in the moment. In the kitchen . . .

Panting and sweating, he saw his mum, Grammy, and Marvin gazing at him, wide-eyed.

'Tyrese, why?' his mum simply whispered through tears.

Tyrese looked around. Only then did he realise what he'd done. Two of the kitchen chairs were knocked over, and the legs of Grammy's footstool were upside down, poking through the smashed plates and saucers like shoots of grass. Curry and plantain was splattered over and up the cream kitchen cabinet doors, and in his hand he held the smashed handle of Grammy's favourite cup.

'I . . . I . . .' His own shock silenced him. He hadn't meant to. He really hadn't. He didn't even know he'd done it, although the small cut on his palm from where the broken piece of porcelain had nicked his skin told him different.

'I'm sorry. I'm so sorry, Grammy.' He couldn't bear to look at her; the hurt was thickly painted on her face, her mouth was open but she stayed quiet.

'Mum . . .'

But his mum just blinked, turning away.

Shame splashed over Tyrese. What was happening to him? How could he have ever done this to Grammy?

His mum echoed his thoughts.

'How could you, Ty?' Her lip was quivering. She covered her face with the checked tea towel she was holding, as though it were a mask covering her wounds. She wept, wailing, a long drawn-out note of pain, a sound that cut right through Tyrese, sharper than any blade could. 'Your dad wouldn't have wanted this from you, Ty.'

'Patty, *no*, it's OK,' Grammy murmured. But then she frowned and took hold of Tyrese's hand and stared at the pus-filled blisters on his finger. 'Tyrese, what happened?'

He tried to pull his hand away from Grammy but she held on to it.

'Tyrese, how long have you had dem? When did dat happen?' She spoke firmly, but let his hand go.

Tyrese shrugged. Seeing his mum looking, he put his hand behind his back.

'Ty,' Grammy continued, 'why don't you go and rest in your room, I'll come and see you in a minute.'

He nodded at Grammy and turned away, not wanting to see the hurt he'd caused his mum.

—

'I'm so sorry for what I did, Grammy, I didn't mean to break your stuff, I didn't even mean to get angry. I . . .' Sitting on his bed, listening to the storm, Tyrese shrugged, still unable to look at Grammy. He sniffed hard. His nose blocked from tears.

'Tyrese, there's no right or wrong way to grieve, but grief is a criminal, him a robber, a *tief*, snatches away the heart of us. But like a wound, you need to heal it, otherwise it can become infected. You know people sometimes fight so hard not to hurt, not to feel pain, dem live in the darkness and push everything away.'

The storm whipped around the house and, sullenly, Tyrese shrugged again. 'Sounds OK to me, it would be better than this,' he muttered. 'I just hate the way I feel, Grammy. I'd give *anything* not to feel like this.'

The moment he'd said it, Grammy quickly put her hand

over his mouth. Her eyes darted around as if there was someone in the room, filling Tyrese with dread. 'Sshhhh, Ty, be careful what you say, you never know who's listening.'

She moved her hand away and Tyrese's gaze – just like Grammy's had done – flitted around the room. 'What do you mean?' His fear caused him to whisper.

She gave the tiniest of head shakes, looking like she was too scared to reply. There was a long beat before she finally spoke. 'Listen to me, Ty, to only have darkness, is to have nothing. Just promise me you'll *always* remember what me keep telling you: darkness can't drive out darkness, only light can do dat.'

The storm rattled outside and Tyrese looked down, fiddling with his top, feeling the tension in his shoulders growing, like someone was pressing down on them. He rolled his neck from side to side and she took his hand again and stared at his finger. Then her eyes searched his face. 'Ty, what you said about the rhyme and the Shadow Man . . .' She sucked in air noisily, as if she had trouble saying the name.

He blinked, surprised at the direction of the conversation.

'Tell me the rhyme, Tyrese.'

He took a deep breath, realising how uneasy he felt:

'Shadow Man, Shadow Man, him come get you,

Shadow Man, Shadow Man, him come take you.'

Grammy held on tighter to Tyrese, her face drawn, pinched in anguish.

'Grammy, are you OK?'

She shook her head and gestured for the glass of water

on the bedside cabinet. Tyrese handed it to her and, shaking, Grammy drank it down in noisy gulps. Placing the glass in her lap, she stared at Tyrese and terror cut into his bones.

'It's happening again, Ty. Him awakened, something must have awakened him.'

Tyrese struggled to speak. 'Who . . . who, Grammy?'

She stared straight at him. 'The Shadow Man.' Looking drawn, she rubbed the side of her head. 'Dat's why if you listen carefully enough, Ty, you can hear the screams coming from the mountains.'

'I've heard them – I heard them, Grammy!' Tyrese nodded, quickly recalling earlier. 'When we were showing Ellie how to ride a bike, I heard them then.'

And although it was sticky and hot in the room, Grammy visibly shivered. 'Dem is duppies, celebrating his return, though some people say they're actually the screams of the missing.'

'The missing?'

She dropped her voice. 'The pickney, the teenagers dat are already lost, the ones him have already taken. Over the years, for as far back as me can remember, he's taken the children, Tyrese.'

Tyrese's stomach knotted. 'How, why, I mean, what . . . what happened to them?'

Grammy shook her head. 'No one knows. But dem gone.'

'What do you mean, *gone*? Didn't anyone look for them, or . . . or report them missing?'

Grammy nodded slowly. 'People did both, Tyrese, though

not everyone took it seriously, some just put it down to the pickney running away, or the ones dat did take it seriously were too frightened to find out. No one wants to go poking their noses in duppy business.'

Trying to keep his voice steady, Tyrese asked, 'But how did they know it was him then?'

Grammy's eyes were clouded with concern. 'Because all the signs were there, like the signs are here now.' She rubbed her throat. 'No one knows why the Shadow Man disappears, only to return again. But him back, him *back*, Ty, and for some reason, him want *you*.'

Instinctively, Tyrese scrambled backwards on his bed, clasping his knees up against his chest. Grammy took his hand and once again she looked at his finger. 'And this, Ty,' she swallowed, looking like she was doing it with some difficulty. 'The Soucouyant, Ol' Higue – they do his bidding.'

'The who, Grammy? The *who*? I don't know what you mean.' Fighting back tears, Tyrese frantically searched her face for answers. 'What's my finger got to do with this? Grammy, you're frightening me.'

Grammy swayed, looking like she was going to topple forward.

'Grammy! Grammy, are you *sure* you're all right? You don't look very well.'

She squeezed her eyes closed. 'Just give me a minute, Ty.' Grammy's words trembled out, a rasp of terror in her quickened breath. 'You have to try protect yourself, Ty. Me should a told you all this before, but me did hope dat

I was wrong. But now, now, Ty, me know for sure it's started again.'

Her eyes were wide, love and fear rooted in them. She paused again, studying his face. 'Me need to tell you a story, Tyrese, but you must listen carefully.' She took the last sip of water. 'What you will hear will sound very strange, but all of it is true, Tyrese. True and so very tragic . . . Way back, almost at the end of the nineteenth century, there was a man called Levi Campbell, him family came from around these parts. Well, Levi, him worked hard, even though there were terrible hardships at the time, him managed to rise up, found himself travelling all over the world, educating himself, and before not too long he became a rich man, man come good. He did love him family a whole heap, Ty, and him loved this island too, and even though he went to other countries, this was his home. Jamaica was where his heart lay and so he came back.'

Her eyes glowed. 'Imagine, he even managed to purchase some land and build a home here, which let me tell you, wasn't easy in those days . . . For a long time, everything was fine, *criss*, but what happened later . . .' She shook her head, visibly struggling to tell the story. 'What happened later, what happened later to him was terrible, such a tragedy . . .'

'. . . That's quite enough!'

Tyrese jumped. His mum stood at the door. Her voice sharp. Her face pinched. 'Do not fill his head with all this stuff, please.'

'He needs to hear it, Patty,' Grammy urged.

'No, no, he doesn't. What he needs is to get some rest, and from what I've just overheard, he won't be getting that from your story, he'll be getting nightmares. You saw what happened in the kitchen. Jonathan said—'

'Oh my God, Jonathan this, Jonathan that!' Tyrese shouted. 'That's all you ever say!'

'Tyrese,' Grammy was firm, 'there's no need to be rude . . . Be kind, Ty. Your mum is doing a wonderful job. Try not to be cross with her, don't forget, she lost him too, we all did.' She smiled sadly at Tyrese.

His mum looked flustered. Upset. 'Tyrese, go to bed,' she raised her voice, clearly struggling to hold back her tears, 'just go to bed!'

'But, but, Grammy was telling me—'

'I said, bed! *Now!*' his mum interrupted angrily, her voice soaring.

The shutters banged, the wind slamming them against the walls outside.

'Do as your mother says, Ty.' Grammy stood up with some difficulty from the bed, looking like she was straightening her spine, bone by bone.

Tyrese glanced at his mum and threw her a cold stare. 'Good night, Grammy.'

'Good night, Ty.' Grammy looked like she was going to say something else, but instead she kissed him on his head and he watched her follow his mum out of the room, leaving him trembling and wondering what it was that she'd been about to tell him.

17

The morning sunrays danced on Tyrese's face. He opened his eyes. A moment later he let out a scream. Slithering on the pillow towards his face was a large centipede. He scrambled up quickly just as his mum walked in, carrying a pile of towels in her arms. 'What's all the shouting about, Ty?'

There was a sigh to her voice and Tyrese noticed how pale she looked. 'Nothing.' He kicked his pillow off the bed, watching the insect scurry away.

Wearily, his mum placed the towels on the chest of drawers, rubbed her head, frowned. 'Well, as long as you're not frightening yourself after that silly story Grammy was telling you.'

'It wasn't a silly story,' Tyrese bit back. But his mum was right. He *was* frightened. Terrified. And he knew it was stupid, it was crazy to get spooked by talk of duppies and the Shadow Man. How could he take that stuff seriously? Though that hadn't stopped him spending most of the night lying awake, listening to every creak and groan from the storm. It had sounded like someone walking, *prowling* about outside on the porch, but he'd been too frightened to look and too frightened to call out.

'Actually,' his mum continued, 'thinking about it, from what I overheard last night, it wasn't only a silly story, it sounded like a really horrible one too. All that stuff about the Shadow Man or whatever his name is, returning and coming to get you, that would give anyone nightmares.' She rubbed her head again, looking paler than ever.

Not replying, Tyrese grabbed a towel for a shower, but he stopped and glanced at his mum. He really didn't want to be mean. 'Are you OK, Mum?'

She smiled. 'I think the heat's finally got the better of me, or maybe it's something I ate, I don't know. Grammy isn't feeling very well, either. She's gone back to bed to have a lie-down, so don't disturb her please, let her rest.'

Not really wanting to have a full-blown conversation with his mum, Tyrese went to go but she gently held his arm. 'And, Ty, we still have to talk about what happened yesterday in the kitchen, but for now, I want you to promise me you're not going to fill your head with any more talk of the Shadow Man. That's the very last thing you need.'

—

The mid-morning's searing sun was already high in the sky. It dripped down heat, melting the energy away of anyone who walked under its path. Even the trees by the fence stooped and bowed, looking as though they were searching for shade.

Powderpuff clouds drifted lazily across the crystal-blue skies and Tyrese walked with Marvin to the end of the gravel track, waiting for Ellie by the blue mahoe trees as arranged. He glanced at the blisters on the tip of his finger. They felt hot and he could see pockets of yellow pus under the thin layer of skin. All he'd really wanted to do was go and speak to Grammy, but he didn't want to disturb her if she was feeling unwell.

He'd just have to speak to her later, even if his mum had tried to make him promise not to. And although so much of what Grammy had said had sounded like some weird, creepy kind of fantasy, Tyrese still felt it was important to find out what she had been going to tell him. After all, there'd been nothing unreal about the fear Grammy had shown, and there was nothing unreal about the terror he felt when he thought about the old man's words: *him come take you.*

'There she is.' Marvin waved.

Seeing Ellie, Tyrese refocused his thoughts and watched her get out of her father's car, which sped off as quickly as it had arrived.

'Hey, Ellie!'

She waved back at them. 'Hey, Ty . . . Hey, Marvin.'

'*Weh yuh ah sey, yuh gud?*' Marvin called to her.

Nearing them, she nodded. 'Yeah, sorry I'm late, Daddy had some business he had to deal with first.' She pulled a face.

'Was he impressed dat you learned to ride a bike?' Marvin asked.

'Nope. I mean, I tried to tell him when we drove back home last night but he was talking on his cell, too busy, same thing this morning,' she said flatly. She shrugged. The disappointment was easy to read on her face. 'Anyway, I'm here now.'

Marvin linked arms with her. 'Why don't we go and get some water bottles and then we can ride down to the river on the bikes? You can ride my bike, I'll ride Ty's, and we can make him run all the way.' Marvin winked at Tyrese and laughed.

A spark came back into Ellie's eyes. Grinning, she nodded enthusiastically. 'Awesome. And thanks. Thanks for everything, I'm real glad I'm here, guys . . .'

Tyrese walked ahead, listening to Marvin and Ellie chattering behind him. He made his way into the house and as usual was grateful to feel the cool.

Walking down the hallway, a large moth fluttered into his face.

He swiped at it but immediately found himself having to swipe another moth away. They were huge. Disgusting. The same size as the ones he'd found in his bed.

Shuddering at the memory, his attention was drawn to the window where he heard a soft tapping. More moths banged themselves against the glass pane. Where had they all come from? He quickly looked away, hating how the markings on their wings looked like eyes staring back at him.

He wrapped his arms tightly around himself when he noticed that several other large dark grey moths had attached themselves to the wall. He'd never seen so many in just one place. He felt his heart begin to beat quicker as a thought came to him, and he forced himself to look again at the moths at the window.

Were they actually even there? Was he just seeing things again? He didn't trust himself any more. Would it be like the other things, just in his imagination?

'Ty, wait for us!' Marvin shouted cheerfully, making his way into the house with Ellie. 'Maybe we could . . .' He trailed off. Tyrese watched his cousin's expression tighten as he looked around the hallway, his eyes darting around. '*Me Raah!* What's happening, Ty? Where've *they* come from?'

Tyrese exhaled. He held his hands on the top of his head and turned around on the spot. 'You can see them too? You . . . you can *actually* see them? The moths?' Relief poured from him.

Marvin gave him a strange look but he nodded whilst Ellie just stared wide-eyed at the insects spread across the wall and window.

'Cuz, you don't know how happy you've just made me,' Tyrese whispered.

'What?' Marvin frowned. 'What are you talking about?'

Tyrese didn't have time to explain. He didn't even know if he wanted to try to tell Marvin how with each passing moment, he felt like he was losing touch with reality.

Suddenly wondering where his mum and Grammy were, Tyrese began to creep slowly along the hallway, pushing away the feeling there was something else in the house with them. The sweat trickled down his forehead and he clenched his fists tight, resisting the temptation to turn back and run.

The light above him flickered on and off and, even though there were windows along the hallway, dim and dark shadows twisted across the ceiling. The walls were now completely covered with moths, vibrating their wings, producing a low unending hum.

'*Tyrese, Tyrese.*'

Tyrese jolted, spun round, his terror so sharp it was if he'd been stung.

'*Tyrese, Tyrese.*'

He flicked his eyes to Marvin and Ellie. 'Can . . . can you hear that, Marv? Can you *hear* it?'

'Hear what, Ty?' Marvin looked puzzled.

'Ellie, can you? Just listen! Listen!'

Looking drawn, she shook her head. 'I can't hear anything, Ty.'

'*Tyrese, Tyrese.*'

His name filled the hallway, getting louder and louder and Tyrese covered his ears. He stumbled backwards, fighting for air. *Breathe.* He had to breathe. He had to focus on something else.

'*A. B. C. D. E . . .*'

But no matter how much he tried, no matter how hard he attempted to recite the alphabet, Tyrese couldn't concentrate on what Jonathan had taught him to do. He couldn't find the breath he needed to take into his lungs and that feeling gripped him like claws, scraping, sinking into his body.

He dropped his hands away from his ears, leaned on the wall, hearing the crunching of the moths' bodies crush against his back. His legs began to give way but he felt arms around him, then heard the familiar voice of his cousin: 'Me have got you, Ty, it's OK, me got you.'

Tyrese's breathing began to steady. He glanced gratefully at his cousin, looked around at the mass of moths, then his gaze moved towards the room opposite. The blinds were closed in the bedroom but he could still see, and he quickly moved from Marvin's hold, pushing him gently aside. 'No, oh no! No! Oh my God, no!'

Lying motionless on the twin beds in Grammy's room were Grammy and his mum. He dashed towards them, skidding on the polished floor. 'Mum! Mum! Grammy! Mum! Oh my God, they're not moving! Marvin, they're not moving!' He held his mum's shoulders and gently shook her. 'Wake up! Wake up, Mum! Please, wake up!' But then Tyrese noticed their eyes. He flinched, stepped back quickly . . . That didn't make sense. Why were their eyes open like that? Unblinking. Just staring at the ceiling?

He felt lightheaded. The room started to whirl. Panic clutching at his chest. He gripped Marvin's arm. 'Can you see them? Can you?' It was the same question as before but this time his voice was tinged with a scream.

His cousin gave the tiniest of nods, his forehead breaking into a frown.

'Marvin! Just tell me! *Talk* to me, Marvin!'

Marvin threw Tyrese and Ellie a worried look. 'Me see them . . .' He touched Grammy's hand gently, blew out his cheeks, closing his eyes for a moment. '. . . It's fine,' he uttered breathlessly, 'it's OK, Ty . . . Me think dem a just sleeping.'

Tyrese stared at his cousin. He didn't have words. Marvin couldn't be serious. Sleeping? There was no way Mum and Grammy were *just asleep*. '*What?* What are you *talking* about? Sleeping? Look at them!'

Marvin glanced at Ellie, who glanced back nervously at him. 'I think I know what's happened . . . It would make sense,' he said, sounding like he was talking more to himself than to Tyrese or Ellie.

Once again, Tyrese couldn't believe what he was hearing. Make sense? How did *any* of this make sense? Nothing around here made sense any more. Then with the quickest of movements, Tyrese touched his cousin's arm for a second time, making sure that this was real, *he* was real, Marvin was real, that they were really present in the moment.

A rage flared in his chest. 'To you! It makes sense to *you*, because I don't know what the hell you're talking about . . . So, go on then, tell me what's happened!'

'Duppies.'

Tyrese shrank back. 'Ghosts?' He shook his head, glanced at his mum, his mind a jumble of thoughts. 'Are you friggin' kidding me?'

'No,' Marvin said firmly, and Tyrese spotted that panic had darkened his cousin's eyes.

'Why would you say that, Marvin?' Ellie murmured.

Tyrese rubbed his face. 'Exactly.' He pointed at his cousin. 'That's crazy talk, you do know that, yeah? I get that you and Grammy believe in them, but this is nothing to do with any duppy!'

Marvin jerked his head in the direction of the hallway. 'Then if it isn't, how do you explain the duppy bats, Ty?'

'Bats?' Agitated, he licked his lips. 'What bats? What are you going on about?'

'In the hall. Those bats only come when there's a soul not at rest, Ty. Dat's what duppies are, troubled or wicked souls. They're the undead.'

'Oh my God,' Tyrese began to pace. He glimpsed Ellie, who looked as shocked as he felt. 'First off, they're moths, *not* bats, and secondly, who even said that?'

'Grammy. Dat's what she's always said to me. But everyone knows dat. Everyone in Jamaica knows about duppies.'

'Listen to me, Marvin, there are *no* ghosts here, just Mum and Grammy, and I reckon they must be sick. Mum said she didn't feel well earlier and neither did Grammy,' Tyrese said quickly. He turned to Ellie. 'We just need to go and get some help for them, yeah?'

'We should call an ambulance,' Ellie suggested, her face paler than ever.

Marvin raised his eyebrows in surprise. 'You don't get it, do you? No one will come. Not once dem know it's duppies.'

Tyrese wiped away his tears. He kicked the chair hard, causing it to tumble and clatter on its side. 'Stop saying that, yeah, we're wasting time! Come on, let's go! *Hurry* up!'

Blocking Tyrese from leaving, Marvin's eyes brimmed with tears as well. 'There's nothing anyone can do.' Marvin paused, the room falling into a tense silence. 'Don't you see, Ty, they've been cursed by something!'

Tyrese raised his voice. '*Stop!* Can't you hear what you're saying is crazy. *Cursed?* Look around, cuz, we're not in a castle, there is no prince, no spinning wheel, no witch and this is definitely *not Sleeping Beauty*! So *shut up* and come on and let's go and get some help!'

The corners of Marvin's mouth drew downwards. 'No . . . *Look* at dem. Look 'pon dem properly, Ty. This is real.'

Tyrese stepped in closer to his cousin. He clenched his fists again, trying to fight the burning inside him, which had started to feel so familiar. 'Like *normal* real, Marvin. Not duppies,' he hissed through gritted teeth. 'Like, I dunno, maybe this is some kind of gas poisoning or something, what's that stuff called . . . *monoxide*? You hear that kind of thing all the time on the news.' He stared at his cousin, who didn't look at him. 'Anyway, even if *you* don't want to, *I'm* going to go and find someone, because no matter what you think, this isn't about the undead or some stupid *duppy bat*.' Tyrese's words spat out. He turned to go.

'You're right, Ty. It's not about dat, it's about *you*!' Marvin called after him, sounding angry. 'I think this is about the Shadow Man wanting you.'

Tyrese's knees buckled, his chest tightened. Slowly he turned back round to face Marvin. Save the rhythmic sound of the grandfather clock, silence once more surrounded them. The tension between Tyrese and Marvin crackled in the quiet as Ellie watched on.

Recovering, Tyrese flipped, yelled at his cousin, panic

propelling his voice louder, 'What? Why would you say that? How do you know about that? Who told you?'

'Last night, I heard a *liccle* bit of what Aunt Patty and Grammy were talking about in the kitchen. Your mum was upset, she was worried Grammy had frightened you, but Grammy said she didn't want you to become *one of the missing*.'

Tyrese edged away. He shook his head. 'Don't say that, that's just a stupid story, yeah.' He lifted his glasses, wiped his tears, covered his face with his hands. 'This is crazy. *I feel* like I'm going crazy. It's just one big nightmare, so many weird things have been happening. I hear voices calling me all the time, I see things nobody else does, like the old man from the beach and . . .'

'. . . What old man?' Ellie asked.

Tyrese dropped his hands. 'That's the thing, I don't even know if he was real or not. I saw him at Buff Bay . . . then under my bed.'

'For real?' She sounded stunned.

'I don't know, I don't know! It could all be in my head, because when Grammy looked, he wasn't there, so what does that say about me?' He tapped his temple. 'I think I'm losing it.'

Marvin's bottom lip was trembling and he gave Tyrese a quick hug. 'Ty, please, it's OK, look – maybe you imagined some stuff, maybe you didn't, but if it was completely in your imagination then you wouldn't know the rhyme. Grammy told Aunt Patty you knew the rhyme of the missing.'

Tyrese felt like he was about to throw up. He didn't want

to start thinking about it. 'But that doesn't mean what's happened to Mum and Grammy has something to do with the Shadow Man . . . I still think they're just ill, and . . . and anyway, it was just a stupid rhyme . . . wasn't it?' His voice was small.

It was a beat before Marvin answered. 'No, Tyrese, it's not just a stupid rhyme . . .

"Shadow Man, Shadow Man, him come get you,

Shadow Man, Shadow Man, him come take you."'

He repeated it then stared at Tyrese.

A sound escaped from Tyrese's throat and Ellie flinched. 'Marvin, please, this is just too freaky, you're frightening me. Look, I think we really need to go and tell someone. We need to go and tell my dad, if we . . .' Her unsaid words hung in the air as she gasped loudly. Tyrese and Marvin looked in the direction she was gazing.

Ice ripped through Tyrese's veins as, open-mouthed, he watched Grammy and his mum – who still lay on the bed staring unblinkingly up at the ceiling – slowly bringing their fingers to their lips to make a loud shushing sound.

Ellie held on to Marvin's hand. 'What are they *doing*?'

'I think . . . I think,' Marvin stammered, his voice low, 'whatever's possessing dem is warning us. A warning for us to tell no one.' He turned to look at Tyrese. 'Now do you believe it, Ty? Do you believe dat this is the work of the undead?'

18

The minutes slipped by to the sound of the deep, rhythmic ticking of the grandfather clock in the corner. Tyrese's panic began to rise. He quickly turned away. 'So now what? What are we supposed to do now?'

'We need to get out of here,' Marvin said.

'But we can't just leave Grammy and Mum, that's crazy.'

'What else are we supposed to do? If *we* don't help, no one will.' Marvin looked between Ellie and Tyrese, bringing his voice to a whisper. He grabbed Tyrese's hand. 'The rhyme says the Shadow Man is coming to take you.' He looked confused. 'But *why*, Ty . . . ? We need to find dat out before it's too late. Maybe finding out why this is happening is the way to save Grammy and Aunt Patty, otherwise they may never wake up, and they'll just stay there asleep, frozen in time, eventually rotting away . . . it might also be the only way to save *you*.'

Tyrese pulled his hand away but in that moment he realised it felt wet. He glanced down and saw the painful infected pinpricks on his finger were beginning to drip with blood and pus again, and quickly he put his hand behind his back, not wanting Marvin to see.

'God, Marvin, can you just stop saying that, how would you feel if I kept saying stuff to freak you out?' Tyrese snarled. 'Nothing's going to happen to me, OK?'

Marvin stared at his cousin. 'OK, Ty, whatever you say.' He gave Tyrese a sympathetic smile which only made Tyrese feel worse.

'Can we just go?' Ellie pulled on Marvin's arm.

'We need to, but remember, when we leave here, we can't tell anyone, understand? Not even your dad, Ellie.'

Her eyes were wide and she chewed on her thumb. 'Yeah, I know, but if we can't, how are we supposed to find out what's going on?'

'Well, we can look for the old man in Buff Bay, find out more,' Marvin said, grabbing a small red tin off the top of Grammy's chest of drawers and pushing it in his pocket.

'No. No way.' Tyrese shook his head. 'We can't, it's not safe, Marv. You don't know what he's like. You haven't seen him.'

Marvin flinched. 'You think he's a duppy?'

Tyrese rolled his tongue round his mouth.

His stomach knotted.

He stared at his mum and Grammy, whispering his words. 'Yeah. Yeah, Marvin, he's definitely a duppy.'

Marvin nodded, the implication of Tyrese's acknowledgment not lost.

'OK, then we just scout out the place where you first saw him . . . Sorry, Ty, but *bad things a gwaan* and we don't have any other way to find out more . . . Come, let's go.' Marvin gestured to Ellie and Tyrese, who followed him out of the room.

They crept along the hallway, keeping close to each other.

The tension in Tyrese opened up. He could taste the dryness in his mouth as he fought to quell the fear whirling in him.

Ahead, he watched the front door begin to creak shut, then abruptly, it slammed closed.

He quickly reached for the doorknob, turned it, expecting it to pull open, but it was stuck. He pulled again, rattling the handle hard. It *still* wouldn't open.

He heard a bang.

Glanced around.

Another bang.

'What was that?' Ellie uttered.

Pushing himself against the wall, it took Tyrese only a moment to realise what the noise was. His blood chilled. One by one, the house shutters were closing on their own, plunging them all into darkness.

Ellie screamed, grabbing on to Marvin and Tyrese, who both yelled just as loudly.

'How are we going to get out of here?' Ellie's words tumbled out.

'This way . . .' Marvin pulled Ellie, and Tyrese hurried after them, racing along in the near darkness.

Trying to ignore the sense that someone else unseen was behind him, Tyrese charged into the bathroom after the others.

Marvin pointed up to the ceiling. 'The loft. We can go

out dat way. There's an air vent at the end of the roof space. Ty, you want to go first? You're taller.'

Without answering, Tyrese quickly clambered on the edge of the bath and stood on tiptoes, careful to keep his balance. He reached up to the loft hatch, pulled at the handle to open it, hooking his fingers on the ledge. 'I need you to push me up,' Tyrese said, struggling to get a firm grip.

Marvin sat on the edge of the bath. 'Stand on my shoulders, Ty. It'll be easier.'

'I'll hold your legs,' Ellie added in a whisper. 'But can we hurry, I don't have a good feeling about being in here.'

With Marvin and Ellie's help, Tyrese slowly managed to haul his body into the loft. Dragging himself inside, something squelched under his hand. He wasn't even going to try to look. But whatever insect it was, he knew it had a hard shell, he'd heard the crunch.

The dust and dampness hit him and sweat dripped into Tyrese's eyes. He wiped under his glasses with the top of his T-shirt, spun around, looking back down to Marvin and Ellie, keeping his focus firmly on them, uneasy about being alone in the loft.

He frantically swiped at his face as a thick sheet of cobwebs dropped on to it. He spoke in a rush, reaching with his arms: 'Ellie, give me your hands, I'll help pull you up, then Marvin, we'll help you afterwards. But come on, Ellie's right, I just want to get out of this place . . .'

. . . It took a couple of minutes for Ellie and Marvin to be pulled inside the roof space. And scrambling on his hands and knees, Marvin led the way through the attic, Ellie behind and Tyrese last.

The roof was too low for them to be able to stand and Tyrese crawled along in the semi-darkness, blowing the dust from his nose while he ducked away from the thick layer of spider webs which hung like paper chains from the ceiling.

Getting to the large air vent grille, Marvin quickly smashed it aside with his foot, revealing the way out. 'Ellie, come, you go first, but be careful,' he said, moving out of her way.

Tyrese could see the drop down to Grammy's garden wasn't far – it was only a single-storey villa – but still high enough to do some damage if they landed badly.

Without saying anything at all, Ellie hurried forward. She hesitated only for a second, then jumped out on to the soft earth below.

'You OK, Ellie?' Tyrese whispered loudly, breathing in a mouthful of dust.

'*Yeah, fine.*'

Tyrese glanced at his cousin. 'You go next, Marvin.'

'You sure, Ty?'

Tyrese forced a smile. 'Yeah, yeah, go on,' he said, just wanting Marvin simply to hurry up.

His cousin didn't have to be asked twice, and he leaped down.

'*I'm good*,' he shouted. '*Come on, Ty.*'

Relieved it was his turn, Tyrese went to follow.

Then stopped.

He shivered, touched his neck. What was that . . . A draught? There it was again . . . Cold air on the back of his neck.

'Tyrese. Tyrese.'

Tyrese shot backwards against the loft wall, his scream catching in his throat. A centipede scurried over his hand.

'Tyrese.'

He felt the word breathed on to the side of his face.

Someone was there in the corner.

'Tyrese. Tyrese.'

He pressed himself further against the wall. His body rigid, he glanced to the side.

A huddled form.

Two glints in the dark.

Cold eyes staring back at him.

Tyrese knew he needed to get out . . . *Now.*

19

In the furnace-dry heat, Tyrese sprinted towards the soapwood trees which stood like watchful giants. He glanced over his shoulder and saw Marvin racing towards Grammy's shed.

'Marvin! Marvin! Come on, what are you doing?'

His cousin didn't turn to answer and Tyrese continued to head to where the bikes were still leaning against the flaking white-painted fence. He swiftly wheeled one across to Ellie, who was standing by Grammy's vegetable patch, but a cold chill ran through him when he saw what she was doing. 'Ellie! Ellie! Who were you talking to? *Ellie!*'

Holding her mobile phone, looking upset, Ellie turned to Tyrese. He saw her press *end call* on the screen and Tyrese could see she was shaking.

'I'm . . . I'm sorry, Ty, but I had to call him. I had to speak to Daddy.'

'Tell me you didn't, Ellie. You saw what happened, whatever it is that's taken them over – *possessed* them – was warning us. We told you not to. You might have made everything worse.'

Her face flushed. 'I just panicked, and I'm scared, Ty.'

Tyrese put his hands on his head and turned away.

He could feel his temper rising and rushing through him. 'What did you say to him, Ellie, *what did you say*?'

'Not much, the signal went.'

Tyrese raised his voice. 'Just tell me!'

Ellie's words rushed out. 'I told him about Grammy and your mom, and I told him about the Shadow Man, but he could hardly hear me, and he wasn't even sure what I was talking about, he didn't really get it, and then that's when the signal went, Ty, I'm—'

'Guys!' At that moment, Marvin called to them, hurrying over with a rucksack. He paused only to quickly grab some clothes off the washing line.

'What are you doing?' Tyrese stared at his cousin.

Panting, Marvin pushed the clothes in the blue rucksack, put it on his back and grabbed his bike. 'We don't know how long we're going to be, Ty. We might need dem. I also grabbed Grammy's flashlight as well as my savings.' From his pocket, he pulled out the red tin he'd taken from Grammy's room. 'At least now we'll have some money.'

'And I've still got the money Daddy gave me the other day.' Ellie's voice cracked and she began fidgeting with her fingers.

Marvin looked between Tyrese and Ellie. 'Are you two all right?'

Tyrese didn't trust himself to answer, so he just nodded.

'Yeah, but I've got no signal on my cell at all now, so I'll have to go and see Dad.'

'You really think that's a good idea?' Tyrese looked at her accusingly.

She held on to Tyrese's arm, imploring him. 'If I don't, he'll come here to try and pick me up later . . . I'll just say that I'm having a sleepover with you tonight. He never listens to me anyway, but if he asks about what I was talking about, I'll just make something up.'

Tyrese glanced at his watch. 12.14 p.m. Then he glanced back at the house, his stomach knotted once more. He felt a sudden breeze get up, the tops of the trees beginning to sway. He shivered, looked away, feeling like the house had a life of its own. 'OK, fine, yeah, you take my bike, Ellie, and I'll run by your side. It'll be quicker and then we can catch the bus to Buff Bay . . . You guys ready?'

They nodded.

Then they sped down the hill, going as fast as they could, and Tyrese ran by the side of Ellie. He welcomed the burn from his lungs, the sting from his out-of-condition muscles, the discomfort from his feet in the pair of trainers he wore, and he'd greeted the veneer of sweat covering his body like an old friend. Familiar. A semblance of normality within the winds of fear, helping relieve some of his tension.

He could hear the sound of his own panting in his ears and the thud of his feet on the ground. Too terrified to glance towards the dark, twisting forest on either side of him, Tyrese concentrated on keeping up with Ellie whilst the sun scorched a pattern of fire on his back as he ran. His infected blistered finger throbbed painfully, as though it'd been caught in a door, and a piercing headache danced around in spikes, sending shooting pains to the back of his eyes.

—

Exhausted after the twenty-minute run, his sweaty clothes sticking to his body, Tyrese slowed into a walk as Ellie's dad's construction site came into view.

'That's weird, why are the gates shut?' Frowning, she put her bike down, making her way over to the main entrance of the building site. 'It's Wednesday, it shouldn't be closed and Daddy *never* stops work for anything.'

'Is there another way in?' Marvin asked, resting his bike by Ellie's.

'Yeah, round the side . . .' She quickly turned to run, disappearing through a small gateway.

'Ellie! Ellie, wait up! Oh my God, Ellie, *wait*!' Tyrese shouted, alarm bubbling within. He whirled around to Marvin. 'I don't want her to say anything else to her dad.'

'What do you mean, *anything else*? She's spoken to her dad?' Looking worried, he kissed his teeth.

'Yeah, when you were in the shed, she called him. Look, come on, I'll fill you in later.'

Tyrese and Marvin dashed along the sandy track, through a small metal gate and on to the construction site where a forest once grew and where now the sprawling hotel was being built. Large bulldozers, cranes and dump trucks were parked and dotted around, though the whole place was completely deserted.

Wiping away the sweat from his forehead, Tyrese forced himself to keep looking ahead. On the track. On the stones. On the back of Marvin's head. Anywhere which wouldn't take his mind to a frightening place. He battled to silence the creeping suspicion that someone was hidden, waiting, watching their every move.

'Something doesn't feel right, I don't like this.' Tyrese whispered to Marvin as he tried to spot where Ellie had gone.

'Me neither. The sooner we get out of here, the better.'

They continued to run, searching for Ellie, but the further they went, the more edgy Tyrese started to feel. The unsettling quiet wrapped round them, and even the birds in the trees, looking down at them from their branches, were muted.

'Look, there she is! Quick . . . Ellie, wait! Ellie, *please*!' Tyrese yelled, and he picked up his pace, easily catching up as she headed across the ground floor of the partly built hotel, making her way through one of the large empty rooms.

'Ellie, please don't say anything else to—'

'. . . Daddy! *Daddy!*' Cutting off Tyrese, Ellie pointed to her dad at the far end of the corridor which led off from the room they were in. 'Dad?' Her voice sounded thunderous in the quiet. 'Dad?'

There was no reply.

'*Dad?*'

Unease settled in Tyrese's chest and he heard the sound of his own quickened breathing. He followed Ellie towards Mr Thomas.

'Daddy! No!' Ellie let out a scream and rushed towards her dad.

Mr Thomas stood facing the wall, statue-still, mouth half closed, his eyes blank, wide open, unblinking. 'No, Daddy, no! Wake up, wake up!' She tugged on his jacket but he didn't move. 'Please wake up, *please*.'

Marvin stepped forward and stared at Mr Thomas. He gave the tiniest shake of his head. 'Him won't wake up, Ellie,' he mumbled, 'it's the same as Grammy and Aunt Patty.'

'What are we going to do?' Ellie spluttered. 'This is my fault, isn't it?' She spoke so fast, her words sounded jumbled. 'Y'all told me not to say anything. Ty told me, we . . . we . . . we were warned, but I ignored all that, and now look what's happened. Whatever it is – a ghost, a duppy, the Shadow Man, has done this because of me . . . I'm so sorry . . . I'm so sorry, Daddy.'

'Ellie, Ellie, listen, yeah? This is no one's fault,' Tyrese said, trying to sound stronger than he felt. 'You were scared, I get that, and that's why you told him, but it's going to be OK. Like Marvin said, we just have to find out why this is happening, right? You hear me?'

She pushed her hair behind her ears. 'But any one of us could be next, Ty.'

'Ellie, he's not after you.' Tyrese swallowed hard, finding it difficult to speak the next words: 'The rhyme says it's me, the Shadow Man wants *me*.' As he spoke, he abruptly remembered how the old man had referred to him as the *child of the Shadow Man*, *child of the darkness* . . . What did that even mean? He didn't know, though it did feel like something bad, something evil was coming his way.

'I just don't think any one of us is safe, though.'

'Then this time,' Tyrese said, still struggling to contain

his fear, 'we don't say anything to anyone, maybe *that's* what's going to keep you safe.'

She stared at him for a moment. 'But what about you, Ty? What will keep you safe?'

Tyrese cricked his neck, trying to undo some of the tension. 'Look, let's just listen to the warning.' He was too fearful to answer her question. 'Agreed?'

She gave a small nod. 'We really are on our own, aren't we?'

Neither he nor Marvin replied.

From underneath her white floppy hat, Ellie gazed at her dad. 'I'll be back, I promise.' She wiped her tears, then frowned. 'What's that noise? Listen.'

Tyrese looked around, then his stare fell and stopped at Mr Thomas.

The tiniest of pitter-patters, like a dripping tap, was coming from him. In the quiet, Tyrese crept slowly forward to get a better look. He stared up at Mr Thomas, still not quite understanding what the noise was.

His gaze wandered over his face.

'Oh my God!'

Tyrese shrank back, watching a moth crawl out of the side of Mr Thomas's mouth.

Ellie let out a distressed squeal, turning away.

'Let's go, let's go! Come on, come *on*! Run!'

And as Tyrese pulled the others with him, he wondered if any of them would ever make it back home . . .

20

The bus down to Buff Bay had driven at speed, taking them along the winding roads. The engine had clattered and grinded in and out of the different gears while Tyrese had filled in Ellie and Marvin on some of the other unexplained events which had happened to him since he'd arrived on the island. Though most of the journey had been done in silence, and Tyrese had watched out of the window with his mind flitting from Ellie's dad to his own.

Panic had sparked inside him like a match as he'd scrambled around in his memories. He could see his dad's favourite socks, remember the threads on the heel giving way, the dots of blue so vivid, the spots of green so vibrant, but he couldn't really picture his dad's face any more. It was as though his dad was out of focus, fading away little by little. He'd slammed that thought down like a gavel.

At just gone four o'clock, having found himself squashed up against a window next to a large woman, Tyrese gratefully stepped off the bus in Buff Bay. The warm ocean air lapped over him as he stood beside a yellow-painted wooden hut on the side of the road.

Fanning himself with nothing more than his hand, he glanced up towards the craggy slopes and mountains which towered over the coastline. A blue mist coloured them. He thought about his mum and Grammy back there in the mountains; their stillness, their staring eyes. He was so far from the safety of everything he knew, it made him feel like he was a stranger in his own life.

'Hey, Ty! Hey, you OK?' Marvin, who'd ended up a few rows behind him after giving up his seat for an elderly lady, stepped off the bus looking as hot and uncomfortable as Tyrese felt.

Tyrese rubbed his chest, kneading away the panic, the cold sense of being hunted down sitting within him. 'Yeah . . .' His throat was so dry, the words got caught. 'Yeah, fine.'

'Ellie, *yuh gud*?' His cousin glanced over his shoulder at Ellie and threw a smile.

Ellie, whose eyes looked red raw from crying, nodded. Tyrese thought she looked far from all right but he didn't comment, and focused his attention on his cousin instead. 'OK, so what's the plan?'

'What you say we buy enough food for the next couple of days from one of the beach huts? At least then if we need it, we won't get hungry? Then we make our way to where you saw the old man, look around . . . Come.'

Under the greying skies, Marvin began to hurry away but Tyrese quickly gripped his cousin's arm, stepping in close, bringing his voice to a whisper. 'I know we need to do this, but why does it feel like the worst idea ever?' He could see the reflection of himself in Marvin's fearful eyes. 'I don't think this is safe, Marv.'

His cousin held his stare before he replied. 'It isn't, but like me said before, what other choice have we got? There is no other way . . . now, let's go.'

—

Having bought enough food to last them, they hurried in the direction of the beach, cutting through the small, busy covered market. Boxes of sweet potato and green banana piled high, with peppers and cho-cho and jackfruit laid in colourful rows, stalls full of scallions, avocados, breadfruit, kola nuts and yam, and a milling hubbub of voices and music filled the air.

Tyrese felt drops of rain from the beginnings of the summer storm which had been threatening since they'd arrived in Buff Bay. He led the way, running down the narrow sand path by the beach hut cafés and kiosks and on to the deserted section of the beach, looking behind him occasionally, making sure the others were keeping up. He headed towards the palm trees, ducking left down another small sandy path and through the grove of palm trees.

Seeing the brightly painted beach diner in front of him with the deserted track behind it, Tyrese slowed, and dread pricked at him like pins.

Unlike last time, the diner was open and a handful of customers sat outside at the tables.

He felt Ellie try to clutch his hand but he pulled away. He saw the hurt flicker over her face. He didn't want to upset her again but he had the most intense itch on his blistered finger which continued to ooze and bleed; it burnt, stung, though it was too painful to scratch. It was driving him crazy, as though he had thousands of bugs crawling underneath his skin.

'Whereabouts did you see him, Ty?'

Tyrese gestured with his head. 'Over there by the palm tree, after I'd banged my foot on the box, that's where he was.'

She nodded and gave him a cautious smile.

'Let's have a look about, see if there's anything else we can find,' Marvin said, sitting down at one of the chairs to tie his laces.

Tyrese felt himself sway, as though he were surfing on crashing waves of panic. He sat next to his cousin, breathing in deeply, slowly. He could feel his cheeks flush and he gripped the edge of the metal table, hoping to stay in control. He drew his hand back quickly at the sight of a long centipede darting across the table.

'How can me help you?' A waitress appeared behind them, long braids down to her waist, wearing a white flowing maxi dress, a matching head wrap, and holding a pen and notepad to take their order.

Marvin glanced at Ellie and Tyrese. 'We don't have time.'

'I really need to get a drink though,' Ellie said, looking hopeful. 'I should've got one at the kiosk, sorry.'

'But we—'

'. . . She *needs* a drink, Marvin,' Tyrese cut in. 'Five minutes won't hurt.'

Marvin, visibly agitated, nodded. 'OK . . . Can we have three sodas, and a large bottle of water, please.'

The waitress nodded. Her face was pretty, with thick black

eyelashes framing her brown eyes. She scribbled their order on her notepad and smiled. '*Dat* all?'

'Yes, thank you,' Tyrese replied politely and she smiled again before going back inside.

Another sharp pain pierced through Tyrese's head. Rubbing his temples, he glanced around: a whirl of wind, sand twisting towards them like writhing snakes, the leaves on the palm trees snapping and cracking like flags in a storm, bringing a sudden chill.

'You know, I was wondering, Marvin,' Ellie mused. 'If we went to . . .'

'. . . Wait, look . . .' Tyrese scraped back his chair, stood up, willing his legs not to give way underneath him.

Marvin frowned. 'What are you doing?'

'He's there . . . He's there . . . The old man, I've just seen him, he was looking straight at me. He's inside the diner.'

Face pale, Ellie swivelled around in her chair. 'Where? I don't see him.'

Tyrese didn't move his gaze from the diner but he did bring his voice to a whisper. 'A moment ago, I swear he was there, staring right at us out of the window.'

'Then come, let's go and see.' Marvin got up but Ellie held on to the hem of his top.

'Marv, *don't*, please. It's not a good idea to follow him . . . Ty, tell him.'

'Ellie's right, it's a stupid idea, let's just scout out the area instead, like we agreed.'

'This could be our chance, Ellie, think about it, this could be the way of helping Grammy and Aunt Patty, *and* you dad.' There was an urgency to Marvin's words. 'Don't you want to help your dad?'

'Of course she does,' Tyrese snapped angrily at his cousin. 'But that doesn't mean we have to be dumb about the way we go about it.'

'We're wasting time, Ty!' Marvin's eyes blazed.

Tyrese looked around before bringing his voice to a whisper, making sure the other customers didn't hear. 'Cuz, have you forgotten it's *me* the Shadow Man wants? Don't you think I should decide what we do or don't do? And I'm not looking to follow no duppy.'

Marvin glanced around as well, then he brought his focus back on Ellie and Tyrese. 'Look, it's light, there are people around, there's the three of us. What can happen?'

Ellie shook her head. 'I don't know, Marvin, but that's exactly what I'm afraid of.'

'*Rahtid*, then you stay here with Ty.' Annoyed, Marvin headed towards the diner but Tyrese ran in front of him.

'Marv, listen, we all need to stick together, don't do this, this is stupid.'

Marvin quickly wiped away the beginning of his tears. 'Think what you want, Ty, but *wid yuh or widout yuh*, I'm going to do everything I can to help Grammy . . . She's all I've got.'

He pushed Tyrese out of the way and continued to march towards the door of the diner, giving Tyrese and Ellie no other choice but to follow . . .

21

The bell over the door of the diner rang as they walked in. The ceiling fan spun the hot air around at speed, the glowing blue flytrap buzzed in the corner. The seated customers – some were eating, some were just playing dominoes – glanced up curiously, but within moments they'd lost interest and continued minding their own business.

Angry at his cousin, Tyrese slowly walked towards the back of the long diner with Ellie close behind, trailing Marvin. He stood by the restroom sign, peering around the corner. Immediately he spotted the waitress coming towards him, carrying a plate piled high with steaming hot food.

'Well?' Marvin asked.

'I can't see him.'

'Are you *sure* it was him?'

Tyrese gave the smallest of nods, aware how much his heart was racing. 'Yeah, totally . . . unless . . . unless it was in my head.' He shrugged, sounded less certain, and massaged his throbbing temples. 'I dunno, maybe he's in the ba—'

But when Tyrese started to say his next word, Marvin gave him a hard dig in the ribs with his elbow and shrank back against the wall.

'Ty, *don't* . . . whatever you do, don't say another word. We need to get out of here. *Now*.'

His breathless whisper chilled Tyrese.

'Why, what's happened?' Tyrese rubbed his side. 'What's the matter?'

Marvin flashed a glare at him. 'Keep your voice down and just start heading for the door . . . Try . . . try to look natural, OK?' Tyrese could see his cousin's body beginning to tremble.

'I don't get it.'

'Ty . . . Ty, we just need to leave.' Looking like he was going to cry, Marvin seemed to struggle to speak. 'It's La Diablesse.'

'I flopped French, dude, what the hell are you talking about?' Tyrese hissed, trying not to own his cousin's fear.

'The waitress, *she* is La Diablesse.'

Tyrese glanced at her but Marvin quickly pulled him back around. 'Don't look! Don't let her see dat you know it's her.'

Even though Tyrese didn't quite understand, that didn't stop panic clutching at him.

'La Diablesse is a duppy,' Marvin continued. 'She's well known on the island. She was born human, but dem say she befriended the devil, making deals with him and over time she got her wish and him turned her into a demon. La Diablesse, it means, the devil woman . . . Apparently, she roams the nights, screaming, hides along dark paths, covering her face and body which isn't human. She waits for people to walk by, to drag dem to their death.'

'Hold on, how can it be her if we can see her face? She's real pretty,' Ellie whispered, almost too quiet to be heard.

'Grammy once told me dat, like a lot of duppies, La Diablesse shapeshifts, she can change her looks . . . But dat's not all. It's not the worst part.' Marvin gulped, looking like he was having trouble saying the words. 'Rumour has it, La Diablesse not only works for the devil, but she's also connected to *him*.'

'Who?' Ellie blinked away some tears.

'The Shadow Man.'

Tyrese felt Ellie jolt and noticed a couple of the diners looking up towards them.

'Yeah, but, Marv, like Ellie says, how can you be sure it's her?' he murmured, hoping – desperate – that somehow his cousin had made a mistake.

Marvin gave a discreet sideward glance to the waitress, who was taking an order from one of the customers. 'Weirdly, there's one part of her body she can't ever change. The part dat stays a demon . . . Look down at her feet. When she moves, you'll see it under her clothes.'

Tyrese and Ellie glanced towards the waitress, their gaze travelling down her long white dress. Ellie put her hand over her mouth and without even realising it, Tyrese leaned against the tiled wall, steadying himself, staring mesmerised at her feet . . . Her left leg ended not in a foot but a thick, yellowing brown hoof which was stained and crusted with what Tyrese thought looked like blood.

He reached and grabbed Ellie's hand. 'Let's go! Let's get

out of here!' He glared at his cousin, muttering, 'I told you it was a stupid idea to come in here.'

Keeping his voice down, Marvin retorted angrily, 'Why don't you save telling me dat for when we actually manage to get out of this place, huh?' He glanced quickly again at La Diablesse, who was busy laughing with one of the customers. 'Ty, just go, move. But listen, we need to make it look like we haven't noticed her, like there isn't anything unusual. *Yuh* ready?'

Tyrese didn't say anything, and with his eyes down, not looking left or right, he walked towards the door of the diner with Ellie so close behind him, he could feel her breath against the side of his cheek.

'Ty, hurry up,' Marvin whispered again.

'I am!' Tyrese's heart hammered; he only had a few more steps to go but it felt like a thousand. His footsteps, however quietly he trod, seemed loud, banging, as if the soles of his shoes carried a marching band.

He reached out to push the door open but he stopped, frozen, resting his forehead on the glass of the door.

'*Rass, wah yuh ah duh, Ty?* What are you doing? What are you waiting for? Move!' Marvin poked him hard in the back.

Without moving, Tyrese continued to stare out of the door, then turned slowly to face Marvin and Ellie. 'We . . . we can't go this way.'

'Why not?' Ellie asked, her lip quivering.

'Because of who's out there.'

Tyrese gazed at the old man standing outside the diner,

laughing, waving slowly to him. He tilted his head, his face covered in streaks of dirt, twisting up into a toothless grin, his whole neck covered with writhing black insects. His colourless eyes stared intently back at Tyrese.

It felt like the diner had cranked up the heat, the sweat dripped off Tyrese, the perspiration on his face like a mist of rain as his fear rose. 'It's the old man. He's tricked us. We're trapped.'

Marvin reached for the door but the grey blind on the glass pane rolled down at speed all by itself. He leaped for the handle.

Too late.

The door was locked.

Blood drained from Ellie's face. The place became quiet. The chattering stopped. Tyrese whipped his head around, quickly glancing at the other customers. Like his mum and Grammy had, the diners brought their fingers to their lips, sitting motionless, unblinking, making a loud shushing sound. But La Diablesse was nowhere to be seen.

'Oh my God,' Tyrese uttered and he fought hard not to scream. Marvin and Ellie stepped in closer to him and in that moment, it seemed like all their hearts were beating fast as one. 'What are we going to do?'

Without saying anything, Marvin gestured to Tyrese and Ellie. Silently, they hurried after him towards the back of the diner, following the sign for the restroom round the corner.

'It's a dead end,' Marvin said.

To the side of him, Tyrese saw the kitchen door begin to swing open.

La Diablesse.

He grabbed Ellie and Marvin, pulling them backwards into a room marked *Private*, shutting and locking the door behind them.

'Do you think she saw us?' Marvin turned to Tyrese.

Before he had time to answer, the door handle rattled.

Once . . .

Twice . . .

A sickening surge rolled through Tyrese. He stared transfixed at the door.

Just waiting, trying to quieten his breath.

The handle rattled again.

Then it stopped.

Now there was nothing but silence . . .

Tyrese moved only his eyes. 'That can't have been her,' he whispered in barely a murmur. He glanced behind him . . . What was this place? The windows were boarded, the heat stifling. He could taste the dust in the air. The only noise was the constant patter from the large black flies hitting the flickering light bulb and the sound of his own breathing ringing in his ears.

They were in a storeroom. Tins and packets of food rammed the shelves, boxes of vegetables and fruit occupied the floor, crates of drinks and wooden barrels and sacks stood to attention, and over in the far corner, Tyrese spotted something like hope.

'Look, over there. Come on, this way.' He pointed and ran across to the other side of the room. 'Hurry!'

Ellie shook her head, backing away. She gazed at the stairwell Tyrese was pointing at, leading down into an unknown darkness. 'Not the basement, anything but the basement, Ty. We can't go down there.'

Tyrese rushed up to her, grabbed her hand. 'Listen to me, unless we just want to wait here for La Diablesse to break through that door, we've got no other choice.'

A thud came from behind them.

A gasp bolted out from Ellie. 'That's her! That must be her! She's coming! She's coming!'

'Then let's go . . . Marvin, come on, what are you doing? *Marvin!*'

He watched his cousin grab a pocketful of dried rice from one of the large hessian sacks. 'Marvin, come on! Marvin?'

'OK, all right!'

Marvin ran to join Ellie and Tyrese. To the sound of a blood-chilling scream behind them, they began to descend the steep flight of wooden stairs into the darkness . . .

22

The sound of the door being smashed open followed them into the darkness as Tyrese hurriedly tiptoed down the stairs, each one creaking underfoot. The further he descended into the blackness, the more the temperature changed. The air turned into a chilly dankness and the smell of wet earth sat in his nose.

Above them, he could hear someone walking with one foot heavier than the other: the sound of La Diablesse's hoof thudding on the floorboards.

With his eyes closed, the noises from upstairs seemed more intense. The chilling unearthly shrieks, the haunting, angry howling cries seeped through him, knotting him with fear.

Tyrese heard something being dragged across the floor. Then another loud thud, sounding like something was being chopped up. A whirl of metal on air. Scraping, dragging. He didn't even want to imagine what that was, though his mind flooded with ideas.

He took a deep breath, slowly opened his eyes, focusing on the entrance of the stairwell. He could sense La Diablesse standing there, waiting, just as still, just as quiet as he was.

A light was switched on at the top of the stairs. The naked bulb, covered in dust, cast a dim glow throughout the basement.

Ellie turned to Tyrese but seeing her about to say something, he put his hand gently over her mouth.

Like statues, they stood under the stairs.

'Tyrese. Tyrese.'

He whipped round to look at Marvin and Ellie, speaking in a hurried whisper: 'She's calling my name. She *knows* my name.'

Whispering back, Marvin looked doubtful. 'Are you sure?'

'Yeah, yeah, can't you hear it?' Tyrese's voice was quiet, urgent, breathless.

His cousin shook his head.

'Tyrese. Tyrese.'

The sound of his name being screamed out was so high-pitched, so shrill, that Tyrese covered his ears, and not thinking, he stepped back.

The moment he did, Tyrese regretted it.

His foot struck the ground, the noise echoed around the basement, and he glanced up to the top of the stairs, terrified she'd heard. But he suddenly realised: when he'd stepped back, the floor had felt different. It had *sounded* different too.

Instantly, he dropped quietly to his knees, brushing away the film of mud and soil on the ground. His nose itched from the dust and he quickly pressed his lips tightly together to stop the cough tickling his throat. 'Marvin! Ellie, look! There's a hatch in the floor.'

He tugged on the looped handle of the wooden flap cut into the ground, feeling the rope pull the heavy trapdoor which looked like it hadn't been opened for years. The rope carved into his hand.

The hatch began to lift.

A rancid, decaying smell hit him.

He stared down into the darkness. 'It must be the sewers! They probably run right under the road behind the diner. It must—' He heard a movement above him. 'She's coming! Oh my God, she's coming!'

Tyrese gazed through the gaps in the bannister to the top of the stairs, though he heard her rasping chant before he saw her.

'Shadow Man, Shadow Man, him come get you,

Child of the Shadow Man, him come take you.'

A new terror began to grow inside him. The chant had changed. She had called him *Child of the Shadow Man*, just like the old man had done. And he watched as the bottom of her long, white dress appeared. La Diablesse was slowly making her way down the stairs towards them.

Unexpectedly, Marvin ran towards her.

'Marvin, no! Stop! *Marvin! Marvin! Don't!'* Tyrese yelled, unable to work out what his cousin was doing. 'Marv, don't be stupid. Marv!'

But Marvin stood at the bottom of the stairs. He dipped his hand in his pocket, bringing it back out to throw a handful of rice at La Diablesse. She screamed, recoiling, as though the dried grains were made of billowing flames. Her eyes turned bloodshot and yellow, and dark black froth oozed out from the side of her cracked mouth. She dropped to the floor, grunting and scratching, bloodstained fingernails scrabbling to collect the grains.

'Marvin, run! *Run!*' Tyrese beckoned his cousin, who sprinted back over to them.

'How deep do you think it is?' Ellie asked quickly, looking down into the hatch. 'How far?'

Tyrese glanced over to La Diablesse, who was still writhing and clawing the ground to collect the rice. 'Who cares, Ellie? Just jump. *Jump!*'

And without hesitation they threw themselves down into the dark, stinking tunnel below.

Marvin landed hard and awkwardly. He let out a yelp, and Tyrese quickly scrambled to switch on the flashlight. He glanced at Ellie, checking she was all right then he waded through the dirty, shallow water towards his cousin, who was holding on to his leg, clutching it in pain.

The fetid, malodorous air was so putrid, it was as though they'd dived into a pool of rotting eggs and Tyrese was sure he could even taste it. He swallowed with difficulty, struggling not to be sick.

Crouching, he gently touched his cousin's ankle. 'Are you all right, Marv? You think it's broken?'

'No, but it hurts bad,' Marvin said, his whisper high with pain.

'Here, let me help you up.' Tyrese stood, reached out for his cousin, pulling him up and out of the foul-smelling water.

'Lean on me, Marvin,' Ellie spoke quickly.

'I'll be fine, me don't want to slow you down.'

'I'll be fine too! Come on!'

Marvin gave her a grateful smile. He put his arm over Ellie's shoulder, resting his weight on her, as Ellie switched on her phone light. 'Oh dat's right, me forgot, you're the Blue Mountain Wrestling Queen,' he whispered, sounding like he was trying too hard to be cheerful.

'You guys go first, I'll keep a watch behind,' Tyrese muttered, glancing back up into the hatch. He could hear the scraping and snarling sounds from La Diablesse like a hungry rabid wolf, just metres above them, and he ran to catch up with Ellie and his cousin.

The network of sewage tunnels all looked the same. The dripping water echoed and black rats scurried and squealed in the darkness. Tyrese shone the flashlight around as he walked slowly through the fetid, decaying water filled with waste and rubbish. He was too afraid to turn around. The squealing of the rats made it seem like someone was walking behind him. And he tried *not* to wonder if they were going round and round in circles. He tried *not* to lose hope as one long sloping tunnel led on to the next. And he tried *not* to think that they could be stuck down here for ever.

No one to find them. No one to hear them scream.

He stopped.

His breathing quickened and he gazed intently at the wall of the tunnel, lit up by his flashlight beam.

Ellie turned, looked over her shoulder and called to him in a hush. 'Tyrese, what are you doing, *Ty!*'

He didn't answer, though he continued to stare at the walls.

'Tyrese!' Marvin's voice echoed. '*Ty!*'

Ignoring them, Tyrese lurched forward. He started to tear at the sewer walls, fiercely pulling down what was plastered all over them. Marvin limped back through the water towards him. 'Ty? *Wah gwaan*? What is it?'

Tyrese stepped away from the wall and, as though someone had their hand over his mouth, he slowly panted his words: 'That's me . . . that's me!' He pointed the beam at the poster-size photographs stuck all over the sewer walls. There was someone else in the photo, standing next to him, though only one side of their face was visible, the other had been rubbed away. There was something familiar about them, as if the person was someone he used to know.

'Dat's the photo from Grammy's guest room! The one which was by your bed, Ty. But hold up, why half of him face missing?' Marvin stared in disbelief. '*Jeesam pees,* Ty, what's it doing here though? What's going on?'

'What?' Tyrese blinked. 'I've never seen that photo before . . . I mean, who's that guy with me?'

Marvin gazed at Tyrese strangely. 'Ty, are you kidding me, what are you talking about? Ty, look at it properly . . .'

Tyrese stared at the lit-up poster again. He shrugged.

'Ty, dat's your *dad*. It's a copy of the photo you said you took out of the frame and threw away.'

'Wait, what? That's . . . that's my dad?' The word cut at his tongue. It felt like he was looking at a stranger. He backed away from Ellie and Marvin, holding his head. 'No, don't say that, don't try to trick me . . . Just tell me who the hell it is. *Please, just tell me!*' He raised his voice and Marvin took the flashlight from him, pointing it at the wall. 'Look, Ty, it *is* your dad. I wouldn't lie to you. But hold up, why can't you recognise him?'

'I don't know, I just can't, but . . .'

'But what, Ty?' Ellie urged. 'Go on.'

Tyrese hesitated; the itch in his finger had subsided but the excruciating pain still lingered, shooting up his arm. He quickly glanced towards the dark tunnel, and whispered, 'I've started to forget things, small things at first, I didn't think it was a big deal when it started. But it's gotten really bad. Things fade in and out, and I can't hold on to them. I don't feel in control any more, and now nothing's really clear in my head about Dad . . .' Upset, Tyrese struggled to speak. '. . . he's disappearing, a piece at a time, just like that photo.' Tears lodged in the back of his throat. 'What's happening to me, Marv? I feel like I'm going crazy, I . . . I . . .'

A sharp twinge rushed and twisted into Tyrese's chest, the tightness so great it choked him. No matter what he did, he couldn't stop the surge of panic. It felt like he was being held underwater with no way of coming up for air.

Ellie kneeled in the foul water and took Tyrese's hand, looking up at him while he gulped and bent over. 'Breathe,

Ty, breathe . . . That's it . . . That's it, Ty . . . Way to go! That's it, you got it.'

Concentrating on Ellie's voice, clutching her hand, Tyrese began to feel calmer. He breathed in and out deeply several times, then flicked her a warm glance. 'Thank you . . . Thanks, yeah.'

Marvin looked nervously back down the tunnel. 'Ty, if you can, we need to go.'

Tyrese didn't move; instead he threw the briefest of glimpses at the poster. 'I know, but all this is just messing up my head more.'

'Maybe that's the point, someone or something is playing with us, Ty. They're toying with us . . . or rather they're toying with *you*.' Ellie glanced at the poster as well. 'It's like they're *trying* to send you kooky. Playing games with you, like when you thought you saw your dad's jacket in the wardrobe.'

Tyrese wiped the water away from his face which had dripped down from the ceiling of the tunnel. 'I'm really scared, guys.'

Looking anxious, Marvin whispered, 'Me too, but we really need to get out of here.'

'Will your ankle be all right?'

Marvin nodded at Ellie. 'It hurts but there's no way I'm staying here.'

They continued hurrying along the water-filled tunnel, which sloped gradually uphill. As they ran, Tyrese heard another screech coming out of the darkness behind them. He saw Ellie and Marvin slowing and he pulled them along with him while the screams and shrieks followed them, filling the air.

'Look! Look!' Tyrese pointed. 'Up there! At the end! Can you see it?'

There was a stream of moonlight.

The night sky was like a beacon, calling them to safety. They sprinted up the slope of the tunnel to meet the outside world. They found themselves on a ledge on the side of a hill.

'Where now?' Ellie stammered.

Marvin peered back at the tunnel as a piercing howl, like an animal caught in a trap, tore through the air. He shuddered. 'Anywhere but here.'

23

It was late, past midnight. Exhausted, they'd stumbled along the single mountain track in the wind and rain, trying to put enough distance between them and the tunnels to feel as safe as they could.

Eventually, under the troubled night sky, they'd come to rest at the edge of the forest which ran along either side of the winding path. The trees stretched out over them like giant umbrellas, and using the bright flashlight to see, Tyrese sat rinsing his T-shirt and joggers by the small bubbling stream, washing the sewer water out. He wiped his glasses and the wet from his forehead, feeling the specks of dirt mixed in, scratching against his skin.

Marvin sat huddled opposite against the trunk of one of the trees, massaging his ankle. 'Ty, you seem quiet. You worried about what happened in the tunnel with dat poster of your dad?'

'I don't want to talk about it.' It was a sharp reply. 'Sorry, I'm just tired, and—' He stopped. 'Actually, nothing, it's fine.'

'And what? Go on, Ty, what were you going to say?' Ellie asked kindly.

Standing to squeeze the stream water out of his top, Tyrese

grimaced at the pain in his finger. He looked over to Ellie. 'I was thinking about the others. *The missing.*' His voice was strained and his stare darted around the dark forest.

Ellie shrugged. 'I'm not following.'

'I was wondering what happened to them. The other kids.'

'What? What other kids?'

'The Shadow Man. That's who he wants, that's who he goes after. Kids. Teenagers. No one knows why though, they just disappear.'

Ellie and Marvin's faces reflected how Tyrese felt.

'How . . . how do you know? Who told you?' Ellie mumbled.

'Grammy.' Tyrese looked at Marvin. 'But you know about them, you even told me that the chant was called the rhyme of the missing.'

Looking stunned, Marvin shook his head. 'I only know what I overheard from Grammy, and a bit of stuff friends told me. But me never knew who the missing *actually* were.' Looking pensive, he added, 'Too afraid to ask, I guess . . . I never knew it was kids, Ty.' He visibly trembled. 'Why didn't you say anything before?' He suddenly sounded annoyed.

'I don't know, I'm sorry, everything's just happened so fast. I'm just trying to get my head around it . . . You know, when Grammy talked to me about the Shadow Man, I was really surprised because when I first mentioned him, do you remember how cross she was, Marv?'

Marvin gave a small smile. '*Grammy nuh easy at all wen shi a bringle.* Grammy's not easy when she gets angry,' he said warmly, though sadness tinged the warmth.

Tyrese smiled but then he shook his head and looked at Ellie again. 'But I know now she wasn't cross, she was scared, like she was taking a risk. But she was desperate to tell me this story.' He paused, thinking about the terror he'd seen in Grammy's eyes.

'What story?' Ellie leaned back against the tree.

'She started telling me about this guy called . . . Levi. Levi something . . . she did tell me his second name but I didn't really take it in, I was too freaked out. Anyway, Grammy said the only reason she hadn't told me the story earlier was because she was hoping that she didn't have to.'

Swirling her hand in the wet ground, Ellie said, 'So what *did* she actually say?'

'That's the other thing, she didn't have time to say loads because Mum overheard and got mad. Mum said she didn't want Grammy filling my head with frightening stuff and then after that, I never got the chance to ask her about it, it was too late. But Grammy did manage to say this Levi guy had done well in life, and he loved his family and everything, but one day something really bad happened. Like something terrible happened to Levi.'

They fell silent, deep in thought.

'Maybe your grammy was telling you the story of Levi because the Shadow Man did something to *him* as well,' Ellie suggested after a moment.

'Yeah, but Grammy also said, it was teenagers, kids who were *the missing*, not adults.'

'I don't mean like that, kind of like what's happened to

Grammy, and your mom and my dad . . . but only worse. Maybe something much worse than being held in sleep happened to Levi . . . But I think we really need to know his last name. It might help.'

'How?' Marvin asked.

'Well, what happened to him must be important, otherwise why would your grammy start to tell the story to Ty? And think about it. No one wants to talk about the Shadow Man because they *know* something real bad will happen, like they'll be possessed or something and—'

'. . . but why not us?' Marvin interrupted. 'We haven't stopped chatting about him.' Like Tyrese, Marvin stared into the darkness of the forest. 'Why haven't *we* got this sleeping curse as well, especially as the Shadow Man obviously wants to stop people talking?'

Ellie looked thoughtful. 'Perhaps . . . perhaps it's a different rule for them. I dunno. It's like what they say about poltergeists: they focus on kids and teenagers. They don't really haunt adults unless they get in the way. Maybe it's kind of the same thing. Like maybe the Shadow Man can't get to us the same way . . . or maybe the point is, he doesn't *want* to get to us the same way. I actually don't think he *wants* to put kids to sleep at all . . .' She looked at Tyrese a moment, before continuing, '. . . for some reason he wants to actually *take* them, like the rhyme says, and that's why each time it's the kids, the teenagers, who become the missing.'

'Can you just stop, yeah?' Tyrese responded angrily. 'Are you trying to scare me or what? Have you any idea what it feels like to know someone, *something* is out there, playing with you, just waiting to take you? Look, just stick to talking about Levi, OK.'

'But wait, hold up, so we agree the Shadow Man doesn't take adults, but I don't get why he's *only* going after Tyrese. And why not take Ty straight away?' Marvin questioned.

'God, what did I just say?' Tyrese growled at Marvin. 'And . . . and anyway, you don't know he won't come after you as well, there's always time,' he added defensively.

'I don't know why, but there must be a reason,' Ellie answered Marvin quietly but gave Tyrese a small, apologetic smile. 'Look, perhaps this Levi, maybe he knew too much about the Shadow Man. Maybe he tried to *stop* the Shadow Man. Maybe he was the only one brave enough to try.'

Marvin stared at Ellie. 'So this Levi was a *victim* of the Shadow Man too.' It was a whisper, a statement, but it was loud with fear.

Ellie nodded, 'So if we find out Levi's full name, we can find out more about him and the reason the Shadow Man did something terrible to him. Perhaps if we do, we can work out the story Grammy was going to tell Ty. Then maybe, *hopefully*, it'll lead us to the answers we need. What do you think, Marv?'

'Agree. I think it's the best chance we've got . . . as long as we know his surname.'

'And how do we do that?' Tyrese said, feeling the pressure and suddenly aware of how noisy the rain was as it fell heavily on the leaves.

'If you still haven't got a signal on your cell, you can use mine,' Ellie said. 'It's in the outside pocket of the rucksack. Let's just scroll through surnames, there's like A to Zs of them, you might recognise it when you see it.'

'And if I can't?' Agitated, Tyrese waved his hand in the air. Marvin grabbed it, pulling it closer to the flashlight.

'What's dat? What's dat on your finger?'

Tyrese pulled his hand away. 'It's nothing. I mean, I know it looks disgusting but I think that's because it's infected.'

'When did it happen?'

Tyrese frowned. Grammy had asked him the same thing. 'On the morning we went to Buff Bay, I woke up and it was there . . . Why, what's the problem? What are you looking at it like that for, Marv?'

'Ty, dat's the bite of the Soucouyant.'

The Soucouyant. Tyrese had forgotten until now but Grammy had said that too. He stared down at the painful infected blisters. They made him feel sick. His skin had begun to discolour and it felt constantly hot now. He'd never experienced anything so physically excruciating, not even when he tore his hamstring running. That pain was nothing compared to this. And if he put his nose close enough to the blisters, a foul odour came from them.

'Who are the Soucouyant?' Ellie asked, staring at Tyrese's finger with as much revulsion as Tyrese felt.

Marvin's lips were dry, he spoke in a hoarse whisper. 'Duppies. People sometimes call dem Ol' Higue. Dem a supposed to be the gatekeepers of evil. They suck blood, trade it with the devil for power, dat's why they bite the skin.

Three pinpricks, just like you've got, Ty. Grammy once told me they're like the workers of the duppy world, they do what other duppies tell dem to.' He paused before continuing, 'But to have their bite . . .'

'. . . To have their bite, *what*?' Dread gripped at Tyrese. He closed his eyes for a moment, his voice tight. 'What's going to happen to me?'

'I don't know, Ty, because most of the time when someone gets bitten, the Soucouyant would be coming back night after night whilst you sleep, taking your blood until . . .' Marvin paused again.

Tyrese opened his eyes to look at as his cousin, who shrugged nervously. 'Until? Marvin? *Until . . . ?* Just tell me, yeah!'

'. . . Until you're dead.'

'No, no, no . . . Don't say that.' Tyrese began to back away, his voice shaking, 'Don't you dare say that. That is not what's going to happen to me.' A pain like the bone in his finger was being snapped in half tore through him. He stared down at his hand, then yelled out in agony as a vein in his arm started to pulsate, getting larger, larger, until eventually he could see a long lump forming underneath his skin. It moved down his arm, to his wrist, across his palm, along his finger and towards the blisters.

He screamed, shrieking in terror.

Bursting and puncturing through the thin layer of blistered skin was a long, black antenna, then the head and legs of a centipede came wriggling from out under his skin. 'Get it out! Get it out, get it out! *Please*, get it out!' Tyrese scrambled, falling backwards as if he was trying to get away from his own hand. Tears streamed down his face. 'Get it out!' He banged his hand against the ground, trying to kill the insect, which writhed and squirmed under his flesh.

'Ty! Ty! Ty! Stop, you'll hurt yourself. Ty! Ty, you're making your hand bleed. Stop!' Marvin crouched next to Tyrese, holding on to his cousin's hand. 'Ty, Ty, please calm down, what are you talking about? There's nothing there . . . See?'

'What?' Tyrese panted heavily.

'Look.'

He slowly turned to look. The only thing he could see were the three blisters on his finger, oozing but largely still intact.

Ellie crouched as well. 'Your mind's playing tricks on you, Ty.'

'I'm going crazy, aren't I?' Shaking, Tyrese wiped his runny nose on his top.

'No, no, of course you aren't. Maybe it's more of the Shadow Man's sick game or . . .' Ellie trailed off, looking puzzled. '. . . I dunno, Ty, I wish I could tell you why this stuff is happening, but just try to hold on to what's real. Like, try to fight what's happening to you.'

'What do you think I'm trying to do? But when you don't know what's real, yeah, it's not that easy. Thanks for nothing.' Angrily, Tyrese sniffed, stood up, swiped away the wet earth from his damp trousers.

Still tense, he frowned and opened his mouth to say something else but Marvin got there first: 'But how did they get to you, Ty? The Soucouyant usually enter houses at night. I don't understand. Grammy *always* sprinkles rice around the house to make sure we're safe and nothing can get in.'

'That's just dumb, Marvin, rice isn't going to stop duppies getting into a house. It sounded like some joke when Grammy said it, when she asked me to—' He stopped, suddenly remembering. The rice. He'd thrown the rice away, hadn't he? Could it really be that? He hadn't bothered sprinkling it around like she'd asked him to, then the very next morning he'd been bitten.

'Asked you to do what?' Marvin stood up as well, stepped in closer to his cousin.

A wave of shame passed over Tyrese. 'On the first night, Grammy asked me to sprinkle rice around the house.'

'And did you?'

Tyrese didn't say anything.

'Did you?' His cousin raised his voice.

'No!' Tyrese felt anger surge inside him. 'No, I didn't, OK! But . . . but it seemed . . . it seemed ridiculous.'

'Ridiculous? Think about it, Ty. Dat's when this all started. I remember when you came to breakfast, you thought Aunt Patty had opened the window but she hadn't, none of us had. It must have been dem. It must have been the Soucouyant opening it and coming in.' Marvin paused and stared hard at his cousin, then he shook his head slowly. 'By not sprinkling the rice, Ty, you made it easy for dem . . . I think the

Soucouyant helped the Shadow Man get to you. Get inside your head.'

A flame switched on in Tyrese. He clenched his jaw. 'Are you saying this is my fault?'

'I'm saying, maybe you shouldn't have messed with things you don't understand.'

Stressed, Tyrese wiped his face. 'For God's sake, it was rice, Marvin! *Rice.* Maybe next time I'll throw a can of spaghetti hoops around the house whilst I'm at it, hey?' He snarled, but he knew it was guilt which was making him be so harsh.

Tyrese saw a flicker in Marvin's eyes, wounded from his words.

'Why are you making fun, Ty? You saw what happened to La Diablesse when I threw the rice at her. It *works*.'

Tyrese knew he should just back down and agree but he couldn't, he didn't want to admit what had happened to everyone was somehow his fault. It made him feel sick. He could feel a muscle twitching on his face, pins and needles shooting through him. 'So let's get this clear, Marv. You're saying it's because of me that everyone's in this mess?'

Marvin gazed intently at Tyrese. 'I'm just scared, Ty, I'm scared for all of us. All me want to do is to work out why this is happening and make everything OK again. I want to work out *how* to wake everyone up and keep *you* safe, to *save* you, Ty, before you become one of the missing. I know you don't want to hear it, but it's *you* the Shadow Man seems to want, and it was only *you* dat the Soucouyant attacked.'

'I know, OK! I know that, because *you* keep reminding

me that any minute now something could happen to me,' Tyrese screamed.

'Ty, please calm down. But Marvin's right, Ty, we just need to find the answers, it's like those fairy tales,' Ellie said softly. 'Find the key, lift the curse.'

'Well, it sounded like he was blaming me. Like I've done something wrong. Well, I haven't, I *haven't*, OK!'

For some reason Tyrese felt like he was overheating. He scratched and pulled at his wet clothes as though he wanted to jump out of his skin. His finger felt like he was holding it in a flame, his head was throbbing so hard, and his sinuses shot out a hot pain, as if he were breathing fire. 'And who do you think you are trying to bl—'

Then Tyrese blinked and he could hear his own words continuing in the distance without him, though he couldn't make out what he was saying.

He gazed at the storm wafting the leaves above, and it felt as if he were being picked up by the wind, floating, his body hovering over the forest, allowing him to see the tops of the trees. But little by little they started to change into waves of colours, moving, shifting into a fountain of shapes which danced and drifted around him until he was back in his bedroom again. He could see his wallpaper, his bed, his bookshelf, his TV on the wall and he reached out his arms and felt the weight of nothingness as the sound of a voice, of crying in the distance, soared towards him on the wind . . .

'Were you really going to throw dat at me, Ty? What's *wrong* with you?' Marvin pushed him.

Snapping back to reality, Tyrese stumbled, falling against a tree. He shook his head, feeling strange, like he'd just walked in on something he wasn't part of, and he wondered why he was holding a stone in his hand, so tightly that it dug into his palm. He stared at his cousin, who was standing over him. 'What the hell are you doing, Marv?'

'Me?' Marvin glared at him, an angry expression sliced across his face.

Tyrese stood straight. 'Yeah, you, what did you go and push me for?'

'Because stones *hurt*,' Marvin raged.

'What? No, I . . .' Tyrese glanced at the rock in his hand and dropped it. He caught sight of Ellie over Marvin's shoulder. 'What's the matter, Ellie, you OK?' He could see tears running down her face. 'Ellie?'

Ellie turned away and Marvin continued to glare at Tyrese. He poked him in his chest. 'Of course she's not OK when you swear at her like dat. Why do you have to be so nasty and screw face? She's done nothing wrong. Say sorry.'

'What do you mean? I don't know what I said.'

'Don't play games, Ty, don't lie!'

'I'm not lying, *I have no idea* what I'm supposed to have said or done. Marvin, please, don't you see, this must be part of it too, this must be part of what the Shadow Man's doing to me.'

'You're lying! And don't try to use dat so you act bad-minded, me ashamed to call you my cousin right now.'

Tyrese's shoulders drooped, pushing the air out of him.

'Please, please, guys, I'm telling the truth. Ellie, you know I wouldn't want to swear at you, or say anything horrible. I would never want to do that.'

He rubbed his head, watching Marvin hand Ellie his T-shirt to wipe her tears.

'Whatever I said, Ellie,' Tyrese continued, 'whatever I did, Marvin, I'm sorry, I'm so sorry, I didn't know . . .' But he didn't bother saying any more. His mind was numb, it felt there was so little of his true self remaining. Nothing seemed real. Not where he was. Not *who* he was, as though he were no longer a part of his own body.

He rolled his tongue round his mouth, wanting to get up enough saliva to take away the sticky dryness. He blew out, steadying himself, trying to avoid being sick. Ashamed, he sat by the tree and kept quiet, watching Marvin try to comfort Ellie.

24

The night passed uneventfully, but Tyrese didn't sleep much. The rains had stopped and the sky was black as ink, the moon so vast, and sitting so low, it felt like he could've reached up and touched it. He'd woken up several times thinking about Grammy, his mum and even Mr Thomas. He'd tried to fill in the blanks of what had happened with Ellie and Marvin, hoping to somehow remember what he'd done to them. His restlessness had prodded at him, though it didn't help that his cousin had snored loudly, but in a way, it had been comforting to know Ellie and Marvin were there.

Eventually, the sound of the wind rhythmically striking the treetops had lulled him back into an agitated sleep, then he'd woken up and before the others had stirred, he'd started scrolling through surnames on Ellie's phone, hundreds of them, thousands of them, like some warped version of Rumpelstiltskin trying to work out the name.

And now at just gone six in the morning, with the rise of the early morning sun, Tyrese had whittled it right down.

Yawning, he spoke to Ellie, noticing the crease line on her cheek from where she'd lain on Marvin's rucksack and the angry red mosquito bites on her legs. 'Carter, Clarke,

Campbell, Cook, Cooper. They were the surnames that seemed to click with me. Though one minute they all seemed right, then none of them seemed right. But the more I thought about it, yeah, the more Levi Cooper or Levi Cook, just didn't land.'

'But that still leaves us with Carter, Clarke, or what did you say, Campbell?' Ellie looked despondent.

'No, because all night the name *Randall* kept popping into my head, maybe because it was similar in sound, and that's what jogged my memory in the end, I remembered the name began with the letter *C*.' He shrugged. 'Anyway, it's Campbell. Levi Campbell. I just know it is.'

'You sure?' Marvin asked, yawning as well.

'Yeah, though apparently it's the most popular surname in Jamaica, in fact there's supposed to be more Campbells here than in Scotland, and it's a Scottish name!'

'Oh great, so we're stuck.' Ellie sighed.

'Actually, it's not as bad as it sounds. Grammy said this Levi guy was around the end of the nineteenth century. I've done a search, though the signal's not great on your phone, so the pages aren't loading properly, so I can only find three people of that name from around that era. Though only one of them comes from around this parish, which is where Grammy said he was from.' A sharp pain tore through Tyrese's head. 'Here, my eyes are burning, you have a look . . . And, Ellie, about yesterday, I may not be able to remember what I did, but I'm so sorry.'

She smiled warmly. 'How's your finger?'

Tyrese looked at the now mottled grey skin. There was a constant trickle of yellow pus and a sickly, rancid smell coming from it. 'It hurts like crap.'

He gave her back her phone and for the next ten minutes they sat in silence while Ellie stuck her tongue out in concentration as she searched on it and the summer rains started to fall once more. And Tyrese watched her, wishing the sense of impending danger which gripped him would let go, would just leave him alone. Though the twisted knots of anxiety had filled every part of him long before he'd ever heard of the Shadow Man.

'If we've got the right Campbell, there's nothing really much about him. The only thing I've managed to find is that his family home was a place called Hathaway Hall.' She glanced up at them. 'Who knows, his family might still live there? Maybe they kept the house in the family, handed it down to different generations? You think it's worth going there? Maybe someone will talk to us.'

'It's possible,' Tyrese said.

'Apparently the hall isn't too far from Spanish River, which is supposed to be somewhere in the Blue Mountains. Do you know it, Marvin?'

'I know where Spanish River is from Grammy's.' He shrugged and bit into one of the vegetable patties they'd bought in Buff Bay.

'Here, why don't you have a look now, Marv, I've got location on, but it's not making much sense to me? You know the area.' She passed him her phone.

Marvin took it and looked over the map Ellie had brought up on the screen. 'OK, so it's saying we're here . . . and Hathaway Hall is here.' He spoke more to himself. 'OK, yeah, me see how to get there.' He passed it back to her. 'Can you move a mountain, Wrestling Queen?'

He grinned and Ellie giggled. 'What?'

'Well, if you could or you went by how the crow flies over dat canyon, then Hathaway Hall is only ten minutes from where we are now.'

'And *dang it*, as I've got no wings . . .' she drawled in an exaggerated Texan twang. 'And I kind of need more practice at moving mountains . . .'

'. . . Then it's a couple of hours' walk.'

Tyrese and Ellie groaned at the same time.

'There's only one track and we're already on it.' Marvin glanced at his watch. 'It's half past six now; if we're lucky and the weather holds, we'll be there by eight maybe, otherwise in hurricane season, we'll just have to wait it out. Ready?'

Ellie took a deep breath. 'As ready as I'll ever be, y'all . . . Ty?'

He looked at Ellie and Marvin. 'Yeah, I'm ready . . . let's go and find out Levi Campbell's story . . .'

—

The weather was against them and the storm whisked around. Tyrese found it easier to walk with his head down, helping him avoid the sharp sting of the driving rain. He'd also taken his glasses off to stop him feeling like his face was pressed against a water cascade.

Ellie walked next to him, her red hair stuck to her forehead in thick, wavy wet strands. 'I was thinking about those posters in the tunnel of you and your dad, and I was wondering, you know . . . why you don't talk about him?' she asked cautiously. 'I know you said your memory's fading in and out, and I get that, but when you do remember stuff, Ty, or when someone talked about him back at your grammy's, you got really angry, you never wanted to speak about him. I don't understand, Marvin said he was really cool.'

Tyrese turned his head slightly and immediately regretted it when a piece of grit blew into his eye. He thought hard, trying to work out what Ellie was saying. *Dad.* He shook his head as though the word were a complicated maths sum. A foreign language. Then it hit him. He realised what she was saying.

He felt the rain run down his neck and he breathed deeply, for some reason picturing Jonathan. 'Why are you asking me about him? Why does it bother you what I say or don't say?'

Ellie ran in front. 'Because it might help, Ty. Every time he's brought up, you don't want to talk, and now you say you can't because your memories are like –' she searched for the word – '. . . being erased, disappearing. But I think to fight this, you have to *want* to remember, Ty, you have to *want* to talk about him, otherwise it's going to make everything harder. If you talk about your dad, well then, surely it'll be harder for everything to fade. Just try it.'

Tyrese felt a darkness descend on him and torrents of rainwater ran down his face. He gritted his teeth, feeling the pulse throbbing above his eye. 'How do you know what I've tried to do? You don't know what's in my head. And don't you get it, I don't want to talk about him in the past tense, Ellie. Talking about him, or thinking about him, won't bring him back, will it? So what's the point?' He stopped himself from crying as a bubble of snot came out of his nostril. 'But you're wrong to think I haven't tried. I have. But I can't get past all the bad stuff, and I definitely don't want to think about *that*.'

He stared at Ellie. It was weird because it seemed it was all he had left now; bad stuff, sad stuff, stuff that no one would ever want to remember. He couldn't explain why, but the thoughts that made him feel sad were the freshest in his mind. So he guessed that was *one* good thing – the only good thing about what was happening to him. His memory was fading, melting away like the last days of snow, and once that was gone, all the hurt would be gone too.

'What do you mean?' Ellie asked.

Tyrese shook his head, not wanting to say. 'It doesn't matter.'

'No, tell us, Ty. What bad stuff?'

His eyes stung. 'I said it was nothing, didn't I?'

'Ty, I . . .'

'. . . OK, OK, God.' He banged his hand against his head and gulped for air, feeling the familiar tightness return in his chest. '*Bad stuff* . . . The day in March at the airport; the trousers I wore that Mum had bought especially for the funeral that rubbed a little mark on my waist; the rain outside the crematorium, running down the side of his coffin. And the silence, I remember what that sounds like in the house, now that Dad's voice isn't there, so I turn my music loud, right up, to stop me hearing it, but Mum always wants me to turn it down because she doesn't understand . . .'

'. . . Ty, you don't have to do this,' Marvin said, looking upset.

'No? Well, she wanted to hear them,' Tyrese raged, pointing at Ellie. 'Are they bad enough memories for you? Or . . . or maybe you want to hear how I can remember *exactly* the way I treated Dad the last time I saw him. And that, Ellie, *that* moment, messes me up every time . . .'

He swallowed and lowered his head, tears rolling slowly down. '. . . It was the day I was flying to Athens for the athletics championship. Mum had gone to work and I couldn't find my wallet so Dad was helping me find it. He couldn't come on the trip because he was going to have some treatment at the hospital, which wasn't unusual for him. But he was happy, joking, and I remember he was munching on this really big piece of hard dough bread, and . . . and I can't see his face any more, but I do remember that he had these short dreadlocks and they were really shining with oil in the sun . . . I was worried the coach would go without me, but Dad laughed and said that it would be like Man United starting without their centre forward. Then he got all soppy, yeah, telling me he was sorry he couldn't come, but he'd be there in my heart . . . but some of my team mates, well, they were in the house, waiting for me, so I got embarrassed when he gave me a hug and started telling me he loved me. I was like, yeah, yeah, whatever. I . . . I . . .'

He stopped as shame washed over him. 'I . . . I didn't even bother saying a proper goodbye, I just *left*, and he called after me, asking me to phone him. But . . . but I never even bothered turning round.' Tyrese shook his head looking down at the ground, watching the rain bounce back up as it hit the stones. 'And I never did call. I just got caught up with running some stupid race.'

He was trembling so much, the zips on his rucksack rattled noisily. 'And then . . . and then, when I arrived back home, Dad was . . .' He wiped his nose with his sleeve. 'I should've told him I loved him, I don't know why I didn't . . . and now I'll never be able to tell him. He'll have died thinking I didn't love him.'

'Ty, he won't have thought that.'

Tyrese lifted his head up quickly. 'Of course he would've done, and if I'd known – if I'd *known* it was the last time I was going to see him, I would never have left without saying it. But then, I would never have left him at all . . .' He glared at Ellie. 'So that's the thing, there's nothing good in *here* any more. *It's all bad*.'

'Ty, that's not all there is. There are the good memories too, maybe we can help you remember. There's this—'

'. . . You're not listening to me, Ellie. There's nothing there, it's like there's a wall and every brick of it is made up of *bad stuff* . . . And anyway, yeah, I've already told you, how will it help remembering the good things? It's pointless, it'll just make everything worse.' He gulped down hard for breath.

'But maybe it *will* help, Ty,' Marvin suggested. 'Look, you said you can't remember his face properly now, but I've got photos of him on my phone from when he was over here last year, and I've got some dat Aunt Patty sent me of all three of you. I can show you if you like. Help you remember the good things.'

'What part of this are you missing, Marv? What part of *nothing good* don't you understand? I mean, I can get photos, I can get all that, I even have a message on my phone from him which only came through when I got back from Athens. I saved it, but I've never listened to it, cos I can't . . . I just don't want to go there. And I'm not looking for your help on this either, yeah?' Tyrese snarled angrily. 'I had enough of all of that from my counsellor . . . So now can you both just leave me *alone*? . . . I'm going to Hathaway Hall, even if you guys don't.'

And with that, struggling to hold it together, Tyrese turned and marched up the track.

25

'Marvin! Marvin, wah a yuh a duh in this bad weather, huh? Lawd, yuh should be at home!'

The rain had eased only slightly but the wind was stronger than ever. Tyrese watched his cousin run up and greet an old lady who was calling him and standing at the side of the road, carrying a large basket full of callaloo.

'Hey, Mrs Stuart, *wah gwaan*, you OK?' Even though Marvin was soaking and his T-shirt and shorts hung from his body, he grinned.

The woman was wearing a bright floral print dress, a large brimmed straw hat, limp from the rain. She laughed warmly, showing off her gums. 'Marvin! Come, let me see you, let me give you a squeeze. Look 'pon you, you're soaking wet. What did you do, jump in a bucket?' She cackled, opened her arms and gave Marvin a long hug. He gently pulled away.

'Mrs Stuart, this is my friend, Ellie, and this is my cousin, Tyrese.'

Tyrese looked at Mrs Stuart. He'd seen her in some of the photos on the wall at Grammy's house. 'Hi, nice to meet you.'

Mrs Stuart looked back at Tyrese; her grey eyes filled up

and swam with kindness. She opened her arms again. 'Oh Lawd, Lawd, *cum yah now pickney. Me so sorry bout yuh fadda.*'

'Mrs Stuart, him don't know how *fi chat Patois,* remember him a Manchester *bwoy,*' Marvin said, winking at Tyrese.

She roared, and it sounded like a mix of laughter and sorrow. 'OK, sorry, sorry! Come here now, pickney.'

Tyrese felt shy, but he did as he was told and once more Mrs Stuart opened her arms, gave him a hug. 'Me so sorry for you, me so sorry to learn about your father, but me heard dat the funeral was lovely.'

Tyrese pulled quickly away. He gave her a tight smile. 'Thank you.'

'Your grammy, well, to see her so upset, it was terrible,' Mrs Stuart continued. 'But at least you're here, me know dat will mean a lot to her . . . How is she, by the way? She good?'

Tyrese gave a quick glance to Marvin, who shook his head, prompting Tyrese to say, 'Oh yeah, she's fine, thank you for asking.' He knew they couldn't risk Mrs Stuart finding out the truth in case something bad happened to her, or something worse happened to Mum and Grammy and Mr Thomas.

Mrs Stuart nodded, shaking the rainwater off her brim. 'Anyway, what are you doing here so early in the morning? It's a long way from your grammy's house. Not causing trouble, me hope, Marvin.'

'We came out for a walk.'

'At this time? At seven-thirty in the morning!'

Tyrese could see her mulling it over. He watched her

frown and look at Marvin suspiciously. 'You tell me dat you walked all the way from your grammy's mountain to here at Rose Hill Gap? Dat's a mighty long walk, Marvin, a difficult one too. You sure you didn't fly?'

Marvin grinned, Tyrese thought he looked slightly relieved. 'Oh no, we were staying in Buff Bay, we got a bit lost and then we got caught in the storm. Me never realised where we were.'

'Well, now you are here, how about something to eat for breakfast? You can't walk about in this weather, you know it's dangerous.' She smiled, patting him gently on the cheek. 'And me know how much you like to *nyam* my fried dumplings and boiled bananas, and if you're lucky, me do you some salted mackerel . . . Now come, which one of you a strong enough to carry my basket?'

—

Mrs Stuart's house was sweet relief to Tyrese. She'd given them some towels to dry themselves and although he knew they had to make their way to Hathaway Hall as soon as they could, just sitting on a soft chair in her front room looking out through the large open windows, felt like a luxury.

The view saw forest-covered mountains rise and fall in the distance and the air was fresh and smooth as the summer rain continued to fall.

The room was painted in a cream wash, simple white furniture was dotted about, and they sat quietly around a table drinking homemade iced lemonade.

'Tyrese, come and get some more, come fill up the jug,' Mrs Stuart called from the tiny kitchen off the sitting room.

He stood and walked through, taking the empty jug with him. He caught a glimpse of himself in the mirror on the wall and he noticed the rings of tiredness under his eyes. His hair needed a good comb – he could see knotty locs forming in his Afro – and although his clothes looked clean enough, they were crumpled and carried the faint waft of sewer water.

Mrs Stuart smiled. 'It's in the refrigerator, Tyrese.'

He opened the fridge door, carefully spooned the lemonade into the glass jug from the large pan and glanced up at the wall. Like in Grammy's house, photos and pictures were dotted around, but there was also a large framed ink map of Jamaica on the wall.

'Your grammy and the ladies from our bridge club gave me dat a couple of years ago for my seventy-fifth birthday,' Mrs Stuart said, noticing Tyrese looking at it. 'It's an antique, very old, like me!' She laughed.

Tyrese's gaze darted over the beautifully drawn map. Studying it in detail, he read out some of the names. None he recognised. 'Spes Mountain, Ferrum gorge, Anser Hill . . .' He searched the map and pointed: 'There's Grammy's mountain, Clara mountain, but on here it's called Umbra.'

'Tru, tru, dat's what it used to be called. The names of some of dem places on dat map have changed over the years. It's not unusual for places to undergo name changes at some point in time, especially when it comes to an island like Jamaica with its history.'

Mrs Stuart turned, and looked at him strangely. She lowered her voice, talking slowly and Tyrese found himself stepping back slightly. 'Umbra. It means shadow. Darkness. It's the darkest, most inner part of a shadow, where all light has gone, Tyrese.'

There was a tense pause, then she smiled. 'Pass dat pepper, will you?'

Tyrese put the jug down on the side, passing over the container of ground pepper, making sure she didn't see his finger. He watched her grind it into the bowl of the dumpling mixture she was making.

'So, anyway, how are you finding Jamaica, Tyrese?'

'It's cool.'

Stirring the mix vigorously with a well-used-looking wooden spoon, she laughed again. 'One thing this island isn't, is cool. Even I am melting this summer and me live here. But you like it, mmm?'

He smiled. Nodded. 'Yeah, and it's good to see Marvin and Grammy . . .' He stopped talking, not wanting to say any more, not wanting to lie to her more than he had to.

Instead, mesmerised, he watched her spoon going round and round in the bowl, gazing as the flour trickled down the sides. But the contents of the bowl seemed to shift under his gaze, the mixture turning into a mass of writhing maggots.

He squeezed his eyes shut.

'Are you all right, Tyrese? Tyrese?'

He opened them, stared at the bowl, saw there was nothing there, only the dumpling mixture Mrs Stuart was stirring.

Cold sweat ran down his forehead. 'I . . . I . . . I . . .' Unable to get his words out, Tyrese stopped, lifted up his glasses and rubbed his eyes.

'Tyrese, you don't look very well, all dat rain maybe has given you a chill? Why don't you just go and sit down with the others and let me get on with this. Maybe once you have some food inside you, you'll feel better. My fried dumplings are known for getting even a sick man out of bed.' Once more she roared, reminding Tyrese of Grammy.

He glanced again at the bowl. 'OK, I think I'll do that . . . Oh, and thank you, Mrs Stuart.'

Tyrese hurried out of the room, and gave Marvin and Ellie a look, who stared back at him.

'You good, Ty?' Marvin asked. 'Something wrong?'

He shook his head. 'Bit hot, that's all. Maybe I'll go and wash my face in the bathroom,' he answered, trying to sound normal.

He rushed out of the room, into the small hallway, closing his eyes. Leaning against the wall, his thoughts poured into his head like the torrential rain. He was so tired. His *head* felt so tired but he knew he needed to keep strong for his mum and Grammy, but right now he wasn't sure how to.

All this was his fault. He was the one to blame. And he wished, he wished, he wished, he *wished* life could go back to how it was last year. And even though he couldn't remember it properly any more, he knew, somehow he just *knew* everything would be all right if he could go back to before.

He squeezed his eyes and pushed the air out of his lungs. He kicked the skirting board with his heel, over and over again. He didn't want to feel like this. He didn't want to feel like *this* any more. And Ellie was right, there must have been good times, lots and lots of good times, but everything hurt too much, everything was too painful. So if he couldn't picture his dad, if he forgot everything about him, if he even forgot to know how to say the *word*, he'd be fine, wouldn't he? This feeling he hated, couldn't explain, would go. This knot in his stomach getting tighter and tighter would vanish, wouldn't it? And the squeeze on his heart which felt like someone was crushing it between their hands, would disappear. Because he couldn't deal with it, he couldn't deal with it a single moment more.

Opening his eyes, Tyrese took a deep breath, stopped himself from crying and walked along the hall to find the bathroom. He wanted to wash his face, but he also wanted to wash his finger. Apart from the pain, the smell and the blood and pus seeping from it was getting worse.

He looked behind the first door he came to but straight away he saw it was just a storeroom, packed high with various boxes and books. Closing it quickly, he made his way along, peeked around the next door. It was a small, tidy bedroom, but not wanting to look like he was snooping, Tyrese hurriedly closed it.

Entering the room at the end of the hallway, he stumbled back like a gust of air was knocking him over.

His gaze darted left to right.

The walls, windows and floor were covered in thousands and thousands of long, thick, black centipedes, making the room look like it was moving. Then he caught sight of something . . . *someone* on the bed. So still. And like Grammy, his mum and Mr Thomas, the person's eyes were open wide and unblinking.

His legs began to tremble but he stepped forward, hearing the crunch and the squelch of insects underfoot.

Not daring to go any nearer, Tyrese stopped, stared. Although the centipedes crawled over the person on the bed, he could see that their skin had become almost transparent. He could also clearly see who it was . . . Mrs Stuart. But if *this* was Mrs Stuart, who was the person making dumplings in the kitchen?

26

'Tyrese? Ty?' Marvin glanced at his cousin. 'What's up?'

Tyrese took a deep breath.

Glancing across to the kitchen, seeing Mrs Stuart happily frying the dumplings and salted mackerel, Tyrese leaned forward so Ellie and Marvin could hear what he was whispering: 'Mrs Stuart is in the bedroom.'

Marvin's forehead creased. 'What are you talking about?'

'*Mrs Stuart* is in the bedroom,' Tyrese repeated.

'Ty, she's in the kitchen, can't you see her?' Marvin said slowly, frowning.

Tyrese nodded. 'Cuz, of course I can see her, and that's not what I'm saying.'

'Then what?'

Tyrese sat down and lowered his voice even further. 'Mrs Stuart, the *real* Mrs Stuart, is *sleeping* in the bedroom.'

'Are you sure?' Marvin sounded dubious.

'Yes, I mean I was . . . I think I'm sure . . . But then I thought I saw the old man back in the diner, I dunno . . .' Doubt began to descend on Tyrese. He rubbed his head, noticing the whole of his hand was beginning to turn mottle grey as the veins bulged painfully. It made him feel ill and, not wanting to look at it, he placed his hands on his lap. 'Then go and see for yourself, Marv. But I'm warning you, it's not pretty.'

Marvin nodded and quickly left the room, but within moments he returned, tiptoeing in, a strained, pinched expression on his face. He glanced at Tyrese then Ellie, slipping back into his chair, and simply said, '*Bwoy*, dat's not good.'

'Oh Lawd, look at dat, the storm is getting worse.'

Tyrese jumped at *Mrs Stuart's* voice.

'Let's hope it doesn't blow us all away . . . Here you are, Tyrese.'

She stood over him with a plate of steaming hot mackerel and fried dumplings. 'Now, get dat down you, Tyrese . . . Don't look so worried, Marvin, yours is coming. Me know how much you like your food.'

She chuckled to herself and Tyrese let his stare follow her into the kitchen. The minute she was out of sight, he turned to Marvin and Ellie. 'Just *don't* eat it. Whatever you do, don't eat the food.'

'Why? Ty, *why*?' Ellie whispered.

'Is everything all right?' Mrs Stuart called through cheerfully.

'Trust me, I've seen what's *really* in them,' he whispered back to Ellie before shouting through to Mrs Stuart, 'It's lovely, thank you!' and at the same time grabbing the fried dumplings off his plate and stuffing them into his pocket.

Staring at what Tyrese was doing in a mixture of shock

and surprise, Marvin leaned over to Tyrese. 'We need to get out of here.'

Tyrese nodded. 'I know, but—' He stopped talking. Mrs Stuart was coming into the room.

She smiled at them. 'Looks like you'll have to stay here, the weather's too bad for you pickney to try to get back to Buff Bay. Dat's what happens when you come in hurricane season, Tyrese.' Mrs Stuart laughed and watched the rain batter the windows. 'Now, here you go, Ellie, and Marvin, me did some extra dumplings for you . . . Tyrese, what! You finished already, Lawd have mercy, you want some more?'

'*No* . . .' Frantically Tyrese shook his head, speaking quickly, 'I mean, no thank you, Mrs Stuart.'

She stood looking at Marvin and Ellie. 'Go on then, let me see you eat it. I like to see pickney enjoying their food.'

Marvin and Ellie glanced at each other, then they glanced at Tyrese, who gave them a tiny shake of his head, then finally they turned to Mrs Stuart, trying to smile.

'Well?' Mrs Stuart said. 'Go on, eat up. What are you waiting for?'

Ellie and Marvin stared at the plate, picked up their forks and slowly, very slowly, each scooped up a dumpling, bringing it to their lips with trembling hands.

'Oh my God, oh God, look at that! Oh wow, look at that! Mrs Stuart, look!' Tyrese jumped up, pointed out of the window, pulling Mrs Stuart gently over with him.

'Look there!'

'Where?'

'There! Over there!' Tyrese shouted.

Mrs Stuart gazed out of the window. Her gaze darted around then she kissed her teeth. 'What am I supposed to be looking at, child? The only thing me see is rain.'

Tyrese glanced over his shoulder and Ellie mouthed a '*Thank you*' as she and Marvin stuffed the dumplings into their pockets.

'In the trees. I . . . I think I saw . . . er, I saw . . . a . . . a . . . woodpecker.'

'A woodpecker?' Mrs Stuart stared at him and something in the way she looked, the darkness clouding her eyes, made Tyrese catch his breath, step away and shrink back towards the table.

'Yeah, well I thought it was . . . maybe, maybe I got it wrong . . . sorry,' Tyrese said hurriedly.

Mrs Stuart continued glaring at him, holding his stare like she'd done in the kitchen. Shadows flickered through her eyes. Unable to look at her any longer, Tyrese gazed down, tried to stop shaking, clasping his hands tightly together.

Another moment passed, then without saying anything, Mrs Stuart turned, kissed her teeth, and walked back through to the kitchen.

Feeling like he'd been holding his breath, Tyrese hurriedly sat down and along with Ellie and Marvin, emptied his pockets full of food into the rucksack. 'You're right, we need to go, like *now*.'

Marvin glanced towards the window. 'Problem is, look

'pon the weather! We're in the middle of nowhere, it won't be safe to walk. The wind's so strong, it'll be dangerous.'

'I don't care, I really don't, let's just go. You've seen what's in that room.'

'I agree with Ty,' Ellie said, nodding. '*I* don't know what's in the bedroom, but I know I'd rather face the storm than stay with Mrs Stuart.'

Tyrese pointed to the kitchen. 'Believe me, Ellie, that is *not* Mrs Stuart!' He stared at *Mrs Stuart* busying away, noticing a large, thick centipede slithering up her leg. It was like she didn't even notice it was there.

Ellie looked at Tyrese. 'Let's go, now. *Please* . . .'

'But how, it's not like we can drive out of here, is it? It's not like . . .' Marvin paused, leaned back on his chair, throwing a quick glance into the kitchen. 'I've thought,' he said, bringing his voice down. 'Mrs Stuart has an old pickup truck, it's easy to drive, it's automatic. Even Grammy drove it when Mrs Stuart wasn't well. And Grammy, *bwoy*, she is the worst driver *ever*.'

'Yeah, but you still have to know how to drive, Marvin, to *be* a bad driver,' Ellie said, looking more anxious by the minute.

'I can drive,' Tyrese stated. 'I mean, I think I can . . . I . . . oh, I dunno.' He shook his head, trying to get the thought to focus, the memory, having faded in the back of his mind like a setting sun.

'What do you mean?' Ellie asked, sounding puzzled.

Tyrese's gaze darted around. Why couldn't he remember?

Think. He had to think. 'No, it's no good. I don't know why I even said it.'

His cousin nudged him. 'Ty, can you drive or not?'

'That's what I'm saying,' Tyrese hissed. 'I don't know, I can't remember.'

Marvin glanced towards the kitchen then back at Tyrese. 'Why did you say it then?'

He raised his voice. 'I said I don't know!'

'*Everything all right*?' Mrs Stuart called through. '*I hope you pickney aren't arguing*.'

'No, we're not, sorry, Mrs Stuart, we'll try not to be so loud,' Ellie shouted back. She stared at Tyrese. 'How would you know how to drive? Would your mum have taught you?'

Tyrese shook his head. 'No, she's too much of a nervous driver. She's really bad.' He gave a half smile.

'Then maybe your *dad* did,' Marvin said, emphasising the word. He went in his pocket and pulled out his phone, and flicked through the apps. Then he placed his phone on the table. 'There, Ty, dat's your dad. Did *he* teach you?'

Tyrese pushed the phone away, turned and stared out the window. He shook his head again. 'Just leave it, yeah? I don't want to play these games.'

'Tyrese, no one's playing games. Look at it. *Please*. We need to get out of here alive, and we need to get out before dark, dat's when duppies are at their strongest, so *please* just look.' Marvin took his hand.

Tyrese fought back the tears. 'It's pointless, I can't remember.' He continued to stare out of the window.

'Ty, please. Just look. You have to look at it.'

'You've got to fight whatever's going on, Ty,' Ellie whispered. 'I know you can do it. I believe in you, Ty.'

His cousin tapped his arm and slowly Tyrese turned back to look at the phone.

'Really look at it,' Marvin added. 'Him teaching you to drive would be the good stuff, Ty, not the bad stuff, and me know it might be hard, but try, Ty. OK? Really try.'

Tyrese gave the tiniest of nods. He took a deep breath and stared at the photo as though he were falling into it. A strange feeling suddenly shot through him like a spark of light, and he braved through the sharpened ache in his heart, and fought to push away the sense of panic, the feeling of wanting to run as his memory began to rise, as images grew in his mind . . . That was it. Yes, that was it . . . Dad and him, they'd been on the Yorkshire moors, laughing, having fun . . . A *good* day. Yes, that was a good day. The good stuff. 'I remember!' Tyrese blurted out. 'I remember! I mean, I've only done it a couple of times but last summer, me and Dad, we went camping, he taught me how to drive his truck.'

His chest began to tighten and it felt like waves of pain were crashing in and Tyrese pulled back from that summer day, fidgeting with the hem of the crisp white tablecloth. The memory shut down again, then there was nothing but darkness once more, a guillotine cutting off his thoughts.

His cousin smiled at him, slipped his phone back into his pocket. 'So, if Ty can drive, we just need to find the keys,' Marvin said, throwing another glance at the kitchen.

'OK, I'll go and distract Mrs Stuart in the kitchen,' Ellie said, getting up.

Tyrese and Marvin waited, listening for Ellie to start talking to Mrs Stuart before they quietly searched through the small polished wooden writing desk.

'There's nothing here,' Tyrese said after a few minutes. He carefully shut the last drawer, wondering where else they could look. 'What are we going to do now?'

Marvin shrugged as Ellie came back through to join them.

'Anything? How did you get on?' Tyrese asked, hoping she had good news.

Her mouth was drawn into a line and she shook her head. 'No, sorry. I tried to look for them when I was putting the silverware away, but I don't think they're there.'

Marvin sighed. 'So where else?'

'The bedroom, what about her bedroom?' Tyrese suggested.

'No way, Ty. Me don't want to go in there, not again.'

Tyrese brought his voice down into a murmur, shuddering at the thought of Mrs Stuart's room and the sound of the crunching centipedes. 'OK then, I'll go. But you need to keep Mrs Stuart distracted. You and Ellie go back into the kitchen and talk to her, talk about me, talk about Grammy, talk about your wrestling, Ellie, talk about *anything*, but whatever you do, keep her distracted.'

27

It was worse than before. It seemed to Tyrese like the insects had doubled in size and number. The walls, windows and floor were thick with the black, writhing centipedes. Once again he saw them scurry and drop off the ceiling. He shivered, recalling last night, when he thought a long, thick centipede was crawling under his skin, burying into his flesh.

But quickly he shook away that image and hurriedly made his way towards Mrs Stuart's bureau.

Hearing the insects squelch underfoot, Tyrese gulped down hard. He felt like he was going to throw up. He opened the drawer but jumped back at the sight of dozens of centipedes pouring out of it. His legs felt weak, but he forced himself to take a deep breath. '*Come on, come on, you can do this,*' he spoke out loud, trying to boost himself.

He breathed out. His hand hovered above the open drawer before he lowered it, *slowly*, gritting his teeth, feeling around for Mrs Stuart's keys. Though the only thing Tyrese could *actually* feel were the bodies and legs of the scuttling, crawling insects.

'*Oh my God!*' He flinched but he forced himself to continue to root around in the next drawer and shivered in disgust as another wave of centipedes came out of it, splattering on to the floor.

Pushing his hand right to the back, Tyrese winced. Wait, what was that? His fingers brushed against something cold and metal. He grabbed at it, brought his hand out. *It was the keys! He had the keys!*

Not looking at the real Mrs Stuart covered in writhing insects – which made it look like her legs were moving – Tyrese ran out, back along the hallway and into the sitting room.

He signalled to Ellie and Marvin who quickly finished off their conversation with Mrs Stuart and hurried through to join him.

'I've got them!' Tyrese panted, desperate to get out of the house as soon as he could. 'Did she notice anything, Marv?'

'No. Ellie was just talking to her about Texas.'

Tyrese nodded. 'Then come on, let's go – but we've got to be quiet.'

Ellie looked nervous. 'Are you sure this is going to work, Ty?'

'No, but what else can we do?'

They hurried quietly out of the lounge and Tyrese crept along the hallway with Ellie and Marvin so close behind, they were almost falling on top of him. He could hear Mrs Stuart loudly singing an out-of-tune hymn, though she sounded like she was struggling, choking on the words.

He tried to concentrate on nothing else but getting to the door, to the truck, to safety, though he glanced around at

Marvin, stopping occasionally and checking Mrs Stuart wasn't coming. He reached for the door and winced at the sound of the handle creaking. He paused again, trembling at the sea of black insects, seeping out from Mrs Stuart's bedroom like tiny eels.

Pulling open the front door, the storm rushed in. Terrified Mrs Stuart was going to hear, Tyrese signalled to the others and broke into a run, sprinting over to the truck.

The doors were already unlocked and they clambered in, the wind rocking the truck side to side, the rain hammering on the windows.

Tyrese tried to put the key in the ignition but his hands were shaking so much he couldn't fit it in.

'Hurry up!' Marvin shouted.

'I'm trying!' Tyrese concentrated harder on stopping his hand shaking, managing this time to put the key in the ignition.

He turned it.

He heard nothing except a small clicking.

'Come on, Ty, we've got to go! What are you doing? Turn the engine on! I thought you said you could drive?' Ellie yelled. The wind howled around the underneath of the pickup truck and it continued to rock side to side.

'It's not me, the truck's not starting. It's not working. It's not working!'

Tyrese's palms were slick with sweat. He looked towards Mrs Stuart's house and he tried the truck again but apart from the clicking, there was still nothing.

Marvin shook Tyrese's arm. 'Give it another go!'

'I am! I am!' Tyrese yelled, but no matter how much he turned the ignition on and off, it just wouldn't start. 'I think the battery's dead!' Losing hope, he slammed his fist on the steering wheel, which sounded the horn. He jumped, looked towards the house, and gazed through the heavy rain.

He gasped, pushing himself down into the driver's seat: looking right back through the window was the distorted, twisted face of Mrs Stuart.

'She's there! She's there!' Terrified, he jigged up and down in his seat like it was burning.

'What are we going to do? Try again, Ty! Try again!' Ellie leaned over, stretching across to fiddle with the key in the lock. She shook her head, tears threatening in her eyes, then glanced at the dial on the dashboard.

'Ty, look! *Look!* I think that's the problem! You've got the gear in drive. I see my dad do it all the time . . . Put it in neutral, I . . . I think you're supposed to have a car in neutral, otherwise it won't start.'

'Holy crap!' In the side mirror, Tyrese saw *Mrs Stuart* rush out of the house, the speed of her walk not resembling any old lady he knew.

'Go, Tyrese! Go! Oh God, she's coming, oh my gosh, she's coming! Drive! *Drive!*' Marvin hollered, looking through the rear window.

'*Shadow Man, Shadow Man, him come get you,*
Child of the Shadow man, him come take you.'

Tyrese heard the now-familiar chant as Mrs Stuart came

screeching out through the front door. He looked at the instrument dial: like Ellie had said, the truck was in drive. She was right.

As quick as he could, he flicked the column shift lever down one notch, changing the gear into neutral.

'Please, please, please, please start this time!' He held his breath, turned the key, the engine jumped and fired. '*Yes!*'

He released the handbrake, pressed his foot on the accelerator, the windshield wipers going at speed, and began to drive off.

'*Go!*' Ellie screamed. 'Go!'

Tyrese put his foot down hard on the gas, the tyres sped around, sending a mist of mud and rain into the air. He looked again in the side mirror and he thought for one moment *Mrs Stuart* was going to try to run after the truck. He gripped hard on the steering wheel, struggling to stop the pickup truck from running off the road, driving as fast as he dared, swerving and weaving along the winding mountain roads, hoping he wouldn't meet any other cars.

For the next fifteen minutes they drove along, down the mountain pass until Tyrese pulled the truck up to a stop.

'I can't believe I've just done that! I actually *drove*! We actually got away!' He grinned and laughed. It was like a firework had gone off inside him, rocketing through his veins.

He laughed again. He did it, he *really* did it! Then his dad flashed into his mind . . . He could picture him, *properly*. He could see his face. He could actually see his face. *Good stuff.* And this time it didn't hurt as much to think about him, it didn't feel like his heart was full of tiny razorblades. He could see the dimple in his dad's cheek, just like Marvin's. And he could see the way he always smiled at him when he came home from school.

A warm glow rushed through Tyrese as if he'd swallowed the sun. He giggled. What would his dad say? *You see, you did it, Ty. I knew you could. Just remember, you're so much stronger than you know, so much braver than you believe* . . . Yes, that's what he would've said, he always did.

Tyrese's shoulders suddenly slumped. He started to get that knot in his stomach. The memory was beginning to hurt, slashing at his heart, his lungs, his insides. And the more it began to hurt, the more he realised he'd been right in the first place. He didn't *actually* want to think about all those good times they'd spent together, it made him miss him too much. So he wouldn't, he couldn't – he wanted to shut it all out.

And as soon as Tyrese had made that decision, his dad's face started to fade into a blur, a tiny dot in the distance of his mind that faded all the more, until eventually his dad faded to nothing at all.

'Hey, Ty, what's with the long mouth?' Marvin said. 'You were amazing. *Bwoy*, my bredrin didn't ramp there, my cuz, him just burned up some rubber good! Big up, respect!' Marvin patted Tyrese on the back and burst out laughing, triggering them all to do the same.

Tyrese glanced in the driver's mirror. He leaned back on the seat, staring out of the window. 'Marvin . . . ?' he said after a moment. His shoulders tensed and he pushed his glasses to the top of his nose. His chest rose slowly as he got another glimpse in the mirror of something starting to slide down the outside of the rear window of the pickup truck.

He turned around and saw the bottom of a shoe appear, felt something shift on top of the car. 'She's on the roof! She's on the roof! *Mrs Stuart's* on the roof!'

Ellie screamed and Tyrese scrambled to turn on the engine again. He slammed his foot on the pedal and skidded off. The speedometer touched and quivered at sixty and Marvin and Ellie shrieked as Mrs Stuart's gnarled hand banged on the glass. Wind and rain billowed through the gap at the top of the windows and no matter how hard Marvin tried to put the window up, he couldn't, it was stuck.

The engine raced faster than the truck wanted to go and Tyrese saw smoke waft up from the front bonnet. He tried to swerve, hoping to shake Mrs Stuart off the truck, but one side of the road was a sheer drop and he was going so fast, Tyrese wondered if he could actually keep control.

'Get her off! Get her off the roof!' Ellie shrieked.

He gripped the wheel harder. 'I'm trying, but we're too near the edge. It's dangerous!'

Mrs Stuart held on, her fingers poking through the gap at the top of the passenger window. Marvin tried to bang them away but they curled in, gripping the inside of the car. 'Over there! Ty, over there!' Ellie pointed at some trees on the other side of the road. 'Drive through them, you might be able to knock her off! Quickly!'

Tyrese nodded, focusing too much to speak. Desperate not to mess up, he steered the truck towards where Ellie was pointing, feeling the tyres hit a small mound, causing the truck to judder violently.

Hoping it would keep going, he drove through the twisted plants of the banana trees, under the low blue mahoe branches, trying to knock *Mrs Stuart* off. In front of him there was another line of trees.

'*Ready! Close your eyes!*' Tyrese shouted, then drove at them at full speed, hitting the branches, banging and crashing through them. He heard a loud thud and glanced in the driver's mirror once again, heaving a sigh of relief as he saw *Mrs Stuart* finally tumble and roll off the roof on to the ground.

28

After making sure there was enough distance between them and the duppy, they left the truck safely parked on the side of a mountain track, not wanting to be seen driving it. The storm rumbled on but they agreed it was early enough for them to go back to their original plan: Hathaway Hall.

Cold and wet, they hurried along a small road for twenty minutes before stumbling upon a hamlet where, after a short wait, they managed to get a taxi back towards Levi Campbell's family home.

Tyrese had been deep in thought for the whole journey. He was feeling odd, strange. It was hard to describe, but it was as if there was a constant buzz in his head. He was shivering hot and cold, and nausea sat constantly within his throat. It was as though he'd eaten something bad, and he'd been poisoned. He peeked at his finger. Maybe that was exactly what *was* happening. The Soucouyant's bite had infected him somehow, like the bite of a diseased dog.

Watching the taxi drive off, he glanced at his watch. It was barely eleven o'clock. 'The old man, La Diablesse, Mrs Stuart, they must all be part of this same thing.' He looked straight at Ellie and Marvin as they made their way down the small uneven path to Hathaway Hall. 'Whether it's to help the Shadow Man somehow or it's just a game to make me lose it completely, I dunno, but they're definitely working together . . . The rhyme of the missing, that you two don't seem to hear, they've all been chanting it. But the weird thing is, it's changed now, now it's different.' He recited it:

'Shadow Man, Shadow Man him come get you,
Child of the Shadow Man, him come take you.'

Ellie's eyes widened. 'Oh my God, that's horrible. But what does that even mean, how can *you* be the child of the Shadow Man?'

The darkened summer sky stretched out low and heavy above them, thick rain clouds swirling within. Tyrese shrugged, the feeling of disquiet burning away at him. He felt disturbed by the chant. Without saying anything more, he walked up to the tall metal black gates of Hathaway Hall, which were locked with a large rusting chain.

He pushed his face against the bars, icy cool against his brow. It soothed the headache which now seemed constant, raging and pulsing behind his eyes like the storm. He gazed at the unkempt grounds where weeds, grass, trees and bushes twisted together to form a thick blockade, and he glimpsed a wooden sign on the gate which hung broken and rotting:

PRIVATE. KEEP OUT.

'It looks totally abandoned. I really thought there might be someone still living here we could talk to.' The disappointment ran through Ellie's words. 'Maybe we've got it all wrong.'

A loud cracking of thunder came overhead while muddy grey clouds continued to swirl above them.

'Shall we go in?' Marvin asked. 'At least then we can see the actual hall. What do you think, Ty?'

'Yeah, we're here now, we might as well have a look around. We can climb up over that wall. Come on.'

They ran over to it and without too much difficulty they scrambled up, dropping down to the grounds of Hathaway Hall below. And for some strange reason it seemed to Tyrese that the winds had become even stronger on this side of the wall.

'Why don't we try over there?' Ellie suggested. She pointed straight in front of her and they made their way carefully through the dense thicket of wild thorn bushes and trees. Tyrese kicked at the undergrowth, trying to make a path while avoiding the razor-sharp thorns which snatched at his skin. Though each time he managed to stamp down the towering shrubs, it was if another bush or tree sprang up from nowhere. They battled on in silence, using broken branches to smash down the wild scrub, until eventually they managed to push through to a clearing.

The wind raged around Tyrese.

A heavily laden lychee tree dropped its fruit on the ground and the ackee trees' branches shook violently. He pulled a wild bramble thorn out of the back of his hand and rubbed his face, feeling the tiny scratches on his cheek from the bushes.

Although it was warm, he shivered, his clothes soaked through from the pelting rain, and the overwhelming sense of time running out blew around him as strong as any Jamaican winds.

All that remained of Hathaway Hall was an overgrown ruin with a few broken walls, though the brick foundations of the place stretched all around them.

'This must have been such a big house in its day. I wonder why it ended up like this?' Ellie said, looking at how far the ruins of the house went back. 'So where now, guys? You want to keep looking around?'

Marvin squinted through the wall of twisted trees on the other side of one of the dilapidated walls. 'What's dat over there? See it?'

Only just able to make it out, Tyrese saw a sandstone brick building concealed behind some dying breadfruit trees. 'Yeah, I see it – want to have a look?'

Marvin raised his eyebrows. He looked around, the expression deeply carved on his face: fear, dread, panic. It sent a shudder scurrying down Tyrese's spine. 'No, but let's do it anyway.'

As another rumble of thunder filled the air, they hurried towards it.

Nearing the low-pitched roofed building, Tyrese could see two crumbling pillars at the entrance coated with green moss and creeping ivy. Three stone steps took them down to the old arched wooden door. Fallen wet leaves formed a carpet beneath their feet.

'Shall we go in?'

Before Tyrese had given them a chance to answer, he cautiously opened the door, the huge rusted hinges creaking loudly.

He looked over his shoulder, making sure they weren't being followed. Then very slowly he walked inside, his heart beating too fast.

The air was cold, damp, and he found himself standing in a stone room. He heard the sound of his own rushed breathing and, tentatively, he looked around. On one of the walls was a tiny pane-less window cut into the brick, which let in the driving rain. More stone pillars with empty candlestick holders covered in dust and cobwebs festooned the room.

'What do you reckon this place is?' Tyrese asked, tasting the raindrops on his lips and feeling the piercing throb behind his eyes like someone was pressing burning pins into them.

'I think it's a crypt . . . Look at that in the corner, that's a tomb.' Ellie moved over to it, rubbing leaves and dirt off.

'What does it say?' Marvin asked.

She read the inscription on the tomb:

IN LOVING MEMORY OF LLANZO CAMPBELL,
THE BELOVED SON OF LEVI CAMPBELL.
TORN FROM THIS WORLD TOO SOON.
1883–1896

'Oh my god, his son died,' she whispered. 'He was only a teenager . . . what do you think happened?'

Marvin looked at his cousin and then at Ellie. He lowered his voice as if someone else was there. 'Maybe it was the Shadow Man . . . Maybe he did something to Llanzo. Perhaps dat was the terrible thing: Levi's son was killed by the Shadow Man.'

No one spoke but there was a whirl of wind in the darkest corner of the crypt, scattering leaves across the floor. Tyrese stared. Puzzled, he walked across to it.

Crouching, he took off the backpack, pulling the flashlight out. He switched it on, pointed the beam at the ground to where the leaves had been blowing, watching them move. After a moment, he realised there was a draught coming from where the wall should've touched the ground.

Running his hand along, Tyrese could feel a narrow gap there.

He stood and began to examine the wall.

'What are you doing, Ty?' Ellie asked as they walked up behind him. 'What is it?'

Not answering, Tyrese continued to pat the bricks. He stopped, frowned, going back to touch the one he'd just felt.

It was loose.

He pushed it harder.

Then harder still.

There was a loud rumble.

And he was suddenly hit by a plume of brown dust billowing into the air as if from an explosion.

'Ty! Careful, Ty! Run, Ty! *Run!*' Marvin shouted.

Tyrese leaped back, coughing and spluttering from the

dust which he'd sucked down into his lungs. He stumbled, treading on Marvin and Ellie's feet as he pushed back and the wall in front of him appeared to be caving in.

'*Me Raah*! Oh my God!' Marvin mumbled.

Recovering his balance, Tyrese followed Marvin's stare. The wall hadn't been collapsing at all. A door concealed within the wall of the crypt now stood open, leading down into the darkness.

A muscle in Marvin's jaw twitched. 'You're about to say we should go down those stairs and look around, aren't you?'

Trying to raise a smile but unable to do so, Tyrese felt the corners of his mouth trembling. 'Cuz, you read my mind . . .'

29

Careful not to lose their footing, they crept carefully down the steep, narrow flight of stone spiral stairs. The damp and chill rose the further below ground they went and the darkness stretched out in front of them. Each step added to Tyrese's fear. He moved the flashlight round, seeing intricate carvings and gargoyles protruding out from the arched roof, reminiscent of an old chapel ceiling.

The stairs led them into a long, cold passageway which took them to a set of stark, stone empty rooms leading off one another.

Tyrese glanced over his shoulder. 'What is this place?'

'Maybe we've gone back on ourselves,' Ellie whispered. She moved the beam of the phone light above her. 'Perhaps this was a part of the cellars. We're probably standing directly underneath what would've been the house.'

'But why have a hidden door in the crypt?' Marvin whispered back.

She shrugged. 'A lot of big homes back then did. They were often built with concealed passageways and secret entrances into the house . . . Though looking at it, I reckon this could just be the cellar of one of the wings, and the main cellar has been blocked up for a long time, who knows?'

They continued moving forward in silence and Tyrese battled with his thoughts, refusing to let his imagination take hold of what might lie within the walls.

Glancing around, he came to a halt: that was strange. A dark biting smell of wood smoke pinched at the back of his nose. The stench of it was so strong and so crisp, it was like he was standing next to a freshly extinguished fire. 'Can you smell that, Ellie?'

'Smell what?'

'Smoke.'

'Down here? No, the only thing I can smell is dust and damp – it smells like rotting wet clothes, but maybe that's me, maybe I'm just smelling myself.'

Walking on, Tyrese didn't say anything else but he thought back to when he'd been at Grammy's, and how so often it seemed like the air had been punctuated with the same acrid stench.

Getting to the far end of the underground rooms, another black door loomed in front of them. Tyrese stared at it, and even though he knew it was nothing more than a lifeless, splintered piece of wood, he felt as if it was staring back at him, challenging him to walk through.

He turned to Marvin. 'I don't like this, I'm not comfortable being here. I want to go.'

'Me too,' Marvin agreed. 'But we can't, Ty. Think about why we're here.'

And this time, it was Ellie who stepped forward, turning the metal handle.

It took the strength of all of them to push the door open, the bottom edge scraping shrilly against the floor.

Tyrese shone the flashlight around.

Behind the door was just another flight of stone stairs leading ever deeper, darker, into the earth. He began descending them, an eerie, unnerving silence following

'What is this place?' Tyrese whispered as they got to the bottom of the stairs.

Ellie and Marvin moved their phone lights around, and along with the flashlight, the whole room was illuminated.

'Wow, look at it.' Ellie was breathless, as if she was watching the turning on of Christmas lights rather than standing in what felt to Tyrese like the bowels of hell.

The room was vast. Another cellar? Tyrese wasn't sure. Benches and shelves lined the room, with objects lying all about and he could see that dust coated everything, laying so thickly it was as if a snow storm had fallen. He passed the flashlight to Marvin, picked up a heavy book from a large pile on the side, and blew off the dust. Immediately, he began to cough and quickly placed it back. Although he knew, or *hoped*, they were alone, there was a tense atmosphere and he was nervous about making any sound.

His gaze moved cautiously along, landing on a glass vial which he pulled out from a wooden rack as quietly as he could. Like everything else, it was covered in dust, and carefully Tyrese wiped it. It was labelled, though the ink was so faded it made it impossible to read but he could see that inside it, there was a dark reddish-brown, almost black mass, like a thickened crumbling scab. He shook it. It rattled, crumbling even more.

Placing the tube back in the rack, he looked along: there were dozens – maybe as many as a hundred – of glass test-tubes lined up.

'Ty, Marvin, see what I've found.'

Tyrese walked over to where Ellie was standing. Rolled and stuffed inside a tall, dusty wooden cupboard, curiously, there were dozens of pairs of gentlemen's trousers and unbleached cotton long-tail shirts, tattered, stained and torn but with precision, as if someone had deliberately sliced them.

'How old do you think these clothes are?' Ellie asked, stunned. 'It's like some kind of weird dressing-up box.'

Marvin grabbed the shirt out of her hand. He stared at it, and Tyrese watched him examining the dark brown mark on the front. 'Some dressing-up box, dat looks like an old bloodstain to me.' His cousin threw the shirt back into the cupboard and closed the doors quickly.

Turning away, Tyrese picked up a small silver box, pulled off the thick cobweb wrapped round, and opened it.

It was empty apart from a small folded piece of material. He peered through his lenses and absentmindedly moved the fabric out of the way. 'Oh my God!' Thirty or more teeth lay under it, and recoiling, Tyrese dropped the box. It clattered to the ground, teeth scattering all over the stone floor.

Ellie pulled him back towards the stairs. 'Ty, you were right, we shouldn't be here, come on, let's go.'

'No.' Standing in front of them, Marvin shook his head. 'Five more minutes, *please*. We might as well have a proper look around. We still don't know what this place is. And we've got to find some way to save Grammy, Aunt Patty and your dad, Ellie.'

Neither of them said anything and the moment felt strained.

Tyrese glanced towards the stairs. 'OK, but let's just hurry up, yeah? Something feels really wrong.'

Moving further into the long, rectangular stone room, Tyrese could see the dust-covered shelves were full of thick leather books running up each wall to hit the high ceilings. Bottles and boxes were piled on top of the various old cabinets dotted about, and on a wooden stand, metal funnels and rubber tubing caked with cobwebs were stored next to a large set of copper scales.

Steel beakers and bowls lined up along the side, together with a box crammed full of scissors and scalpels, knives, metal syringes and clamps and other sharp instruments that Tyrese didn't know the name of. A cracked leather apron with a large dark brown stain lay across a long metal table.

Tyrese moved across the room to an open steel trunk, crammed so full of strange brass apparatus, the lid wouldn't close. The only pieces of the equipment he could easily identify were the dusty coils and wires and a large brass wheel, bigger than the ones on his bike.

He closed his eyes for a moment, his head feeling like it was being crushed while images he couldn't work out played in his head. He held his hand under his armpit, hoping to somehow soothe the constant pain.

Ellie walked over to an area of the room where objects were draped with thick white sheets forming menacing shapes as if hidden beings crouched beneath, waiting, watching their every move.

She held the corner of one of the dust sheets and Tyrese saw her take a deep breath before lifting it up.

Bats and rats and lizards floated in glass tanks full of dark yellow liquid, preserved for years. Two birds sewn to each other bobbed on the surface in the same tank as a curled large snake.

'That's disgusting.'

She threw the sheet back over the tanks as Tyrese directed his attention to the books on the shelf, reading some of the titles. *The Temple of Nature. Manual of Magnetism.* Books on Plato, Sophocles, Pythagoras. Shelf upon shelf of philosophy and science.

Ellie called over. 'Ty, Marvin, come and look at this, it's some sort of journal. A lot of the writing's faded and some of the pages are stuck together, but from what I can make out, it seems to be some kind of diary of experiments . . . though some of this stuff is so weird.'

Tyrese glanced over her shoulder at the handwritten pages of the diary. He could see the brown leather-bound journal was age-worn – damp and mildew covered the fragile pages.

'Does it say whose it is?' Marvin wondered.

'No, I've already had a look, but these entries are from eighteen-ninety-six, and listen to this . . .

'Twenty-fifth of May, eighteen-ninety-six. The procedure to attach the wires to the jaw of the goat proved simple and after only a moment, the creature quivered, the right eye opened as if observing me. Though I have now decided, I need to extend my research, and build on the extensive knowledge of Dr Ure . . .'

Tyrese glanced back across to the bookshelf he'd just been looking at, where he'd noticed a book written by Dr Andrew Ure. He grabbed it and started thumbing through as Ellie continued to read.

'. . . and using the carcass of a freshly slaughtered lamb, I placed the rods on the creature's neck: the lolling tongue retracted and for a moment, my hopes soared as a loud noise yielded from it, though further investigation brought me to the conclusion it was merely the last of the air from its lungs.

'Wow, what's this guy trying to do?' Ellie asked, looking up at Tyrese.

'I don't know,' Tyrese answered, aware how cold he suddenly felt. Every part of him felt numb, even his tongue felt heavy.

Ellie shook her head, 'And it gets kookier as the dates move on, listen:

'Fifteenth of August, eighteen-ninety-six. Over the course of ten minutes, I observed his chest rise and fall as I connected the rods to the nerves of his diaphragm. I continued to observe the secrets of

death, and made an incision at the neck, hip and calf, exposing the nerves to electrify. The muscles reacted violently, though after I had extracted the teeth to place the rods within the jaw, the fingers moved as if the deceased were playing the keys of a piano.'

Ellie gazed at them. 'Whoever wrote this isn't talking about animals any more, he's talking about actual people.'

A terrifying screech ripped through the air.

They froze in unison, as though they were playing musical statues.

Tyrese watched Ellie's face drain of colour. Shaking, she stared at Tyrese and Marvin. 'What are we going to do?' Then her gaze drifted towards the stairs, to where the scream had come from. 'There's no other way out of here.'

'We just need to go.' Tyrese spoke quickly. 'We don't want to be trapped down here . . . Come on, quick . . .'

'. . . Wait, we should take the journal with us,' Marvin suggested.

Without answering, Ellie hurriedly pushed it inside the rucksack on Tyrese's back.

They switched off their lights, but not before Tyrese caught a glimpse of the floor beginning to squirm with black insects. And as they climbed back up the narrow stone staircase, more shrieks started to tear through the darkness . . .

30

By the time they got to the top of the stairs, the shrieking had stopped but a restless silence filled the air. Tyrese peered through the crack in the heavy door. There was a strange light coming from the far end of the cellar.

He strained to listen, thinking that he'd heard a sound.

'Can you hear something?' he whispered.

Ellie and Marvin shook their heads.

'No, not a thing. You hear the rhyme again, Ty?'

He glanced at his cousin. 'No, it's not that . . . *Sshhhh*, I think there's someone there.'

He froze, rigid with fear.

Marvin pushed him gently out of the way to take a look. 'There's no one there, Ty, it must be in your head again, come.'

'You don't know that,' he said sharply. 'What about that light? That wasn't there before. I don't think it's safe, maybe we should just wait here.'

Marvin checked again, this time pressing his face further into the crack of the door. 'It could be just the daylight coming in from somewhere . . . Ty, look, we need to go.' Marvin squeezed through the doorway, followed by Ellie, giving Tyrese no other choice but to go after them.

Once again, they walked in silence through the stone cellar rooms. The whole place seemed muggier, an oppressive heat sitting thick in the air.

Without warning, Marvin grabbed Tyrese and Ellie, pulling them against the wall to stand in the shadow of one of the stone pillars. 'Ty, you were right, someone's there.'

Terror gripped Tyrese.

Just ahead of them stood a woman, rocking, shifting her weight from one foot to the other.

'Oh my gosh, I see her,' Ellie whispered.

'Get back as far as you can, in case she sees *us*. Keep in the shadows,' Marvin murmured.

Above the woman's head, strange tiny flickers of flame hovered in the air. Tyrese watched her begin to walk back and forth. Wailing. Her shrivelled body was hunched over, her overly-long fingers dangled down by her side. A horrifying shriek rose from her, a sound which ripped through him.

Ellie jerked. 'Oh no, look!'

Emerging from the darkness of the tunnel – which would have taken them back to the stairwell of the crypt – Tyrese saw another woman appear. She was just as old but the skin on her face and arms hung strangely, as though it didn't fit her body. Her eyes were bloodshot, her tongue swollen, too large, lolling over her protruding lips.

Tyrese spoke in the smallest of voices: 'What's wrong with her? Marvin, why are you looking like that?'

'Soucouyant.'

'What?' Tyrese glanced down at his finger. '*They're* the Soucouyant?' He felt sick.

Nervously, Marvin glanced at him.

'Those tiny flames you can see, they're the Soucouyant too.'

'What are you talking about?'

'Those tiny lights are the Soucouyant without their skins, Ty. The skins they're wearing are just a disguise – dat's why it looks like it don't fit. It's hanging off her body, see? She must have collected it from one of her victims.'

Ellie's breathing quickened. 'But . . . but I don't get it, if they're almost invisible, tiny flames, why do they need to hide in an old woman's skin?'

'Because without it, they eventually die. Dem a like a parasite, they can only survive without a host for a small time. They have to feed off blood or live inside someone else's skin.'

Tyrese glanced towards them. They were trapped. He held back the urge to scream. 'Why didn't you tell me this before? Look, how many there are. It's like we're in their *lair*.'

In the darkness, lit only by the flames of the Soucouyant, Ellie grabbed hold and shook Marvin's arm. 'What are they doing, Marv, what are those women doing now?'

Tyrese gazed at the two old women as Marvin barely managed to speak, a whisper on his lips. 'They're shedding.'

The women tore at their stomachs, screeching as their skin split open, the tearing sounding like a piece of wet cloth being ripped apart, though it was bloodless. As they peeled away more of the withered, hanging skin from their arms and legs, Tyrese could smell the decaying, putrid stench seeping from it. It was the same smell which came from his finger. He could almost taste it.

The skin dropped to the floor but there were no bones, no entrails, no beating heart inside, only a cloud of dark insects rose up before transforming into tiny flames. Then just as Tyrese thought it was over, more old women appeared, just as haggard, just as vile, screeching and tearing at their skin, filling the air with screams as they shed.

Then it went dark.

The flames had disappeared.

'They've gone, let's go!' Tyrese switched on the flashlight, leaping forward to run towards the passageway but Marvin yanked him back.

'No, Ty, it's not safe.'

'But they've gone! They must have flown off. And we need to get out.'

'Not until I collect their skins.'

Tyrese opened his mouth to say something else but he *really* couldn't find the words.

'Why?' Ellie whispered, asking exactly what Tyrese was thinking. 'Why would you want to do that? Look, please let's go, I don't want to be trapped down here.'

'We don't know where they are, and we can't risk it. They won't be far away because dem need their skins . . . They could even just be hiding between here and the outside.

And if they do come back, and they put on their skins and find us, then it's over for *all* of us . . .'

'So what are you saying?' Ellie asked.

Pausing, Marvin stared at them. 'If they have no skins to put on, dem can't last forever.'

Ellie shook her head and closed her eyes for a moment as Marvin flicked on his phone torch and ran along the cellar towards the passageway.

'Marv, no! You can't touch it. Marv, don't!' Tyrese called after Marvin in a loud whisper but his cousin ignored him though he called again, 'Wait, Marv, I'll come . . .'

'Ty, wait for me.' Ellie dashed after him.

Catching up to Marvin, Tyrese gazed around. Dotted all over the stone floor were coiled piles of withered and wrinkled skin. 'Oh my God, they're everywhere. This is so gross.' He covered his mouth. Too late. The smell, the way they looked, everything about them made Tyrese vomit.

He retched loudly, bringing up what little was in his stomach. Wiping his mouth on his arm, out of the corner of his eye, Tyrese saw the discarded skins had triggered the same reaction in Marvin and Ellie. He gave them a sympathetic smile. Then with his bare hands, he began to pick one up, feeling the cold, clammy weight of it. He clenched his jaw, lips pinched, swallowed down, hoping it would stop him being sick again. 'Marv, where do you want me to put it?'

'We need to hide dem all. Maybe back down in the other room?'

'Yeah, we can put them in the cupboards, we can dump

them in there,' Ellie said quickly, her stare fixed on the entrance of the passageway.

Tyrese nodded. 'OK, let's do this.'

Over the next fifteen minutes, they ran back and forth, carrying the reeking skins, dumping and locking them in cupboards until they were jammed full, then eventually, sweating and exhausted, they'd collected them all.

Tyrese looked around; he could still smell the skins where they'd rubbed against his clothing and the pain in his finger, in his hand, was unbearable. 'That's it, let's go.'

He and Marvin quickly moved towards the passageway.

'Ellie, come on, hurry up.' Tyrese glanced behind him but not looking where he was going, bumped into Marvin, knocking his cousin's phone out of his hand.

The clatter of it hitting the stone floor shattered the silence, echoing noisily around.

'You idiot,' Tyrese growled at his cousin, his gaze darting nervously towards the tunnel.

'You were the one who—'

Marvin stopped.

Then he began to edge away.

Coming towards them was a cloud of tiny flickering flames.

The Soucouyant were back.

31

The cloud of tiny flames soared towards them at speed. The Soucouyants' force was so great, it brought a blast of air as if a tornado had ripped through.

'Stay still, just stay still!' Marvin yelled.

They were surrounded.

Trapped.

The Soucouyant swarmed in the air in a mass, like a murmuration of starlings swooping and twisting, swirling above them in shape-shifting patterns.

Tyrese felt stinging and scorching as one of the flames struck at his skin. Then more flames began to attack. He swiped the air with his arms, trying to keep them away from his face, from his hair, from setting his clothes alight. His skin felt on fire. He heard Marvin scream in pain, and saw the angry red burn marks on Ellie's cheeks.

'*Where are they, Tyrese? Give them back.*'

He jumped, wincing at the high-pitched whispering rasp in his ear. Trembling, he moved his eyes up slowly and saw a flame hover above his head.

'*Tell me where, Tyrese.*'

He felt something drip on his forehead, down his cheek.

A black, sticky thread of drool oozed out from the flame, down his face. The stench was worse than the skins.

He whirled around, staring up, hitting out at it.

'What are you doing? Ty, no! No! You'll make them angrier,' Ellie yelled to him in panic.

'Can't you hear them, can't you hear them talking to me?'

'Hear who?' Marvin's voice shook. 'Hear who, Ty?'

'*Tyrese, where are they? Give them us!*'

Tyrese ran over, fighting through the heat of the flames as they swarmed around. He gripped his cousin's shoulders: 'Listen, just listen, they're talking, they're talking.'

Wide-eyed and huddled in the corner with Ellie, Marvin gave the tiniest shake of his head. 'No, Ty, no. There's nothing to hear.'

'Tyrese, child of the Shadow Man, tell me where they are.'

Marvin shrieked out in agony again as a cloud of flames dived at him, plunging, blazing sparks.

'OK! OK! Just stop,' Tyrese yelled. '*Just stop!* You can have them, you can have them! You can have them back!'

'Then tell us, tell us, Tyrese, tell us where they are . . .'

'This way, I . . .'

From within the clouds of raging flames, Ellie screamed: '. . . Ty, don't! Ty, stop! *No*!'

'Ty, what are you doing, come back!' Marvin cried out.

'Just go, go without me, just get out of here! Take Ellie and get out of here!' Tyrese shouted.

'Ty! *No!* Wait!'

Ignoring them, Tyrese began to back away, back along the cellars, back to the heavy black door, inciting the flames of the Soucouyant to follow, luring them away from Ellie and his cousin.

'Come on then . . . Come on. If you want them, *this way . . .*' Screaming at the flames of the Soucouyant now, Tyrese walked backwards down the stairs. He felt the blistering heat, almost too much to bear as the wall of flames, inches away, pursued him.

'Tyrese! Tyrese! Tell us, Tyrese!'

Terrified, he led them into the room, wincing at their screeching, furious sounds.

'Where are they?'

He hesitated for a moment and the flames, now merged in a single entity, struck at him. He yelped and jumped back.

'Don't trick us now, Tyrese, tell us where they are.'

Tyrese was trapped, and as he pointed to the locked cupboards where they'd hidden the skins, the room seemed to spin. He had a sense of the floor moving beneath his feet and as if he were being pushed off an unseen edge, Tyrese fell, crashing to the ground while the flames of the Soucouyant began to burn through the wooden cupboards, trying to get to their skins.

He knew he had to get up, get out, but he couldn't think, and disorientated, he lay on the ground, his chest becoming tight.

Smoke began to fill the air, black plumes whirling above him, and the screeches of the Soucouyant bore into his head.

'Get up, Tyrese, get up! Listen to me, you've got to get up!' Coughing, his cousin grabbed him, dragging him on to his feet. 'Ty, run, come on!'

Confused, he looked at Marvin, trying to work out what he was asking him to do.

'Tyrese, what's wrong with you, we've got to go!' Marvin pulled him towards the stairs and taking them two at a time, they got to the top where Ellie was standing.

'Close it! *Close it!* It'll buy us time,' she yelled in panic, and along with Tyrese and Marvin, she threw her weight against the heavy wooden door as a deathly shriek came from the other side . . . Then they began to run.

—

They didn't slow down until they were well away from Hathaway Hall. Wet with sweat and rain, they walked along an uneven path, searching for somewhere to rest.

By a tiny babbling stream running along the track, Tyrese sat at the base of a tree huddled next to Ellie and Marvin, feeling the rain soothing the burns from the Soucouyant as the rough bark scratched his back.

He rubbed his head, shivers hot and cold rushing through his body again. The sense of being watched was stronger than ever.

'Ty, are you listening? This is some freaky stuff.' Ellie

nudged him and he glanced at her, noticing the scorch marks on her face. 'Did you hear what I just read out?'

The rain trickled down his neck, and he realised she had the journal open on her lap. 'What, no, sorry, I was thinking about something else. Read it again, will you?'

Pushing her hair out of her eyes, she gave him an exasperated look and began to read the entry again:

'. . . *a handsome sum exchanged hands but I was not disappointed, for the corpse on this occasion was so fresh, I was able to drain a supply of blood. Eager, I cut off his shirt, wiping the earth from* . . .'

She stopped reading, 'Jeez, I can't get my head round this, Ty. You think that's why all those teeth were there, and those clothes in the cupboard, because they belonged to all these corpses? . . . But where did he even get the corpses *from*, and I mean *why* would anyone want them?'

Struggling to fully focus, Tyrese shrugged. 'Seems like the person paid someone, you know, like a bodysnatcher . . . They probably got them to steal a corpse from a morgue or a grave, I dunno. But way back, I know they used to do that kind of thing so medics could learn about the human body. Do dissections and stuff. That's what it sounds like to me.'

Marvin kissed his teeth, 'Dat can't be normal, Ty.'

Tyrese looked at them both. 'Maybe it wasn't when the person wrote the diary, I don't know much about it, but at one time, all these weird experiments were normal I think.'

Ellie didn't look so sure. She tried to turn over the page but they were stuck together, impossible to prise open. She jumped to another section, much further on in the journal and began to read from the faded ink.

'Thirteenth of November, eighteen-ninety-six. I had believed that this time I would succeed, unfold the mystery of the hidden laws, yet despite all I have learned on my travels, and endless teachings, the wretchedness of my shortcomings have become a familiar affliction. To reverse the eternal rest seems beyond my capabilities and the agony of this failure has shrouded me with such despair, my misery lies next to me. It sleeps when I sleep, awakening when I wake. The burden of knowing Llanzo will think I have abandoned him in death to lie alone, is a weight so heavy, I wish this on no man, neither friend nor foe . . .'

Ellie was breathless. 'Wow, this must be *Levi's* journal. He's writing about his son, Llanzo, who died.' She heaved a sigh. 'I can't even see what he writes next, so many of these pages are too stuck together, if I'm not careful they'll tear.' Once more, Ellie turned to a different section, the spine of the book creaking with age like old bones. 'Look at this page, guys, Llanzo's name is just scribbled everywhere. Don't you think that's kind of weird?'

She showed Tyrese and Marvin, and clear to see on the mouldy pages of the journal was Llanzo's name scrawled alongside other manic, angry scribbles.

. . . They came to me last night, the Soucouyant, so hideous, I feared I might not recover from my shock . . .

'Oh my God, they were after Levi as well. Like they came after you, Ty. Maybe you were right, maybe the grounds of Hathaway Hall was their lair, and Levi didn't know that when he built the house there . . .'

'Or maybe the Shadow Man brought dem there when he killed Llanzo, and they've stayed ever since,' Marvin suggested. 'It's like dem duppies who live in the silk cotton trees.'

Ellie looked at Marvin for the briefest of moments before continuing, '. . . *their screeches* . . . Oh no!' Ellie abruptly stopped as a flurry of rain fell from the leaves of the fruit tree they were sitting under, dropping on to the pages. Without thinking, she wiped the water off with her sleeve, smudging the already faded pages of ink. 'Oh no, I've made it worse! The ink's all smudged.'

Tyrese stared at the page. He felt a raw anger rushing through him. He ground his teeth as his heart beat rapidly. What was wrong with Ellie? It was obvious that would happen, and *now* look. 'That was stupid, wasn't it? See what you've done!' He caught himself. 'Sorry.' He breathed out. 'Sorry, Ellie, I shouldn't have said that.'

Marvin glared at him. 'You don't have to be so—'

'. . . I know, OK, and I don't need you telling me, I said

I'm sorry,' Tyrese cut in quickly. Then he rested his head on his knees. He didn't want to do this any more, everything was such a battle. He didn't know how much more he could take, how long he could keep going. His head was filled with the rhyme, the chant, and it was strange, he knew it was, but it seemed to be the only thing right now which brought him comfort.

Then with his head still resting on his knees, he turned and stared at his hand: green and purple, mottling like an aged bruise. Though the pain was still there, it no longer caused him revulsion, rather it mesmerised him. He was spellbound.

'I'll put it away,' Ellie said, sounding upset. 'I'll leave it until we're somewhere drier.'

No one said anything. They just continued to sit against the tree in silence.

Eventually Marvin spoke up, his tone annoyed: 'Ty, have you got any ideas what this is all about? *Ty?*'

Wearily, Tyrese sat up. He had to focus hard on trying to form his words without sounding slurred: 'I don't think this has anything to do with the Shadow Man. Well, not directly anyway. The Soucouyant maybe, but not Levi's experiments . . . In that journal, Levi mentioned a guy called Dr Ure, well, there was a book by him on the shelves, yeah.'

'Tyrese, Tyrese.'

Tyrese whirled round at the sound of his name, gazing towards the trees beyond.

'Ty, are you OK?' Ellie glanced at him. 'What is it?'

Tyrese shook his head. He didn't want to tell them. Not any more. It was *his* name they were calling, not theirs. And he found it took all his willpower not to get up and walk towards the voices. Because now – although he didn't understand why – it wasn't fear he felt any more. It was if he was being pulled towards the soothing call of his name, like a wolf drawn towards howling. 'Nothing, I . . . I . . . it was just a mosquito, I heard it buzzing in my ear. What was I saying?'

Marvin looked at him oddly. 'The book.'

'Oh yeah, it was about galvanism. From what I quickly read, Ure believed that life could be restored in certain cases through the use of electricity.' He paused, took a deep breath as a rising tide of nausea hit him again. 'I think that's what Levi's experiments were about.'

Ellie stared at Tyrese. 'You mean, he was trying to bring things back from the dead?' She paused, looking around thoughtfully. 'So maybe . . . maybe that's what he meant when he wrote in his journal *reverse the eternal rest*.'

Tyrese was having to work even harder now to hold his concentration. His vision was inexplicably blurred. 'Yeah, everything points to that, and I think that's where the Shadow Man comes into it. Grammy said Levi travelled a lot, got himself a really good education, but she didn't say *what* he did. But if, like Dr Ure, he was a scientist who believed that stuff too, then it would make sense to him.'

'OK, but how's this linked to the Shadow Man, Ty?' Marvin asked.

'So if Llanzo was killed by the Shadow Man, yeah, maybe Levi hoped to use the knowledge he already had to try to bring Llanzo back from the dead.'

'What?' Marvin and Ellie spoke at the same time.

'Llanzo! No way,' Ellie said. 'No way was he doing that. Experiments with sheep and . . . and different animals, maybe, but people? Llanzo? Not that. No way.'

He took off his glasses and rubbed his eyes. 'But if Levi was desperate to bring Llanzo back *and* he believed he could, if he *believed* in the power of galvanism, then perhaps somehow he was preserving his son's body but experimenting on *other* corpses until he worked out how to do it.'

'That's like something out of *Frankenstein*,' Ellie said doubtfully.

'Whatever.' Tyrese shrugged angrily. 'I really don't care.'

'How can you say . . .'

'. . . Don't bother, Ellie.' Marvin gently interrupted her. Standing up, he smiled warmly. 'If my cousin wants to be nasty and bad *mout*, just ignore him . . . Look, I think we should find out how Llanzo actually died. Find out what the Shadow Man may have done to him.'

Getting up as well, Ellie nodded. 'Totally, because unlike the other kids who went missing, Llanzo didn't. We've seen his tomb. And if Ty's right, and Levi was trying to bring his son back to life, he wasn't actually taken by the Shadow Man even though the Shadow Man may have hurt him.'

As anger continued to flow through Tyrese, he followed

on, trailing behind them as they set off along the track, listening to them chatter. It set him on edge.

'There'll probably be records in Kingston library dating right back. It's only three o'clock, so maybe it's early enough to get there before it closes, it's not too far. We can get a taxi or a bus. And if it's closed, we can always rest up in Kingston until tomorrow.' Marvin shrugged.

'I'm cool with that,' Ellie agreed. 'How do you know where all these places are anyway? I know Jamaica isn't a big island and obviously this area of the Blue Mountains is smaller, but I don't think I could even give proper directions from East 32nd Street to 45th Street, and that's not even far.' She giggled shyly.

Marvin didn't laugh back. He spoke slowly, a sadness running through. 'Before Grammy took me in, my dad got married and then had a new family, but him and his wife didn't really want me around.' He tugged on his T-shirt's hem, then folded his arms tightly around himself as he carried on walking. 'In the end it was better to stay out of the house, so me just spent a lot of time walking and cycling around.'

'That sounds horrible. I'm so sorry, Marvin.' She linked arms with him.

'You know, me used to think there was something wrong with *me*, dat it was my fault my dad didn't want me about, cos whenever he saw me, he was always so *vexed* dat I was there. Like I was a mistake he'd made. No matter what me did, how much I tried to please him, he just didn't want to know . . . Not like Ty's dad . . . Ty's dad was different to mine, even though they were brothers, Ty's dad made me feel loved, special. Like I was king of the world.' This time Marvin's giggles exploded. He twirled around to look at Tyrese. 'He was brilliant, the kindest uncle. And the way him chat about you, *bwoy*, you could see how much he loved you, Ty. Grammy said dat when he chat your name, his eyes lit up like he had a *whole* galaxy of shooting stars in dem . . . I wished we could've swapped dads, even for a minute.'

For a moment Marvin seemed embarrassed, but then he grinned, walking tall. 'Anyway, me have Grammy now. And Grammy loves me a *whole* heap. So, things are good. *When cow is in the pasture, he does not think about the butcher*.' Marvin laughed. 'Dat's what Grammy says.'

'What does that mean?' Ellie asked laughing as well.

'She says it means, being content can take your mind off all your troubles.'

Tyrese frowned and watched Ellie and Marvin walk further ahead. Thoughts faded in and out too quickly to hold on to as he struggled to make sense in his mind of who Marvin had been talking about, who this *kindest uncle* was.

32

A bus journey later, they found themselves in Kingston standing on the pavement of Tom Redcam Road. The rains had stopped and Tyrese gazed at the bustling traffic speeding by. So noisy, so busy . . . so normal, something that he certainly didn't feel. He was confused, more confused than ever, a lot of his thoughts no longer making sense.

He watched a man who was carefully balancing a basket of fish on his bike lift his well-worn pork pie hat in greeting to them as he weaved past, his back tyre flattened by the load.

'We need to hurry, it's half past four, so maybe we can still get to the library if we're quick,' Marvin said. 'But let's get a drink first, if dat's OK.'

They headed further down the road to the street stalls dotted along the walkway where music blared out of a radio, and food, trinkets, postcards and posters, and various tourist bits and bobs were being sold.

Tyrese stood back and watched Ellie buy three ice-cold bottles of water from the street seller.

'Dat all?' The man grinned at her, showing off a row of gold teeth. 'Me can't tempt you with some banana chips, spice bun?'

'No, thank you, I'm OK,' she answered politely.

'What about a shrimp bite? Here try one. *Dem gud, yuh nah get better bites than these.*'

Laughing, he reached over with the plate so Ellie and Marvin could try one. As he did, the sleeve on his T-shirt rode up slightly and Tyrese caught a glimpse of a dark, inked tattoo on the upper part of his arm.

'*Wah yuh think? Gud*?'

With their mouths full, Ellie and Marvin giggled. 'Very good. Thank you.'

'That tattoo you've got on your arm,' Tyrese said, stepping forward.

Seemingly proud, the man pulled up his sleeve completely to show it off. 'You like it?'

Tyrese stared at the tattoo: a snake in a circle devouring its own tail. He'd seen that somewhere before but he couldn't quite remember where.

'It's the Ouroboros, apparently it's an ancient symbol. A sign of rebirth, reincarnation, call it what you like.' He looked like he was going to say some more about it but he turned his attention to another customer, waving them off. 'Anyway, pickney, walk gud, yeah.'

'What was all that about?' Ellie asked curiously.

Before Tyrese could say anything, Tyrese's phone beeped loudly. 'Can you believe that, I've *finally* got a signal? I haven't had one since I arrived.' He glanced at the screen and saw an icon showing in the top corner of his home screen. '*And* I've even got a message.'

The glint in Ellie's eyes was as keen as her tone. 'It could be your mom! What if she's all right, what if your grammy's OK?' She stopped, took a breath. 'What if my dad's all right? They could be looking for us? Play it, Ty, quickly.'

'Sure.' Tyrese touched and held down the voicemail icon putting it on speaker . . .

'*Ty, hey, it's Johnny here, I* . . .' Tyrese groaned loudly and quickly deleted it, moving on to the next message. '*Hey, Ty, it's Mr Miller, listen, the athletics team are meeting up at* . . .' Again, Tyrese cut it off. He looked at Ellie. 'It's probably because I haven't had signal in ages, they're just coming through now.'

'So, there could still be one from your mom.' There was an impatience to her tone but it was also fringed with hope. 'We need to know if they're OK.'

'Fine.' Tyrese began to make his way through, deleting the mix of new and old messages and voice notes. He got to the last one, pressing play without thinking.

'*You have one saved message . . .*

. . . Hi, Ty, it's me . . .'

Tyrese suddenly froze.

'*. . . I know you're probably busy getting ready for the race, so there's no need to call me back, OK? Just have fun, enjoy yourself, make the most of being out there . . . It was good to see how excited you were when you set off, let's see if you're that keen for school next week, hey? . . . Anyway, I wanted to let you know that I'm sorry I couldn't fly out to Athens but I'm just going to imagine it. I'm going to imagine you smashing the race like you always do. You've worked so hard for this. But shall I let you into a secret? It's not the race*

I really come to watch, it's the smile on your face when I see you come through that finishing line. Your smile, Ty, beats any gold medal and it always has—'

Tyrese paused the message, his hand shaking. He could feel the rapid beat of his heart. Once again he searched his thoughts, his gaze moving over Marvin's face. He knew he recognised the voice somehow, he knew the caller was talking about him, but he couldn't quite pull the memory out from the darkness of his mind. He stared at Ellie and Marvin.

'Oh my gosh, Ty, is that the message you were talking about that you had on your phone and didn't listen to?' Ellie asked.

Tyrese didn't answer.

'Ty, dat's your *dad*.' Marvin gazed at him. 'Ty?'

Tears quivered at the corner of Tyrese's eyes. His breathing changed. The familiar sense of choking tightened round his throat. Marvin continued to stare at him strangely. 'Look, why don't we listen to the rest, Ty. You might as well. It might help you remember . . . *Ty*? Maybe hearing it, wanting to remember like Ellie said, will help. It helped at Mrs Stuart's, didn't it?'

Still Tyrese didn't move or answer.

Tyrese glanced about, staring at Ellie then at Marvin. The noise in his mind was screaming. He held his head, his hands over his ears . . . His memory coming back like a steaming, screeching train. But he couldn't do it, he couldn't do it. And he felt a pain in his head, a pain all over his body as images of the past became clear . . . Fire burned behind his eyes and he threw his phone on the ground as if it blazed.

'But, Ty, don't you see, that was amazing,' Ellie picked up his phone, holding it out to him.

'I don't want it! I don't want it!'

'But, Ty.'

'Stop!'

'Ty, please? Don't you get it, your dad—'

Traffic rushed behind them on the road chaotically.

'I said stop, stop! Shut up! Shut up! Shut up! Shut up!'

Iced flames blew around Tyrese, he felt like he was diving into the cold, into an ocean of darkness, the world upside down, tumbling, blasting, pushing him to rise and fall to a place underneath where it was dark and there was nothing at all.

High-pitched sounds suddenly rushed at him.

He blinked, unsure where he had been. Unsure where he was.

'Tyrese, just stay where you are! Tyrese, don't move!'

Marvin's voice crashed through the mist, then Tyrese heard horns, saw cars, saw lorries, saw where he was: in the middle of a busy road, speeding traffic all around him.

'Marvin, Marvin,' his call came limply from his lips.

'Ty, *please* don't move. It's OK, Ty. I'll get you back to safety. You hear me?'

Tyrese watched his cousin coming towards him, weaving in and out of the fast-moving traffic, cars swerving, while horns continued to blare.

A van screeched to a stop in front of Tyrese. The driver calling angrily out of the window: '*Pickney move, yuh wah fi get kill? Wah di . . .*' The driver's words faded as he sped away.

Marvin grabbed Tyrese's hand. 'Me got you, Ty.'

'It's getting worse, Marv, it's getting worse, and I don't know how to stop it.' Tyrese trembled.

Waving his arm for the drivers to slow, Marvin led Tyrese safely back to the pavement where he sat on the ground, bent forward, wailing into his hands like a wounded animal.

33

By the time they got to the library it was shut, so they made their way to the beach: the sea in front of them, Kingston behind them, and once again they sat under the protection of the giant palm leaves although, for once, the rain had stayed away.

All night they'd sat huddled together on the beach, though no one had slept or talked, alone in their thoughts, the fears for their families still trapped in the sleeping curse never far away. And now as the sun rose, sparkling across the Caribbean Sea, Tyrese listened to Ellie try to decipher more of Levi's journal.

'Twelfth of January, eighteen-ninety-seven. I am no further forward in my quest, Llanzo still no longer lives. I am tired and I have given up all hope, darkness has become my friend. I scarcely leave the cellar, the light, once a precious pleasure, now only burns, the weight of memories carried in it, blinding me with an ache I did not realise the human heart could withstand. My heart still beats but I am dead to any form of beauty, to the fragrant smells and sound of life as grief crawls over me like a beast, as I awake with wild cries and the name of Llanzo on my lips . . .'

'Fifteenth of March, eighteen-ninety-seven. Last night the Soucouyant came back as though they were invited guests, yet this time, curious, I was moved to speak with them . . .'

'Oh my God, what are you doing, Levi?' Ellie had been poring over the journal, careful not to get it covered in sand. She stared at the page, speaking in a whisper as if she was talking to Levi directly. 'Why are you getting involved with *them*?' She lifted her gaze, then quickly looked back, flicking through, continuing to read aloud from the pages which were still legible.

'Twenty-eighth of June, eighteen-ninety-seven. I wager my time in Hathaway has come to an end, they are coming for me and I believe I am to be taken away any day now . . .'

'Taken?' Marvin asked. 'Taken by who? Where?'

Ellie simply shrugged without stopping:

'. . . and though I am now resigned to this fate, the pact I have made has brought me peace.'

Ellie stared open-mouthed at Marvin and Tyrese. 'Pact? What pact? What kind of pact is he talking about? Made a pact with who?'

'What else does it say?' Marvin asked hurriedly, though Tyrese just sat motionless watching Ellie try to peel apart the pages which were firmly bonded together with damp and mildew. 'I don't think I'm going to be able to pull them apart, and the rest of the writing is so faded.'

'Give it another go,' Marvin urged, grabbing for the journal.

'Don't, you're going to rip it. It needs more time to dry out.'

Just then it began to rain, a rumble of thunder rolled overhead. Quickly Ellie snapped the journal closed, pushing it back into the rucksack. 'The rain's just going to make it worse. I think we should go to the library. We have to find out how Llanzo Campbell died. We need to know *exactly* what the Shadow Man did to him. Come on . . .'

Tyrese got up slowly, watching the waves crash and break on to the shoreline, feeling an ever-growing affinity towards Levi Campbell. Despite the passing of many years, it was as though there was a curious connection between them. He reflected on the entries in the journal about Llanzo and how the words were filled with so much pain; it was as though Levi had dipped the nib of his ink pen into the very centre of his heart.

'Ty, come on!'

He nodded to Ellie, but he didn't answer as he walked along the beach. His mind was still on Levi, because he understood. He understood how right Levi was: the light *did* seem to hold nothing but pain.

—

It was still early, only 9.25 a.m. and inside Kingston and St Andrew parish library the air was cool, the sound of the fan on the ceiling whirled round and round, mixing with the murmuring quiet. Row upon row of brown wooden bookshelves filled the large pale-green painted room. Tables and metal chairs were dotted about and the highly polished tiled vinyl floor squeaked underfoot.

An elderly librarian stood behind a burgundy service desk; a large black oscillating fan – set to high – stood on duty next to him. A pile of books balanced on the edge of the desk, threatening to topple.

Stamping one of the books with enthusiastic vigour, the librarian glanced up, smiling warmly as they walked up to him.

Exhaustion sat within Tyrese, his mind a land of confusion, but he tried to smile back, distracted slightly by the ballpoint pen pushed into the man's long grey dreadlocks.

'*Gud* morning. How *yuh* stay?'

Marvin grinned, nodded. 'We're good, thank you.'

Seemingly satisfied with the answer, he nodded back to Marvin. 'So how can me help you, are you looking for something in particular?'

'Yeah, we'd like to find out about how someone died.'

The librarian shook his head. 'You'll have to speak up, my hearing isn't what it used to be.'

'The register of births and deaths. How do we look at it?' Marvin shouted, causing the other people in the library to turn round and stare at them.

'If you want to see dat, you'll have to make an appointment with the town hall. We used to have it here.' He ended his sentence with a shrug.

For a moment Marvin looked disappointed, then continuing to raise his voice, much to the clear annoyance of the lady sitting a few tables away who kissed her teeth almost as loudly as Marvin was speaking, he asked, 'What about stuff on Jamaica?'

'We've got a large collection. Over in section five, there's all the history books and over by the computer in section three, there's the contemporary books about Jamaica, and if you go through there and downstairs –' he pointed to a glass door by the exit – 'we've got all the old archives. Is it just general or something specific?'

'We need to find information about a boy called Llanzo Campbell.'

Looking mystified, the librarian pulled a face and shook his head.

'Or about Levi Campbell, him was the owner of Hathaway Hall, at the end of the nineteenth century.'

The librarian sighed, crossing his arms. 'No and no.'

Looking desperate, Marvin rubbed his head. 'Basically, what we really . . .' He paused a moment. The librarian frowned, looking slightly impatient. '. . . *Who* we're actually trying to find out about, and . . . and we're finding it really hard to do, is the . . .' Marvin stopped, glanced around then gazed at Ellie and Tyrese. 'I don't think it's a good idea to let everyone know what we're asking about, do you?'

'No,' Ellie agreed. 'Maybe write it down or something.'

'Have you a pen and paper, please?' Marvin yelled.

Not saying anything, the librarian uncrossed his arms and

reached into his pen pot behind the desk and passed Marvin a red pen as well as a small piece of scrap paper.

'Thank you.' Immediately, Marvin began to write. Then he pushed the piece of paper across the desk to the librarian. He had simply written: *Shadow Man*.

The librarian glanced down at the paper. Then, as if it were a fly, he flicked it off his desk. 'Take dat away! You need to go! *Go!*'

'Sorry, I . . .' Marvin muttered, backing off.

But Tyrese stood and stared at the old man.

'Ty, *come*,' Marvin said.

The librarian's brown eyes hardened, then caught sight of Tyrese's hand, swollen and discoloured, his finger now crusted with yellow pus. He whimpered, stumbled away. '*Yuh need fi go!* Now! Get out! *Get out!*'

Tyrese continued to stare, his mind spinning, and the rhyme of the missing rose again in his head:

Child of the Shadow Man, him come get you . . .

'Ty!' Marvin gently tried to pull Tyrese away. 'Ty, *please* don't, *yuh nuh fi eat hot rice*, calm down before you say anything. Don't get angry. Just come. *Please*.'

Tyrese blinked, then simply nodded and they headed for the exit, hurrying out the doors of the library.

'Now what?' Ellie seemed distressed. 'Where now?' She put her head down and slowly began to walk off.

'Hold up, Ellie . . . Ty, wait on. We should try to go back in, maybe there's something down in the archives which might help us. If we just hang around here, we can wait for the librarian to leave his desk, then we can make our move.'

'OK, yeah, sounds like a plan.' Ellie still sounded a little crestfallen. She looked at Tyrese. 'Ty, you haven't said much . . . I'm worried about you.'

Tyrese glanced at Ellie. Her voice mixing in with the rhyme, which chanted louder and louder in his head. He gave a tight smile. 'Everything's fine. I'm good.'

She frowned and, like Marvin had done before, she gave him an odd look, though she didn't comment. Then they watched discreetly through the window until finally the librarian left his desk, allowing them to slip back inside without being seen . . .

34

Ellie and Marvin rushed down the stairs with Tyrese slowly walking behind them. The dusty, gloomy room held boxes and files; row upon row of bookshelves lined the numbered aisles and a pile of broken chairs filled one of the corners. Tyrese threw a gaze at the others, noticing the twisting shadows dancing on the wall as the cobwebbed light bulb flickered. The boiler at the far end of the room made strange noises, creaking and groaning as if it were a creature waiting to fire up as it crouched in the corner.

Marvin looked around. 'Where do we even start?'

Ellie began to look along the shelves. 'The librarian said there was no birth or death certificates held here, but that doesn't mean we can't get information on the Campbells of Hathaway Hall or . . .' she dropped her voice, '. . . the *missing*.'

Marvin looked surprised. 'What?'

She squeezed the ends of her hair, getting out the excess rainwater which was trickling down the middle of her forehead and into her eyes. 'I've been thinking more and more about the kids who disappeared, there must be some sort of record of it, maybe not for all of them, but for some . . . Ty, what else did your grammy say about them?'

Casually Tyrese trailed his hands along the books, feeling them rise and fall over the spines, feeling the blisters on his finger pull open as they rubbed raw against the leather binding. 'I don't know.'

'What do you mean, you don't know? Ty, what's got into you, why are you behaving so weirdly?'

'Like I said, Ellie, I don't know.'

'Fine, whatever. Be like that then.' She turned back to Marvin. 'There's got to be something, Marv. Like back in Austin, if a kid goes missing, even if they run away, it gets in the local paper most of the time.'

She looked around.

Large blue books reminiscent of encyclopaedias were crammed on shelves. She pulled one out. It was awkwardly large and it looked heavy as she opened it with some difficulty. 'Marv, Ty, look at this. This is cool. These are all the archived newspapers.' She continued to study it for a moment before putting it back, then glanced along, reading out loud some of the dates printed in gold on the spines of the hard copy bound volumes, '. . . Eighteen-forty, eighteen-forty-one, eighteen-forty-two. Wow, they go right back.'

'So are we just supposed to start looking through dem, from eighteen-ninety-six, when Llanzo died?' Marvin asked, raising his eyebrows at the sheer number of books in the room.

'No, that could take us like, forever. Trying to do it manually or on the microfilm we'll be here till next week. Maybe they've scanned them, digitised them.' She shrugged.

'And if they have, we can just do keyword searches . . . Ty, can you see any computers back there?'

Tyrese didn't answer; instead he walked away from Ellie and Marvin, continuing to gaze along the bookshelves, not really focusing on anything much as he wandered down the aisles.

He couldn't find the energy to think straight, though he felt a strange heat rising within him and he pulled at the neckline of his T-shirt. '*Child of the Shadow Man*.' The words played on his lips as he walked along the rows, and he was aware of a sense of comfort as he said them. He rubbed his finger, peeling the crusted pus off, which only generated a new trickle of fresh pus to appear.

Casually he pulled out a book at random off the shelf, flicking through it, pictures of old Jamaica whizzing past him at speed.

He placed it back on the shelf.

Something warm touched his hand.

Tyrese held his breath, his heart racing, and slowly he glanced up through the gap on the bookshelf across to the darkness on the other side. He tilted his head, stepping closer, staring harder, and whispered breathlessly, 'Are you there?'

'Ty? Ty, we've been calling you.' Ellie suddenly appeared. 'Who were you talking to then?'

'What . . .' Tyrese pulled his gaze away and looked at Ellie, then glanced back at the gap, not quite sure what he'd been doing. 'Er, no one . . .' He shrugged, looking back at her. 'You've finished already?'

Ellie gave a sideward glance to Marvin. 'You're kidding me, right? We've been at it for almost an hour.'

Marvin glowered. 'Whilst you've been doing nothing.'

'An hour?' Tyrese shook his head, glanced at his watch.

'Don't worry about it.' She smiled through her frown. 'Marvin brought something up about Hathaway Hall in one of the papers, we haven't read it because we wanted to wait for you, and I've managed to find a few things as well. Come on.'

They walked towards the library's computers which were neatly placed in the space under the stairs. Sitting down, Marvin spoke as he stared at the screen. 'It didn't come up with just Hathaway Hall, so I had to put a whole heap of different keywords in. Anyway, me find this. It's from the main Jamaican newspaper of the time . . . listen:

'Thirtieth of April, eighteen-ninety-six. On Sunday a tragedy occurred at the great house, Hathaway Hall, Portland Parish. The hall, owned by Mr Levi Campbell, was badly damaged by fire. Witnesses say the fire started when lightning struck the trees, and was quickly made worse by the wind coming off the mountains fanning the flames, causing it to set alight and race uncontrollably through the nearby buildings. Only a small part of the main house remained intact but was badly smoke damaged. Mr Campbell's son, Llanzo, was found dead, having suffered the effects of the smoke. Mr Campbell, already a widower, was . . .'

Marvin stopped reading.

'Oh my gosh.' Ellie paled. 'We were wrong, it wasn't the Shadow Man who killed his son, it was a fire. It was just an accident.' She sounded stunned, though yet again Tyrese thought about the smoke he'd been smelling, the sharp bitter stench that only he had noticed, but he continued to say nothing.

'I *really* thought it was the Shadow Man who killed Llanzo.' Ellie shrugged, looking upset. 'So none of this helps us. None of this fits with the Shadow Man. How are we going to help Dad, and your grammy and Ty's mom?' Her words ran out and she wiped away her tears. 'I'm so tired, guys.'

'Ellie, listen.' Marvin looked at her, squeezed her hand. 'OK, we were wrong to think Llanzo was killed by the Shadow Man, but dat doesn't mean the Shadow Man didn't do *something* to Levi. Don't forget it was Levi dat Grammy started to tell Ty about, not Llanzo. We'll find the answers . . .'

He glanced back at the digitised newspaper on the screen, scrolling through what the keywords had brought up. 'Oh wow, what, wait . . . listen to this, listen to this! There's a small article dated second of August, eighteen-ninety-seven . . .' Marvin became animated as he read:

'. . . *Mr Levi Campbell of Hathaway Hall, Portland Parish was committed last week to the Scarlett Hill asylum . . .*'

'They *committed* him!' Marvin looked stunned. 'Maybe dat's what he meant when he wrote in the journal "they were coming" for him . . . But why?'

'Does it say how long he was there for or what happened to him next?' Ellie wondered.

'No, there's nothing else about Hathaway Hall, apart from it saying the estate remained in disrepair after the fire, which doesn't really help us.' Marvin spun round in the chair and turned to Ellie. 'What about the stuff you found?'

Ellie glanced between Tyrese and Marvin. 'In math, when you're working things out, you've got to find the pattern. Finding patterns is at the heart of any math problem, and it's the same thing here.' Her eyes became brighter. 'And I think I've found the pattern. For the kids, for the *missing*. Or at least, I hope I have. It goes right back. And no way can it be a coincidence, not when there's so many. I get that sometimes kids and teenagers run away, but like I say, *not* so many and *not* all around the same age and *not* all with the same circumstances.'

'Circumstances?' Marvin raised his eyebrows.

Ellie sat down in front of the other computer. 'I bookmarked some of them, and you know what's so sad is that there are photos of some of the kids, and none of these kids were ever seen again . . .' She let out a long sigh, rolled the tension out of her shoulders and looked back at the screen. '. . . Anyway, listen to this . . . *a thirteen-year-old from the Stony Hill area went missing yesterday, she was last seen* . . . then it goes on to say a bit more about her . . .' She scrolled down, picking up a sentence half way through the article, '. . . *after losing her mother to a short illness three months earlier* . . .' She moved to the next bookmark. '. . . *a fourteen-year-old boy from the Cassava river area went missing, his parents had been killed in a car crash in the January of the previous year . . .*' Once again, Ellie paused and moved the mouse along the screen, '*. . . a twelve-year-old girl from Buff Bay went missing last night, the disappearance follows the tragic death of her younger sister who drowned in the summer . . .*' She clicked to another page. '*A search is underway for a missing fourteen-year-old boy from Portland parish. His father had been involved in a fatal work accident . . .*'

She stopped and like Marvin had done, Ellie spun round on her chair to look at them. 'It just goes on and on, there are so many, and it goes way back, we're talking right back to *years* and *years* ago. And it's all the same, teenagers going missing, never seen again. But do you see the pattern, y'all?' She stared at Tyrese. '. . . They're like you, Ty.' A slight sense of alarm crept into her voice.

'What?' Tyrese clapped back.

'The Shadow Man is targeting kids who are already hurting, maybe it makes them more vulnerable to him, maybe it's like . . .' She broke off and thought. '. . . I dunno, maybe it's like, it's easy to haunt kids that have lost a loved one. Perhaps that's why the Shadow Man targeted *you* and not us, Ty. But the question now is why. What does he want you for? What did he want all those other kids for?'

'So what do we do now?' Marvin asked nervously.

'We need to go to Scarlett Hill asylum.' It was Tyrese who spoke, with such clarity, such forcefulness, it surprised not only himself but Ellie and Marvin.

'Ty, no, *no*. Dat place, well . . . Grammy always warned me never to go there, it's a bad place.'

Tyrese worked through the haziness of his mind. 'But if we need to find out the rest of Levi Campbell's story, I just know that's where we need to be . . .'

35

In the back of the large eight-seater taxi, Tyrese gazed at the rain battering the window. He rocked side to side as the wheels drove over potholes and stones. He glanced at his watch. It was later than Ellie had wanted to be – three o'clock – but they'd had to wait for the heavy rains to pass before any driver would agree to take them up the uneven mountain track beyond Grammy's house and towards Scarlett Hill asylum.

The wind howled, snapping around the old vehicle, and Tyrese listened to the windscreen wipers going at speed. The deep rumble of thunder rolled off the mountains and he saw the lightning crack through the clouds.

The cloying sickly smell of the car freshener filled the air, mixing in with the stench of their wet clothes and his rotting finger.

Pulling the neck of his top again, he scratched his throat frantically with both hands. He had an uncontrollable itch, burning deep under his skin like fire, and his whole body had begun to twitch, tightening and untightening into painful spasms. Everything felt too much, like an overload of mind and body. How could he feel in so much pain but still be numb?

In front of him, he stared at the back of Ellie and Marvin's heads bobbing about as they pored over Levi's journal. He leaned forward slightly, watching Ellie flick to an earlier part of the diary which she'd finally managed to prise open. Even though the taxi's privacy screen was closed, she still spoke quietly; he strained to hear her over the noise of the loud engine and the rain.

'. . . There's so much I can't make out. I think even if we left it to dry for days it wouldn't make a difference . . . I can't even see the date on this, it's too faded, but we know it's been written after the entry in March when the Soucouyant revisited him and before he wrote about the pact which was in the June.' She shrugged and began to read:

'. . . Time is running out and I believe I have no other choice but to look elsewhere for my purpose, and I have now formed the conclusion that the secret of death which I yearn to discover, is held only by the creatures of darkness, as only they can traverse the realms of life and death. I believe it is safer to confide in no one about my new understanding, I dare not, except for the attentive ear of . . .'

Ellie stopped, 'Oh wow, I *think* that says La Diablesse, I dunno, I can't be sure . . . I can't read it properly. Marv, can you see it?'

Tyrese watched Marvin lean over, studying the text.

'It could do, it's so scrawled though, I don't know. But . . . but does dat mean Levi was getting help from dem? He's getting help from the duppies with his experiments?'

Ellie twisted round in her seat and opened her mouth to say something to Tyrese, but seemingly thinking better of it, she quickly turned back and continued talking to Marvin. 'I mean, that's what it sounds like, though I guess it could've all been in his mind, and that's why they took him to Scarlett Hill. Like, if someone found out that he was doing all those weird experiments on all those corpses, trying to bring the dead back to life, maybe they thought he was better off in the asylum.'

'Maybe, but we both know the duppies weren't in his mind, we've seen dem ourselves. We know exactly what they're like.'

Marvin's words hung in the air, then after a moment, Ellie looked down at the book again, flicking forward to the last few pages. She read slowly, working out what the faded scrawled writing said. 'This entry's from July eighteen-ninety-seven, tenth of July, which is less than a month before he was taken to the asylum:

'. . . The days are painful and I have found myself begging for her help, and she is happy to oblige, and with the assistance of the . . .'

Ellie gasped.

'. . . Soucouyant, she holds me away from the light, filling my mind with the darkness which soothes me. It is time.'

'Nineteenth of July, eighteen-ninety-seven. My suspicions were correct, I know now that my dealings with the creatures of darkness have

come to the attention of the authorities from Scarlett Hill and thus, I have taken Llanzo's body away from harm and hidden it high on the mountain where the shadows live. There he can be watched over and I can be with him without fear of them finding me . . .'

Ellie turned to Marvin and Tyrese could see the strain on her face. 'But they *did* find Levi, didn't they? They took him to the asylum . . . He was so desperate, wasn't he . . . Though something still doesn't feel quite right about this whole thing, and I can't find anything more about this pact . . . but then, there's so many pages ruined and stuck together, we'll never know.' She sighed deeply, adding, 'But what's weird, Marv, is that there's no mention of the Shadow Man in any of his entries.'

Marvin shrugged and glanced out of the window. 'It's probably the same thing, those entries are just too faded to read.'

The taxi came to a stop. The driver opened the privacy screen and swivelled round in the seat to look at them. 'This is as far as me can go.'

Ellie slammed the diary closed, causing the driver to look at her, then the journal suspiciously.

He rubbed his goatee, his hat almost pulled over his eyes. 'The place you're looking for should only be a minute's walk up dat small track, just past the stone well over there, but the road is almost flooded, so me can't drive up. Not dat I'd go there even if I could.' He kissed his teeth, his gaze moving along them. 'It's a bad place. No one goes there. You sure you should be out here, pickney? How you going to get back, you want me to wait here for you all? Mind, me can only stay ten minutes.'

'It's fine, thank you,' Ellie answered. 'We don't know how long we'll be.'

Marvin gave the man the last of the money they had for the fare, smiled and stepped out of the taxi, followed by Ellie and Tyrese.

The wind slammed the breath out of Tyrese as if it were fighting him, and he bent his head, holding on to the side of his glasses. The rain swirled round his feet and he found himself walking through mud. Marvin walked backwards to speak to them, yelling to be heard. 'If this storm gets worse, we'll have to sit it out before we can leave here.'

'What did he mean about it being a bad place?' Ellie yelled back.

'All I know is what I told you: it's been shut for years, a long time before Grammy was even born, and since I was little, Grammy has always warned me to stay away from the place.'

They continued up the stony track which wound round a corner, protecting them slightly from the cutting wind. The small, secluded grey building of the asylum came into view. It stood on its own on the top of a mound behind some low rusting metal railings. The windows were broken and an old wooden door flapped back and forth in the wind, hanging precariously off one hinge.

Tyrese stared at how bleak, how isolated the asylum was.

The contrast of the grey, desolate building against the green of the forest emphasised the building's misery. He couldn't imagine that there'd ever been a time in its history when the sense of despair hadn't oozed out from its walls.

Briefly, he squeezed his eyes shut. His mind was a jumble – screeching sounds and rhymes playing over and over in his head, and his body no longer felt like his own, but the overpowering sense that he needed to be here sat within him.

'Why don't we walk through the asylum, have a look around?'

'Are you sure, Marv?' Ellie stared at the building. 'Ty . . . *Ty*? What do you think?'

'What do I think?' Tyrese tipped his head to one side to look at her. 'We go in.' He smiled, but suddenly Ellie appeared ill at ease and stepped away from him. He touched his face, and realised he hadn't smiled at all, he was simply staring at her.

Under the dark grey skies, Tyrese walked towards the asylum, squeezing past the door, careful not to knock it off its last remaining hinge and make a noise. There was nothing much to see. The rooms were boarded up and most of the corridors were blocked off. Their footsteps echoed around the abandoned hospital as the broken windows let in a sliver of light, throwing dark shadows on the walls. The peeling ceiling sagged, spots of water dripped on to metal pipes, sending a strange clanking round the whole building.

They walked straight through the asylum, finding themselves at the back entrance of the building where the only evidence that a door had ever been there were the two, large rusting hinges.

The rain had eased slightly, though the winds still howled as Tyrese stepped outside where he stopped, and did a double take, staring around the asylum's cemetery in disbelief. Each grave had an upside-down tree buried in it. Most of the trees inverted in the graves looked old and dead, broken and decaying, though there were a few trees where their roots had grown back down into the earth and spread around, looking as though a giant knotted spider's web surrounded the grave.

Ellie and Marvin caught up with him.

'Oh my gosh, what is this?' Ellie whispered.

'*Wah yuh ah duh here?*'

Tyrese watched as a short, rounded man dressed in an oversized rain mac which trailed almost to the ground came from behind the trees. The large wheelbarrow he pushed was piled up with leaves and branches, and he bellowed angrily while marching across the wet grass towards them. 'What's your business here, hmm?'

'Sorry, we were just looking around, we just wanted to see it,' Ellie replied politely.

'Now you've seen, now you go. Don't let me catch you snooping when me come back, you hear? This is private property, it isn't a public cemetery. And anyway, you pickney should be at home, dat's exactly where me go now, only a fool would be out in this weather.'

He began to move away.

Tyrese flinched at the pain in his head but he called after

the man anyway: 'The trees. Why are they all upside down in the graves?'

The man turned slowly, stared at Tyrese, looking like he was wondering whether or not to give time to the conversation. 'Dat's just what they do.'

'Who does it, and *why*?' Tyrese asked, a flicker of annoyance in his voice.

'Pickney, you not a Yard man? You not know about it?' the man said, sounding rather scornful.

'Him both a Yard man and a Manchester *bwoy*,' Marvin said defensively. 'And me a Yard man, and me not know about dem trees.'

The man nodded, slowly digesting this information. He glanced at them all and pushed out a loud sigh. 'Dem used to say if you buried a person with their belongings and have a tree or a bush buried upside down in their grave, it would be enough to stop the undead from rising up.'

Ellie gazed around. 'And . . . and did it work?'

The man laughed loudly, showing off stained teeth, as if Ellie had said something amusing. 'See dat stone plaque on the wall?' The man nodded towards the side of the asylum. 'See what it says: *ubi lux est spes est* . . . by all accounts it means, *Where there's light, there's hope*.' Like the taxi driver, the man kissed his teeth, shook his head. 'In this place, let me tell you something, hope never stood a chance.' And with that, he picked up his barrow and moved on.

—

The rains had started again and the grey sky seemed to sit lower than ever. They'd spent the last twenty minutes wandering the cemetery, keeping an eye out for the gardener, though it seemed like he really had gone home.

Tyrese had wandered along, reading the inscriptions on the headstones, some dating back to when the asylum first opened in 1841. He'd noticed a lot of the burial plots weren't actually filled to the top with soil like they'd usually be, rather, they were filled with the trunk and the spreading branches of the tree buried upside down in it. And he found he could actually look right down into a few, through the screen of twisted dead branches to where the thin layer of soil covering the coffin actually began.

'Hey, Ty, over here! *Ty!* You've got to come and look at this! *Ty!*' Ellie shouted, and Tyrese made his way across to where she and Marvin were standing.

'Look.' She pointed at a single grave, the headstone large and chipped. Like all the other graves, it had an upside-down tree buried in it, though it hadn't re-rooted itself in the surrounding earth, instead the narrow trunk of the tree leaned limply to one side, dry and brittle, the dead branches thin and spindly.

LEVI CAMPBELL
DIED DECEMBER 1897

There was nothing else on the inscription and Tyrese thought how abrupt it was. Moreover, Levi had died only a year or so after his son, and only a few months after he'd been brought to this place.

'I can't believe he died here. This was it. This was where it all ended for him.'

Ellie stared at the headstone whilst Tyrese moved to the edge of the grave and looked down, squinting, pushing his glasses up. 'What's that? Can you see that? There's something there . . . Look through the branches.'

Ellie and Marvin moved around to where Tyrese was pointing. He crouched, leaning over slightly to get a better look. It was almost covered by the tree but he could just make out what he *thought* looked like a corner of a box, or a small chest.

'A couple of the other graves over by the hill were the same.' Marvin pointed towards them. 'They had things in dem as well.'

'I guess it's probably their belongings, like the guy said, they were buried with them,' Ellie replied. She looked around. 'But then how come this stuff hasn't been taken, especially if any of it's worth money?'

Marvin raised his eyebrows and kissed his teeth. 'No one in Jamaica I know would ever *think* about getting into a grave, *what*! *Bwoy*, no! And definitely not a grave in *this* place.'

Tyrese stared at Ellie for a moment, glanced back at the grave, then quickly lay down on the wet grass.

'What are you doing, Ty?' Marvin asked.

'Hold my legs, Marv . . . Come on, just do it, yeah?'

'What, no. *No way.*'

'Just hold them, I want to take a look.'

'No, this is crazy, this is just—'

'*Marv*!' Tyrese interrupted, yelling at his cousin.

Marvin glared at Tyrese then begrudgingly held on to his legs, allowing Tyrese to shuffle himself further towards the edge of the grave on his stomach. He reached down through the branches of the upside-down tree, which snapped and cracked as he pushed his hand through.

'Marv, I can't quite reach it from this angle, I'm going to have to turn a bit.'

With Marvin still holding him tightly, Tyrese spun on to his side.

'You good?' Marvin asked.

'Yeah, perfect.' The top half of Tyrese's body was now completely submerged into the grave, helping him to get a greater reach.

The branches poked and scratched at his face, clawing at him as if they were protecting the grave, and although Tyrese couldn't see what he was doing, the fingers on his good hand explored the side of the small chest . . . He moved them slowly, felt a handle and latched them underneath it, pulling hard, trying to drag it up and out from under the branches.

It was stuck. Jammed in.

He gave another hard tug, the muscles in his arm shaking. Though this time, Tyrese felt the chest begin to move. 'I've got it! *I've got it!*'

Watching closely, Ellie scrambled on to her knees, reaching to help Tyrese lift it up. They dragged it on to the grass and Tyrese noticed the chest, which was no larger than half a metre long, had an oval brass plate with Levi's name engraved on it. The outside of it, which Tyrese could see had once been green, maybe leather, was now a stippled brown with broken rusting locks.

Marvin leaned over. 'Ty, I don't like this, can we just hurry up? Are you sure we should even open it?'

Tyrese nodded, but unlike his cousin, he felt captivated. He sat crossed legged, took a deep breath and slowly opened the lid. Hundreds of tiny woodlice scuttled out, but instead of being revolted, he just flicked them off his legs, and stared into the small chest, pins and needles running through his body. His mouth was full of tiny, painful ulcers, his tongue felt large and swollen, and he had a metallic taste in his mouth.

'Oh Jeez, look at this.' Ellie reached for the pile of letters tied in a ribbon. The ink on them was completely faded, impossible to read. Tyrese carefully lifted out a pocket watch from the chest, turning it around in his hand, wincing at another sudden sharp shooting pain driving down through the top of his head.

'There's a photo!' Ellie took it out of the chest gently, staring at it intently for a moment before passing it to Marvin and Tyrese.

Tyrese studied the sepia photograph: a slim, elegant man with dreadlocks wearing a top hat and dressed in a suit, a checked waistcoat with a pocket watch and a white winged shirt and neck tie, stood next to a young boy. Apart from the hat the boy was dressed the same as the man.

Marvin turned it over and read the back.

Levi and Llanzo Campbell,
19th April 1896

'Dat's him! Dat's him! Dat's Levi! Dat's Levi and his son!' Marvin couldn't contain his excitement.

Tyrese took the photo from Marvin, turned it back over, and stared at the picture of Levi and his son again.

'Tyrese, Tyrese.'

His head whipped up and he glanced around, mesmerised, watching the trees moving and shuddering in the wind. It no longer felt cold, rather it was warm and calming like the call of his name.

'Ty, why did you just say "yes"? Yes what?'

He jumped.

Ellie stared at him.

'I didn't.'

'You did. You just looked up and said "yes" . . . Ty?'

He didn't know what she talking about, but it was easier to go along with what she was saying. 'Oh right, yeah, it was just something about the photo, but it's fine.'

He could feel Ellie staring at him but he didn't look at her, instead he just placed the photo back in the chest.

'Can we go now?' Marvin asked. 'I don't want to get stuck here when it gets dark.'

'Wait, what if we've missed something?'

Marvin glimpsed at Ellie. 'Like what?'

'Like, there might be something else in the grave, maybe another box, or something?' She turned to Tyrese. 'Ty, will you have another look?'

'This isn't a good idea.' Marvin sounded as nervous as he looked. 'Can we just leave it now? Let's just go, *please*. Ellie, Ty, come on.'

Paying no attention to his cousin's appeals, Tyrese silently moved over to the grave again and lay on his stomach, shuffling towards the edge. He began to pull and snap the branches – which broke easily – off the dead tree, giving him a better view below.

'There! Ty, I think can see something.' Ellie's words rushed out and she kneeled next to him. 'What's that, there . . . look? Can you see it?'

Tyrese pushed his glasses up, squinting at what Ellie was pointing at: a paper-thin bundle, swathed in a dirty cream linen cloth, lay on top of the coffin.

'Hold my legs. *Marv*, my legs!' He wriggled nearer to the edge, leaned in, but he moved too quickly for Marvin to get a proper grip.

Yelling, he toppled forward, crashing through the remaining broken branches to land square on the coffin, his weight smashing it wide open.

As his panic subsided, he felt something – several

things – slithering against him. In horror he scrambled to his feet and then realised the coffin was filled not with human remains but with scores of dark, writhing snakes. Each one was coiled into a circle, devouring its own tail.

Ellie screamed. 'Oh my God, get out, Ty! *Get out!* Marvin, help him get out! Ty, come on!'

But as the rain poured down and the thunder rattled overhead, Tyrese didn't move. He just watched the snakes slithering around his ankles. His initial fear and revulsion had been replaced by a strange sense of fascination.

'Ty! Ty, what are you doing? Ty!'

He blinked then felt Marvin pull at his shoulder. Grabbing the thin package, Tyrese let his cousin help him up.

'That was disgusting. Are you all right?' Ellie grimaced. 'What is that anyway?'

She nodded to what Tyrese held in his hand and carefully he began to unwrap it.

'I think it's a piece of cowhide.' He felt the soft hair of the cow skin, then he turned it over.

On the smooth underside there were words written in dark red handwriting:

I relinquish the light, I relinquish my soul, to be reunited once more, and I will bring the children unto you. From one soul cometh many.

Then at the bottom, there was a scrawling signature: *Levi Campbell.*

'*Rah!* I think dat's dried blood. It's been written in *blood*,' Marvin muttered.

Ellie stared at the cowhide in Tyrese's hand, and gently took it from him. 'It's a blood oath . . . This is it . . . *This* must be the pact Levi wrote about.'

'And they say a blood oath can never be broken,' Marvin whispered.

Tyrese walked back to the edge of the grave, and stared down at the thrashing snakes. 'There's nothing there, *nothing*. Apart from the snakes, it's completely empty. No bones, no anything.' He blinked, looked up, the rain falling on his face. 'That's why Levi made that blood oath with the duppies, that's why he signed it: it meant he rose from the dead, he could become one of them . . . I don't think Levi was ever a victim of the Shadow Man at all, because . . .'

He stared at Ellie and at Marvin.

'. . . Levi Campbell *is* the Shadow Man.'

36

Tyrese stood in the pouring rain at the end of the track. He looked around as he spoke. 'I need to go.'

Trembling, Ellie said quickly. 'Yeah, I agree, now we know what happened to Levi, what your grammy was going to tell you, we just need to get back to Kingston, work out what we're going to do next. We need to get the heck out of here as quickly as we can.'

Tyrese's head was noisy, the call of the Shadow Man enticing, the rhyme of the missing whirling around. 'I'm not talking about Kingston . . . you go back if you want. Do what you like. But I'm not . . . Marv, how do I get to Umbra Mountain from here?'

Marvin looked puzzled. 'I've never heard of it.'

'It's Grammy's mountain.'

Marvin shook his head. 'No, Grammy lives on Clara Mountain.'

'That's what it's called now, but that's not the original name. There was a map on the wall in Mrs Stuart's kitchen, yeah, and over the years, some names changed. Umbra Mountain was on there, and that's *definitely* Grammy's mountain.' His words rushed out. 'So which way, Marv, it can't be far because we passed Grammy's road on the way to the asylum . . . ?'

Surprise was drawn over both Marvin and Ellie's faces but it soon turned to terror.

Marvin stared at Tyrese. 'OK, dat used to be the name, but so what? Just because it used to be called dat, it doesn't mean you need to go there now, Ty.'

'What aren't you getting?' There was an urgency to his voice as Tyrese started to put it all together. 'The snakes . . . The name, Umbra, it means shadow . . . *High on the mountain where the shadows live,* that's what he said.'

'Snakes, shadow? Ty, you're not making sense. Come on, let's get out of this weather . . . *Ty*.'

'Just tell me which way, Marv.' He couldn't think clearly but he felt a mist rising in him, a sense of being outside his body. He gritted his teeth, hissing through them. He grabbed his cousin's shoulders and shook him. 'Just tell me which way it is, Marv!' He glared at Marvin. 'You know what, fine, if you won't tell me, I'll just have to find it myself.' Tyrese started to jog towards the forest. 'I need to go to him.'

'Ty! Ty! What the hell are you talking about? Ty, no, what do you mean, you need to go to him?'

'Ty, come back!' Ellie yelled.

'Wait! Ty, *Ty*! Ty, you'll get lost . . .'

Marvin sprinted after him, pulling Tyrese back. Out of breath, he spoke, 'Ty, listen, this is crazy, stupid, you're making a big mistake, but me can't let you go on your own.' Marvin paused, glanced at Ellie before he looked back at Tyrese. 'OK, OK, come, I'll show you the way . . .'

The storm raged on.

Tyrese and Ellie followed Marvin, and as they ran further into the forest, screams tore through the darkening day almost as loud as the thunder which rumbled and growled above them. They battled through the winds, through the flooded tracks, racing against the torrents of water which snaked down the paths in rivulets, stumbling through the grove of gnarled banyan trees draped with vines and under the overhanging silk cotton trees, towards Grammy's mountain.

Lightning ripped across the sky and the wind howled, shadows twisting and forming between the silhouettes of the forest, and Tyrese waded through the streams, his feet burning, his skin bleeding as he clambered over rocks that tore at his flesh.

'Tyrese, Tyrese.'

Tyrese heard the familiar calling. He picked up his speed, running ahead of Marvin, following the sound of the screams.

'Tyrese, Tyrese.'

'Ty, Ty! Wait up!' Marvin shouted behind him. 'Where are you going? Ty, don't be stupid! Ty, you'll get lost, you haven't even got your phone on you. Ty, wait, at least take dat.'

Ignoring Marvin, he continued to follow the call of his name, scrambling along the mountain path as he battled the wind and rain which drove down hard, cutting sharply on to his skin, feeling like a thousand pieces of grit were being flicked into his face. His lungs were tight but he kept on running, pushing through the forest, taking no notice of the ants and insects which bit at his ankles and the bugs which stung his arms.

Eventually, he slowed to a stop by a large mahoe tree. Out of the corner of his eye he saw his cousin and Ellie come into sight.

Panting and struggling up the path, Marvin yelled, 'What's wrong with you? Why did you sprint off like dat? I told you not to. You could've got lost, and then what!'

Again, Tyrese didn't bother answering. He actually knew where he was. *Exactly* where he was. He felt the pull of it.

'We stick together, Ty, OK?' Marvin continued angrily as he walked up to Tyrese. 'Don't do dat again, understand? It's stupid, it could put us all in danger.'

'Tyrese, Tyrese.'

Tyrese began to shake, he could feel he was near.

'Marv, where are we?' Ellie whispered, though the groaning of the branches above almost smothered her words.

Marvin shone the flashlight around. 'We're on Grammy's mountain, Clara . . . *Umbra* Mountain . . . But Grammy's house is way down back there.' He turned to Tyrese, the beam of the flashlight lighting up the spark of fear in his eyes: 'How did you even know which way to come, Ty . . . Ty? Ty, are you listening to me?'

Tyrese pushed past his cousin and walked to the edge of the slope, the pain in his head greater than ever, his vision coming and going as though it were a flickering candle.

'Ty, oh my God, are you all right?' Ellie shone her phone light at him. 'Your nose is bleeding!'

Tyrese touched his face, looked at his fingers, saw the blood. He blinked as a sudden warmth enveloped his body again. A stillness sat inside him. A peace. 'I'm fine, I'm fine.' He licked the trickling blood off his lips but he didn't bother wiping it away. 'Down there, down the side of the mountain.' He spoke more to himself but it was as if he didn't recognise his own voice.

Ellie looked at him strangely. She began to say, 'Ty, I think . . .' but Tyrese had already begun to scramble down the side of the muddy slope.

At the bottom of it, breathing hard, he rushed across to the boulder between the fallen tree and rock face.

He crouched, a tingling beginning to move under his skin and through his veins. Then, like he'd done on the first day, he stared at the simple etching of the snake in a circle devouring its own tail on the grave. *Rebirth* . . . Yes, he knew he was in the right place.

'Oh my God, is that a *grave*?' Catching up with him, Ellie shone her phone light on it. 'Ty, we shouldn't be here. Why would you bring us here . . . ? Marvin's right, this is a big mistake. Come on, we need to go.' She began to back away.

'Ty, Ty, come! Ty,' Marvin called. '*Ty*!'

Tyrese didn't move. His breathing slowed down. And as the blood continued to trickle from his nose, he felt the heat of it on his skin, watching enthralled as it fell into the wet earth and disappeared, swirling into the ground.

'Tyrese, *come on*.'

Ellie and Marvin pulled him up to go. 'Just move, Tyrese. *Please*, you've got to move.'

Tyrese shifted his gaze. His thoughts didn't seem to belong to him but he became aware of every cell in his body moving, shifting, like they were changing shape.

'Ty, tell me what's happening to you?' Ellie touched his hand. 'Talk to me.'

The weight of the raindrops on his lashes felt heavy and he leaned his head to one side, staring straight at her. He recognised her face, but he was confused, and as he watched her mouth move, he wasn't quite sure what she was asking.

Marvin shouted, 'Ty, we need to go, but me can't leave you here. Come on, *please*, Ty, come on!' He was almost in tears.

'Oh God!' Ellie and Marvin screamed in terror as two figures started walking slowly through the dark forest towards them. Step by step, the figures moved closer, through the twisting trees until finally they could make them out: it was the old bearded man from the beach, and La Diablesse, their eyes rolled back, showing only the whites. Then others came: grotesque beings drifting out, the twisted creatures of the night.

Insects swarmed on the ground at Tyrese's feet and he felt them curl around his toes, tightening around them, ensnaring him as they writhed in their masses, feeding off each other, feeding off his dripping blood.

The duppies moved towards him. Mesmerised, he watched.

'Child of the Shadow Man, him come find you,

Child of the darkness, him come take you.'

Over and over and over they chanted, their voices rising up into the night sky. Lightning ripped across. It hit the trees, setting them alight, and while the dark clouds swirled, the chanting became louder.

Behind Tyrese came a loud rumble.

The grave was opening.

'Tyrese, no! Tyrese!' Ellie cried, clinging on to Marvin.

The stone slab cracked and splintered apart. Screeching and scraping noises came from within, and, riveted, Tyrese watched as long fingers edged through the earth.

Ellie screamed again.

A boy, his face contorted, his grin manic and twisted, dragged himself up from out of the grave, and Tyrese could see his whole face and body was covered in ash.

The boy stretched out to Tyrese.

'That's Llanzo, oh my God, that's Llanzo!' Ellie shrieked. 'Tyrese, run, *run*! Ty!'

Llanzo's head tilted so far to the side, his neck stretched, misshapen as though it were a winding snake. 'Tyrese, Tyrese, come join Pappy and me.' Llanzo laughed, earth trickling out of the corners of his mouth as his eyes stared unblinking at Tyrese.

Tyrese stepped forward, closer to Llanzo, drawn towards him. He put his hand out, his fingers touching Llanzo's. He felt the warmth, the heat from them. He stared down into the grave, the darkness feeling like a glow of fire.

'Child of mine, you came to me.' A deep, smooth, velvety voice travelled out from the forest. Through the arc of twisted trees, they watched as Levi Campbell appeared.

The Shadow Man.

His face was taut and rigid, the tendons exposed in his neck, and his stare lay intensely on Tyrese as he walked towards him, his eyes endlessly dark. 'Come, come, come be with me.' His fingers grazed against Tyrese's cheek, then he clasped Tyrese's hand tightly, bringing his face close, his breath as cold as the dead. 'Child of the darkness, you came to me.' A torn smile. His voice so silky, so lulling, so tempting . . . Tyrese felt his eyes begin to roll as the Shadow Man squeezed his hand all the harder.

Pain ripped through Tyrese's flesh, his face, his skin, feeling like it was being pulled off. Pain rushed through his bones, his head, too intense to speak of. He was on fire. Although a part of him knew where he was, he felt far away, as though he was somewhere lost in the distance.

He could hear the others' cries, but he couldn't quite hold on to them. He was unable to think straight, the only thing he could see ahead was darkness and he didn't know how to stop himself falling into it.

'I can take it all away, Tyrese, I can take all your pain away . . .' the Shadow Man whispered and as the words hit Tyrese's ear, it felt like something was scurrying and burying down into his eardrum.

Llanzo stepped completely out of the grave. He stood by his father, gurgling as wet earth bubbled out of his mouth.

'It's cold out there, Tyrese. Wouldn't you like to join us in the warmth? Come, feel how warm the darkness is, how safe it feels.'

Tyrese's eyes flicked to the grave. Llanzo grabbed him, pulling him ever nearer to the edge of the darkness as a screech of laughter from La Diablesse cut through the air.

The Shadow Man lifted Tyrese's chin up with his hand, and Tyrese could see his own reflection in the Shadow Man's eyes. 'Come, child of the darkness, come with me, child of mine.'

There was another loud screech.

Shuffling and crawling towards Tyrese, more creatures came: bloodshot eyes and swollen gums, their hanging skin trailing behind them.

It was the Soucouyant.

They circled Tyrese, and somewhere through the fog of his mind he heard voices, rising above the storm. 'Ty, Ty, no! No!'

The Shadow Man's eyes bore into him. 'I was once like you, but they showed me the darkness, they took away my pain. Let dem take away yours, let dem help you forget. Join us, Tyrese, come.'

The temptation, the pull to step into the grave with Llanzo, to become a child of the Shadow Man, engulfed him. The warmth was calling, wrapping around, pulling him down towards a world without light.

'You can feel it can't you, Tyrese? You can feel the warmth, I know it. I can see it on your face.' The Shadow Man stroked

Tyrese's cheek again. 'We'll give you just darkness, no painful light. Come, come, give yourself to us.'

Trembling, Tyrese took another step closer to the grave. But now he was dimly aware of different kinds of screams, of wailing, telling him not to listen: 'They're tricking you. Look at them, look at them, you don't want to be like them. Fight them, Ty!'

The wind howled, whistling round the trees and from down the side of the mountain slope, a procession of figures appeared, their features so faded they were almost faceless. They moved slowly, drifting to stand behind the Shadow Man. Swaying, they chanted quietly and Tyrese watched, and soon he found himself swaying with them.

Then more words came into his head, as if he was hearing a call from far away: 'Oh God, Ty! Ty, they're the *missing* . . . Ty, they're the other children. I get it now, I get it! To be reunited with his son, he sold his soul and agreed to bring them more: *from one soul cometh many* . . . Ty, he wants *your* soul, but it's not too late to hold on. Ty, look at me. Please, look at me!'

Tyrese blinked.

He slowly turned his head and looked over to where a strange girl and boy were calling to him.

'That's it, Ty, look at us, keep looking at us . . . I know it hurts, but it's not too late. Not for you anyway . . . It's too late for them, but it doesn't have to be for you.'

As the wind continued to swirl, Tyrese felt the Shadow Man's hands on his face, turning him back round to look at him. 'Come, it's time now.'

Tyrese stared, locked again into the Shadow Man's gaze, though the cries he could hear kept coming, louder and louder and louder.

'Listen to me, Ty, keep listening, he wants to take you down into the darkness with him, to stay in the darkness forever. He wants you to be like him, but you're not like him, Ty, you're not! You're not! The Shadow Man *is* the darkness, you aren't! Ty, look to the light. They can't fight that, darkness can't fight the light. But you have to want it, you have to want to look into the light.'

'Just play it, Ellie, play the rest of the phone message, play it, *play it*, *play it*!'

And as the Shadow Man's stare continued to burn into Tyrese, another voice tore through the haze, one he thought he recognised . . .

'*. . . but, Ty, I know I couldn't come to Athens with you, but I'm actually calling because I wanted to say, I'm so proud of you. I couldn't be prouder and I couldn't have wished for a better son. And look, what I'm going to say next is really important, OK . . . Always know that I love you. Know I'll always be here. No matter what, no matter how tough things might get, no matter how old and grown-up and grey you get, don't ever forget that. Don't ever let anything get in the way of remembering. Keep that light in your heart. Now have fun, enjoy, you hear me . . . I love you, Ty . . . I couldn't love you more if I tried.*'

Tyrese blinked again.

He stared around.

Then he looked down at himself, at his hands, at his feet,

at *where* he was, and, hearing the sound of his own breathing, he suddenly scrambled back, scrambled away from the Shadow Man. But as he did, he tripped and fell, sprawling across the wet earth.

The Shadow Man loomed above him.

'Child of darkness.' He held his arms open wide. 'Come, Tyrese, you're mine . . . You're mine.'

'No, Ty, no! Tell him, tell him your truth, Ty! Tell him who you are!'

A picture.

An image, rushed into Tyrese's mind, into his heart, a beam of light breaking through.

He pushed himself back on to his feet, shaking his head, edging away, staring at the Shadow Man, whose face twisted and warped, distorting into rage.

Tyrese opened his mouth, blinking, looking around again at where he was. He tried to form the words as he felt the Shadow Man pull on his thoughts, intruding on them with the rhyme of the missing which became louder and louder in his head. He fought against it, wrestling to push it away, to bring back his own thoughts, his own memory, fighting to reclaim them in his heart. 'My . . . my . . . my . . .'

But then it came to him.

Like a crashing bolt of energy, at last he spoke the words he'd struggled to say as his tears cut at the back of his throat. 'My . . . my name is Tyrese Walker, son of Nathan Henry Walker, and I am *not* a child of the darkness.' He looked up to the skies, feeling the rain wash over his face. 'I love you,

Dad, I love you! You hear me, you hear that? Wherever you are, *I love you*!' He stared again at the Shadow Man, raising his voice, tears streaming down his cheeks. 'And I miss him, I miss him, I miss him, I miss him, I miss him, *I miss him*, but I will not live in the darkness any more. I am not yours, and I will never, ever, ever be yours.'

The duppies and Llanzo started to screech, falling back into the grave, gurgling and rasping, turning and twisting. The Soucouyant clawed at their eyes, tearing away their skins, their flames flickering away.

The veins inside the Shadow Man's neck began to bulge, breaking open, pouring out tiny black insects. His body began convulsing, the flesh on his face and his hands disintegrating, and he retreated, crawling, driven back into the darkness of the forest with the other creatures.

A sense of calm fell.

A silence.

Then Ellie and Marvin sat and listened to Tyrese calling out to his dad, his voice loud and strong and brave. Finally saying the things he couldn't before:

'I love you.'

'I miss you.'

'I'll never forget you.'

Today, tomorrow, forever . . .

The Shadow Man had gone.

37

In the early hours of the morning, they ran down the trail path to Grammy's house, passing the grove of rose apple trees which sat alongside the sea of wild ginger lilies, past the fresh water stream which bubbled over rocks. By the stretch of shrubs and plants they saw Grammy's house as it always was; the painted bright-green bricks with sun-bleached pink shutters with the laundry still drying on the swing bench by the broken white fence.

Tyrese looked at Marvin and Ellie. 'Ready?'

'Ready,' Marvin answered.

'Ready,' Ellie said.

Then they rushed into the house, racing down the hallway. 'Mum! Mum! Grammy! Mum! Grammy!' Tyrese could feel his heart racing as he ran to the bedroom. It was empty. They weren't here. And speeding across to the bathroom and then to the kitchen, he tried not to panic.

Dashing back into the hallway, he banged into Marvin who was just coming out of another room. 'Any luck?'

'No,' Marvin said, turning to Ellie, who'd checked the other bedrooms.

'No, sorry, your mom and Grammy aren't there.' Panic rushed out of her. 'I need to go and look for Dad.'

Tyrese stared at Ellie, then at his cousin. Hope was beginning to fade. 'We're too late, aren't we? They've gone.'

'Don't say that, Ty.' Ellie's eyes brimmed with tears.

'We've just got to keep looking,' Marvin said, wiping tears and dirt away. 'Maybe . . . Maybe dem have gone to see Ellie's dad, maybe dat's what's happened.' There was a desperation to his voice.

Nodding, Tyrese hurried out of the house, followed by Ellie and Marvin.

Just as he was making his way to the back of the house, he heard it. He heard the sound he'd longed to hear.

'Tyrese?'

He whirled around. For a moment it felt to Tyrese like his heart was going to explode into a thousand pieces. He gasped out a laugh. 'Mum? Mum, is that you?'

'Yes, Ty. It's me.'

And it was.

He looked at her: she was wearing the same clothes as she had when she'd fallen into the deep, dark sleep, her hair as usual escaping out of its messy bun. He held her tightly, a rush of love and happiness soaring through him like a whirlwind. 'I . . . I thought you'd gone, I thought I'd lost you.'

Then he laughed so loud it caught at the back of his throat as he saw Grammy hobbling around the side of the house dressed in a red head wrap and cream blouse and skirt. 'Grammy! Grammy! Grammy!'

Marvin ran up to her, hugging Grammy so tightly, it looked to Tyrese like he was worried she'd float away. His face ached from his smile.

'Are you all right, Ty?' Mum touched his cheek. Her gaze darting over his face. 'We've been looking for you. I don't even know what really happened. Grammy says she thinks we ate something bad,' she said, shaking her head. 'We've been out cold for over three days! Maybe some kind of food poisoning or something.'

'Well, not from my shrimp curry!' Grammy cackled as she walked up to them, holding hands with Marvin.

'But what I don't understand is why you weren't in the house earlier. Why weren't you there, and—' Tyrese's mum suddenly stopped, looking at Tyrese from head to toe, then she glanced at Marvin, and Ellie, who was standing by the porch. 'You guys look exhausted. You're covered in mud . . . oh my goodness, where've you *been*?'

'Me already told you, Patty,' Grammy said warmly but firmly. 'Dem had gone to get help, hadn't you, Ty? Tyrese knew what he needed to go and do, didn't you, Tyrese?'

His mum's face began to crumble. 'I'm so sorry that you were left to deal with it. You must have been so frightened. I'm sorry, Ty.'

'Mum, Mum, please don't cry, Mum. It's fine, it's all right,' Tyrese said, squeezing his her hand tightly.

'Oh my goodness, what's happened to your finger? Your whole hand looks sore, Ty!'

He looked down, the pain had gone along with the smell,

and it had stopped bleeding and oozing but his finger and hand was still mottled grey and swollen. 'Oh, yeah, I think I got some sort of insect bite a few days ago and it got infected. It'll be OK.'

'We need to get you to a doctor.'

'Patty, don't panic. It'll be OK . . . Tyrese is like his dad, Patty, him brave. Him not afraid . . . Not any more. Are you, Tyrese?' Grammy winked at Tyrese and he tilted his head and looked at her.

She knew. Grammy knew the truth of where they'd been.

'And anyway, dem here now. Safe. Dat's what matters,' Grammy continued and she clapped her hands. 'Me have a feeling dat this is going to be a good summer. And look, the sky has cleared, there's sunshine. *Finally* there's sunshine.'

'I need to check my dad is OK.' Ellie's voice sounded small as she walked up to Tyrese. Her whole body trembled. 'I've got to find him.'

The rumble of a car behind them driving at speed up the sandy track caused Tyrese to turn around before he'd had a chance to answer. It skidded to a halt and Mr Thomas ran out, his cowboy hat falling off as he sprinted across to Ellie.

'Ellie, baby, oh my word, where've you been, darlin'? I was so worried. I don't know what happened to me. It's like I passed out, maybe it was from the heat, sunstroke. But when I woke up I realised I'd been knocked out for three days or so! The site was empty, the men had gone home. Then I looked around for you and you weren't there. I thought something terrible had happened to you. I drove up here but no one was about. The door was locked, the windows shut, you can't imagine what was going through my mind. I've been driving around ever since, and your phone was off, or maybe it was just the signal.'

Ellie blinked. 'You have? You've been looking for me?'

Ellie's dad gave a half laugh and Tyrese could see he was shaking. 'Of course I have, baby. Where've you been anyway, sweetheart, you look exhausted, darlin'?'

Ellie glanced at Grammy.

'Tyrese's mum and I, we weren't well either. They went to get help,' Grammy said.

Ellie shrugged. 'I thought you wouldn't notice I'd gone. You're always so busy, Daddy.'

Mr Thomas's face reddened and Tyrese wondered if he was going to get angry but he just stood, listening to Ellie.

'Anyway, we're fine. Marvin and Tyrese did a good job looking after me. I'm sorry I worried you and I'm glad you're all right because I was worried about *you*.'

'You were?' Mr Thomas looked as shocked as Ellie had.

'Of course, Daddy, I love you.'

He blinked, looking slightly embarrassed. 'I love you too, baby.' And he glanced at Tyrese. 'Then I have to thank you sir for looking after my baby,' he said, his Texan accent like a lullaby.

'Mr Thomas, it's kind of Ellie to say that, but it was the other way round,' Tyrese said. 'She looked after me.'

'And me,' Marvin added.

'I don't know what I would've done without her.' Tyrese smiled, taking hold of Ellie's hand as well.

Mr Thomas turned to Ellie. 'Baby, I'm so proud of you.'

Tears welled into Ellie's eyes. 'I don't think you've ever said that to me before.'

Mr Thomas frowned. 'Haven't I, darlin'? But you've always known that I am, right?'

'No . . . you never say anything to me! We never talk, and I . . . Oh, it doesn't matter.'

For a moment, Mr Thomas stayed silent again but then he bent down, gently held on to Ellie's shoulders and stared at her. 'Tell me.'

Her tears trickled down. 'All I ever do is try to please you and Momma, and you never even notice. It's like . . .' She glanced at Tyrese and Marvin, as if looking for reassurance. They smiled at her, then she looked back at her dad and continued. 'It's like the cheerleading or the beauty contests, they're just not me, I don't like doing them.'

Mr Thomas looked surprised. 'You don't? I thought you loved them, baby.'

'That's because you never asked, and I just did that stuff for you. But I don't want to do it any more, I want to do things that make me *happy*, but I want *you* to be happy for me, Daddy . . .'

'What things?'

Ellie took a deep breath. 'I want to try to get on to the school wrestling team.'

Tyrese saw how taken aback Mr Thomas was.

He scratched his head, chewed on his lip and it took a moment for him to speak. 'There's a wrestling team? For girls?'

Ellie laughed. 'Yes, Daddy, and I've done it loads of times in gym class and . . .'

'. . . And she's a natural,' Marvin cut in. 'She's the Blue Mountain Wrestling Queen,' he said, grinning at Ellie proudly.

Mr Thomas glanced at them all, then shrugged, 'Then, hell, wrestling it is.' He smiled, hugging her tightly.

Tyrese's mum smiled as well. She stroked Tyrese's head, drawing him into her, but he felt his arm being pulled and he turned and looked at Grammy.

'I can see it,' she whispered.

'See what, Grammy?'

She lowered her voice even further, drawing him away from the others. 'In your eyes. You let in the light. I'm so proud of you, child.'

He smiled at her shyly, whispering back, 'I was just scared by the way I was feeling, Grammy. I missed him so much, but I didn't know how to say.'

'Me know, darlin', but now you've let him in, he'll be all around you. He's always there with you. Listen . . . Can you hear him?'

Tyrese listened. He felt the sun, its warmth, then he heard the breeze rustle through the trees, whispering through the leaves, murmuring through the branches as if it was saying, *I'm here.*

Grammy pressed her hands on Tyrese's heart. 'Can you feel dat, Ty? He's there as well.'

A horn in the distance made them all turn and Tyrese saw first a trail of smoke, then a truck hurtling down towards them.

'Who's that?' Tyrese's mum said as she squinted into the sun.

He watched as a familiar-looking truck came steaming down, sand and grit from the track whirling up in the air. The truck's brakes squealed as it came to a stop and the door flung open.

Mrs Stuart stepped out of the car.

Nervously, Tyrese glanced at Marvin. His cousin rushed over to the porch and grabbed the hessian sack Grammy always left there, then quickly racing back, and without warning, Marvin threw a handful of rice at Mrs Stuart's feet.

She stared at him.

Tyrese waited, holding his breath.

She kissed her teeth, stepping over the rice. 'What make you do dat? You think dat's funny, mmm? Always joke, joke, with you, Marvin.' She shook her head. 'Rice a dear enough without you wasting it.'

Then she sighed and relief washed over Tyrese. He glanced at Marvin who seemed just as relieved. It was clearly the *real* Mrs Stuart.

She looked at Grammy. 'Somebody *tief* me car. Dem must have jumped through the window and take me keys!' But then she turned her head, and a wide grin appeared on her face. 'What! Wait! Tyrese? Tyrese, is dat you, child?'

'Yes, Mrs Stuart.'

'Oh Lawd, look 'pon you! Me recognise you from the

photos. Me haven't seen you since you were a little boy . . . Me so sorry about your father. *Bwoy*, you look so much like him. He was a good man, your father . . . Oh, me so glad you're here.'

Tyrese grinned. 'Thank you. I'm so glad I'm here too.'

'Seeing you here with your grammy stops me feeling so *vexed*. Me just don't know *what* happened. I must have been taken ill, eaten something bad, but when me woke up, the truck had gone! I only just got it back this morning.' She pursed her lips. 'If me ever find out who took it, let me tell you, I'll use your grammy's mad hat and put it on.'

Grammy chuckled and looked at Mrs Stuart's truck. 'Where did you find it, then?'

'Can you believe, a whole two mountains away? A whole two mountains! Mr Gregory from the village found it. Him see it driving past him. Him say the truck was going so fast, he swore it was a flash of lightning.'

38

Six Months Later
Manchester, England

'Now don't forget to wear your scarf, Tyrese. You hear me?'

Tyrese balanced his phone on the ledge outside the changing room as he chatted to Grammy and Marvin. Mr Thomas had kindly offered Grammy access to his hotel's Wi-Fi, so now they could FaceTime each other without the signal dropping.

'Grammy, I'll be too hot to wear it!'

His grammy leaned into the phone and Tyrese laughed as most of the screen was taken up by her nose.

'Just show me where it is, Ty, me can't see it.'

Tyrese grinned at the screen, he turned and giggled at his mum who passed him the extra-long, multi-coloured crocheted scarf out of her bag. 'See, Grammy, it's here,' Tyrese said, holding it up.

'Good, just make sure you put it on.'

'Grammy, I can't run an eight-hundred metre race in a scarf.'

'Nonsense.'

He laughed again and Marvin peered into the screen. 'Hey, Ty. Are you looking forward to it?'

'Hey, Marvin. *Wah gwaan?*' Tyrese said in perfect Patois,

which made Marvin burst into a fit of giggles. 'I can't wait, Marv, it'll be the first race I've entered since Dad died.' He glanced at his mum, who gave him a small smile. 'Oh, look what Mum got me. Can you see my T-shirt, Grammy?'

Tyrese stepped back so the top half of his body could fit in the phone screen. 'It's brilliant, isn't it?'

'Oh, Tyrese, dat's beautiful,' Grammy said, looking at the T-shirt which had a large photograph printed on it of Tyrese's dad and Tyrese, arm in arm.

'I think it's going to bring me luck.' Tyrese smiled, watching Grammy wiping her tears. But she looked happy. Everyone did.

'Have you heard from Ellie? I got a voice note from her earlier,' Marvin said.

'Me too. She wished me luck and said she's looking forward to coming over soon with her dad.'

'So am I.' Marvin chuckled. 'You'll have to show me and her around and teach me how to be a Manchester *bwoy*.'

'*Can all contestants for race number three come to the track?*'

Ending the call, Tyrese turned to his mum who took a deep breath and smiled. 'Are you OK, Ty?'

He looked down at the scar on his now-healed finger. Smiling back, he touched the picture of his dad on his T-shirt. 'I am, Mum. I really am.'

Acknowledgements

Life shapes and inspires us, and my journey to write this story was formed and inspired by many things. But inspiration alone hasn't created this book. Without Clare Wallace, my agent, Tyrese wouldn't have been possible. She was willing to see beyond those first drafts, to see potential and to unlock my vision, working tirelessly with me and helping to shape the early manuscript. She not only heard me but listened to why Tyrese was so much a part of my heart. I will be eternally grateful.

I also want to shout out to the rest of the team at Darley Anderson agency, who I know have been rooting for Tyrese from the beginning. I'm lucky to have you all in my corner.

Tyrese was fortunate to come across the editor, Chloe Sackur at Andersen Press. Chloe is simply an exceptional editor who encouraged me to look at Tyrese in a different way, which took me on the deepest and most challenging writing journey of my life, taking Tyrese to another level, helping him to really live on the page. Saying thank you will never be enough. Tyrese also benefited from the talents and insight of Charlie Sheppard, thank you so much. The whole team at Andersen Press have got behind Tyrese and I feel grateful to know that they are helping Tyrese's voice to be heard.

And of course the artist Dananayi Muwanigwa has created a unique and wonderful cover to convey the spirit of Tyrese. Thank you. Plus a huge thank you to Kate Grove, Art Director, whose magical, creative talents and imagination were pivotal in helping to develop and inspire this cover.

Thanks also has to go to Cat Irving, the human remains conservator at Surgeons' Hall Museum, for giving up her time to fascinate me with her extraordinary knowledge.

To my friends, to my family, to my animals, your encouragement and love has carried me when I needed it most. And to my children who somehow have grown into adults, thank you, this journey would be nothing without you.

J.P. x

THE HOUSE IN THE WOODS

YVETTE FIELDING

When Clovis, Eve and Tom decide to play with a ouija board in an old abandoned house on Halloween, none of them foresees the horrors they're about to unleash. What starts out as a bit of fun, soon transcends into something far more terrifying when a distressed and determined spirit follows them home. Before long the friends are caught up in a series of events beyond their wildest imaginings and their journey as ghost hunters begins . . .

'When I grow up I wanna be a ghost hunter!'
KEITH LEMON

'If you're reading this scary book in bed then it might be wise to leave the landing light on'
PAUL O'GRADY